I0817674

CROSSROADS

THE WAR WITHIN ANTHOLOGY

CROSSROADS

THE WAR WITHIN ANTHOLOGY

ADAM CHRISTOPHER

L. L. McKINNEY

ANDREW ROBINSON

Published by Blizzard Entertainment.

Additional Art: siloto/stock.adobe.com (4, 12, 16, 20, 27, 32, 37, 41, 44, 48, 52, 60, 63, 66, 75, 79, 85, 92, 97, 103, 110, 115, 119, 124, 137, 143, 148, 153, 157, 163, 167, 172, 186, 198, 215, 220, 232, 240, 254-255)

Library of Congress Cataloging-in-Publication Data available.

ISBN: 978-1-956916-66-9

Manufactured in China

Print run 10 9 8 7 6 5 4 3 2 1

CONTENTS

HEARTLANDS
ADAM CHRISTOPHER

1
SUMMIT at BORALUS

"I would offer a coin for your thoughts," said a warm voice behind her, "but I fear the price may be too high."

Lady Jaina Proudmoore turned from the view of the city below as her old friend joined her on the parapet. Despite his size and heavy armor, he had somehow made it up the tight and winding stair of Proudmoore Keep's tallest tower without making a sound.

Thrall leaned on the old stone and looked out across Boralus, took a deep breath of the cool air. "I can see why you treasure this spot."

Jaina nodded. The tower offered her the solitude and privacy to think, while the view of Boralus offered perspective, a reminder of where she was—and of *who* she was.

And right now, as the sea mist cleared, Boralus shone like a sapphire in the dawn. A thousand roofs, a hundred spires, all glowing with the promise of a new day. From the tower Jaina could fully glimpse her domain, from the snowy mountains to the great harbor, in which sat the mighty Kul Tiran fleet, with a dozen of its fastest ships ready and awaiting her command.

"I know you thought it would be easy," said Thrall.

Jaina blinked out of her reverie. Thrall's face had lost some of the fear she'd seen the day Dalaran fell. But there was still a shadow over him—over them both. Up here, it was easy to forget the darkness plotting at the heart of the world, a darkness that would soon cast its pall over not only Boralus but all of Azeroth, if they couldn't defeat it.

"Easy is . . . not the word I would use." She sighed. "But yes, I had hoped for more."

She'd counted ten sunrises since that terrible day. And every night since, Jaina had relived the horror of that moment in her dreams, as the city of light and wonder was plucked from the sky over Khaz Algar like a child's toy.

But that nightmare had been real. And Jaina knew that it was just the start.

Something terrible was coming. Another Sundering, another Cataclysm. An evil that had a name.

Xal'atath.

Those ten days since Jaina and Thrall had returned to their respective capitals had been a blur of activity. Couriers had been dispatched to every corner of Azeroth, carrying with them the full authority of both Horde and Alliance within a singular, imperative message: a call to unite, a call for all leaders to meet at Boralus, ready to face this new enemy. They would come, Jaina had been sure of it.

And some had—but many had not.

Perhaps she had been naive, in retrospect, not realizing quite how badly the Radiant Song had affected people across the world. Even now, as she looked across her own city, watching the guards on patrol, workers in the docks, innkeepers sweeping their steps while market traders rolled barrels and loaded carts, she wondered how many of her people had heard the song, unsettled by the vision and the voice. How many were afraid, left wondering what it could mean.

There was a metallic clatter from behind them, followed by muttered curses and the sound of heavy footfalls on the spiral stair. Jaina and Thrall watched as Danath Trollbane emerged onto the roof. He paused for breath, chest heaving under his red tabard.

"By Thoradin's blood," he said, "for such a seafaring people, the Kul Tirans do have a fondness for stairs."

Jaina stifled a laugh—she couldn't help it, despite her foul mood. Danath was the first to respond to her call. He had been in the city for several days already, helping Jaina prepare for the summit. If he was disappointed by the responses from the other leaders as they trickled in, he had never shown it. Instead, he had been a steadfast companion, an excellent sounding board—and a very good friend.

"Have they come up with a solution?" asked Thrall.

"Actually," said Danath, "I think we have." He turned back to the

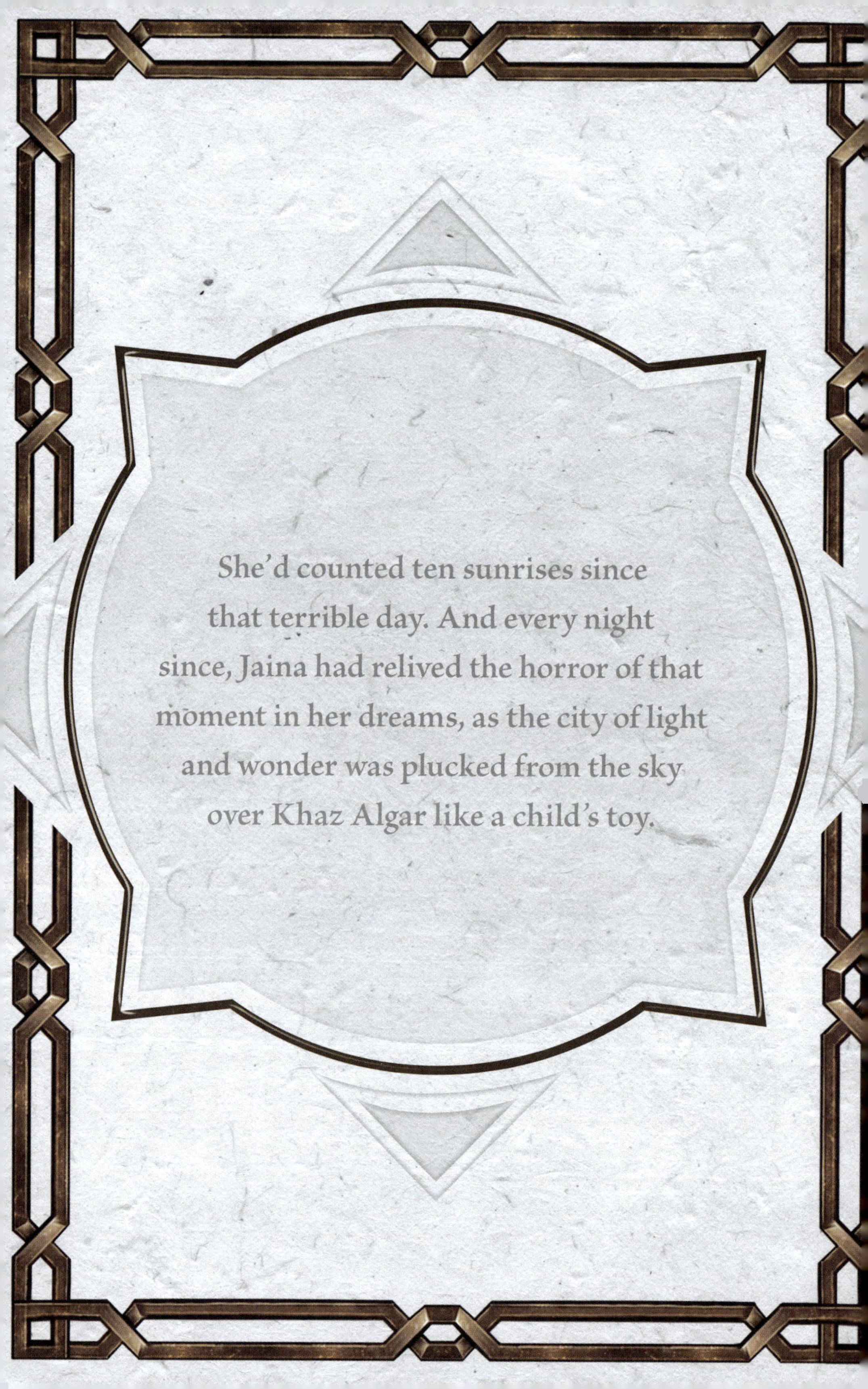

She'd counted ten sunrises since that terrible day. And every night since, Jaina had relived the horror of that moment in her dreams, as the city of light and wonder was plucked from the sky over Khaz Algar like a child's toy.

stairs. "Come, there is much to consider."

Jaina could hear the mumbled discussions as she and Thrall followed Danath back into the meeting room, deep at the heart of Proudmoore Keep. With the return of the trio, those discussions fell into a respectful silence.

The assembled leaders had been locked in conversation all night, trying to overcome both geography and politics to assemble a strike force that Jaina and Thrall could take to Khaz Algar. And now, as the representatives stood around the huge war table in the center of the chamber, Jaina dared to hope that Danath had spoken the truth—that they could soon take the fight to Xal'atath.

The leaders who had answered Jaina and Thrall's joint call were, Jaina reflected, an unusual mix. On the Horde side was Aggralan—Aggra—of the Earthen Ring and Thrall's life-mate; Baine Bloodhoof, the tauren High Chieftain, towering over the slim form of Thalyssra, First Arcanist of the Nightborne, who in turn stood tall over the diminutive Kiro, Caravan Leader of the Voldunai vulpera.

On the other side of the table were the representatives of the Alliance—Shandris Feathermoon, newly risen to leader of the night elves, and Magister Umbric of the void elves stood almost back-to-back, making an impressive, even beautiful pair next to the stout form of Kurdran Wildhammer, the dwarf deputized as Falstad's representative from the Council of Three Hammers.

Finally, Tess Greymane represented Gilneas, a queen in title and, of the group, looking perhaps the most battle-ready in her purple-and-brown leathers. It was she who broke the silence, her warm greeting a relief to Jaina, who didn't quite know what to expect of the assemblage. When they had left the group several hours before, tempers had been high, the atmosphere tense as each leader had argued about their respective burdens of office and the limitations this placed on them to contribute to the strike force.

Jaina approached the table, covered now by a large map that had not been there earlier. She recognized the region at once.

"The Arathi Highlands?"

Danath opened his mouth to speak, but Umbric got in first.

"This is a risk," he said quietly, long blue fingers steepled under his chin. "I need something less . . . *uncertain*."

"So do we all," said Baine. The tauren folded his massive arms and raised his chin, making Thalyssra duck out of the way of his feathered headpiece. "But sometimes what we need and what we have are two different things."

"Agreed." Shandris leaned over the table. "We must take the opportunity offered and use it well."

Jaina looked around the group. "What opportunity? Danath?"

"The 7th Legion." He pointed to the location of his own kingdom on the map of the Arathi Highlands. "There is a considerable force massed at Stromgarde. A ready-made army, awaiting command."

Thrall rubbed his chin. "Interesting. Who commands this

garrison?"

"My niece, Marran," said Danath. "As my diplomatic duties draw me to Stormwind, she stands as regent of Stromgarde. I have had word she has been reinforcing her position with the 7th Legion Auxiliary." He spread his hands. "Her own decision, but I trust she is—"

"Stoking tensions with the Mag'har." Aggra stepped forward, shaking her head. "The Horde granted the base at Hammerfall to the refugee orcs amid the Armistice. After the Fourth War, Overlord Geya'rah and her people had nowhere to go. The lands surrounding Hammerfall are much like Nagrand, a gentle place for their people to make a fresh start on Azeroth." She pointed to the other side of the map, where the orc stronghold lay nestled under the hills, and turned to Thrall. "But the wounds of her Draenor have not fully healed, for Geya'rah *or* her people. The Kor'kron now train in number there at her request, to deter action from Stromgarde." She looked at Danath, a hard expression on her face. "What Stromgarde does, Hammerfall answers."

Kurdran swore under his breath. "An old fight, one we thought long settled," he said, running thick fingers through his beard. "The situation in the Highlands is no good, no good at all."

Jaina watched as Tess and Umbric exchanged a glance, and Thalyssra bent down to listen to something Kiro muttered into her ear. Then Jaina looked at Thrall, but the former warchief was silent, his brow once again furrowed. He was studying the map, not the

Kurdran swore under his breath. "An old fight, one we thought long settled," he said, running thick fingers through his beard. "The situation in the Highlands is no good, no good at all."

people around it.

Danath raised his hands. "*Please*, we have been through this." He sighed and began a slow circuit of the table. "I understand your fears, but you forget, Stromgarde still struggles to recover from the Fourth War. Marran requested aid from the 7th Legion to help farmers fend off predators, to train new soldiers to support the Alliance, to maintain our family's rule while I am absent. I trust she is only doing what she feels she must as leader and that the matter will easily be righted." A fresh murmur spread around the table, but Danath would not be deterred. "*Here* is our strike force. The 7th Legion *and*"—he nodded as he walked by Aggra—"the Kor'kron. Two of the best fighting forces in Azeroth. Trained. Ready! We could not hope for a better army."

He stopped and now stood by Jaina and Thrall once more. He looked at the two of them. "Marran will listen to you, Jaina. I have heard how well she regards you and your mother. I will write to her as well, to tell her of your coming and to prepare the 7th Legion to march. And while I don't know Geya'rah, I know *you*, Thrall. The Horde may not have a warchief, but the Kor'kron are yours to command."

Thrall held Danath's gaze for several moments, then nodded. His eyes found Jaina's. "Perhaps this is our best option, for both rallying a strike force and avoiding a larger conflict."

Jaina considered. The situation in the Arathi Highlands sounded delicate, to put it mildly, but Danath was right. They needed an army, and here was not one but *two*, waiting for a proper target.

Jaina reached for her staff. “Then so it will be. I will order the fleet to sail for Stromgarde. By the time they arrive, the strike force will be ready. Thrall, you will go to Hammerfall and negotiate with Geya’rah for the Kor’kron.”

“I will come,” Aggra said. She stepped around the table to join Thrall. “Geya’rah is as a sister to me.” She laid a hand on her mate’s shoulder. “I promise, she will listen.”

“Agreed,” said Jaina. “Danath and I will go to Stromgarde.”

“I am sorry, Lord Admiral,” said Danath, bowing his head in apology. “I have been away from Stormwind too long already. Turalyon has sent word that I am urgently needed to rejoin his court. But on my honor, Marran will gladly receive you and your word on this matter.” He smiled.

“Very well,” said Jaina. She turned to the assembled leaders. “I thank you all for your courage and candor on this council. We are adjourned.”

As the leaders began filing out, offering their farewells, Jaina turned to Thrall and Aggra.

“Prepare yourselves,” she said, conjuring a portal. “We leave at once.”

Jaina, Thrall, and Aggra had barely stepped through the portal from Boralus to the Arathi Highlands when they sensed the situation had

taken a drastic turn. They had arrived in a hollow, shielded from view by steep hillsides. No sooner had they got their bearings than Aggra rushed forward, cursing under her breath. Jaina watched as she crouched by a body, lying face down.

It was not the only one.

Thrall stepped over a human corpse, the man's armor split by axe blows.

"Oh no," Jaina whispered. She counted the bodies—twelve in total, six human in the colors of the 7th Legion, six orcs in the furs and leathers of the Kor'kron. Casting a wary eye over the surrounding hilltops, she joined the other two. "What happened?"

Aggra pulled a bloodied 7th Legion sword from the nearest Kor'kron. "A fight to the death," she said. She stood and used the sword to indicate several orcs, arrows stuck in the weak points of their armor. "The humans staged an ambush . . ."

Thrall picked up his life-mate's train of thought. "Only to find the Kor'kron a formidable foe." He looked down at the bloody scene, his expression grim. "A battle of mutual annihilation. Two small forces, equally matched in number, perhaps equally—and foolishly—surprised at the strength of their enemy." He looked at Jaina. "I fear we may be too late."

"We *cannot* be too late," said Aggra. She dropped the sword and turned to her companions. "But I agree that time is short. I will go directly to Hammerfall and stay Geya'rah's hand. You *both* should

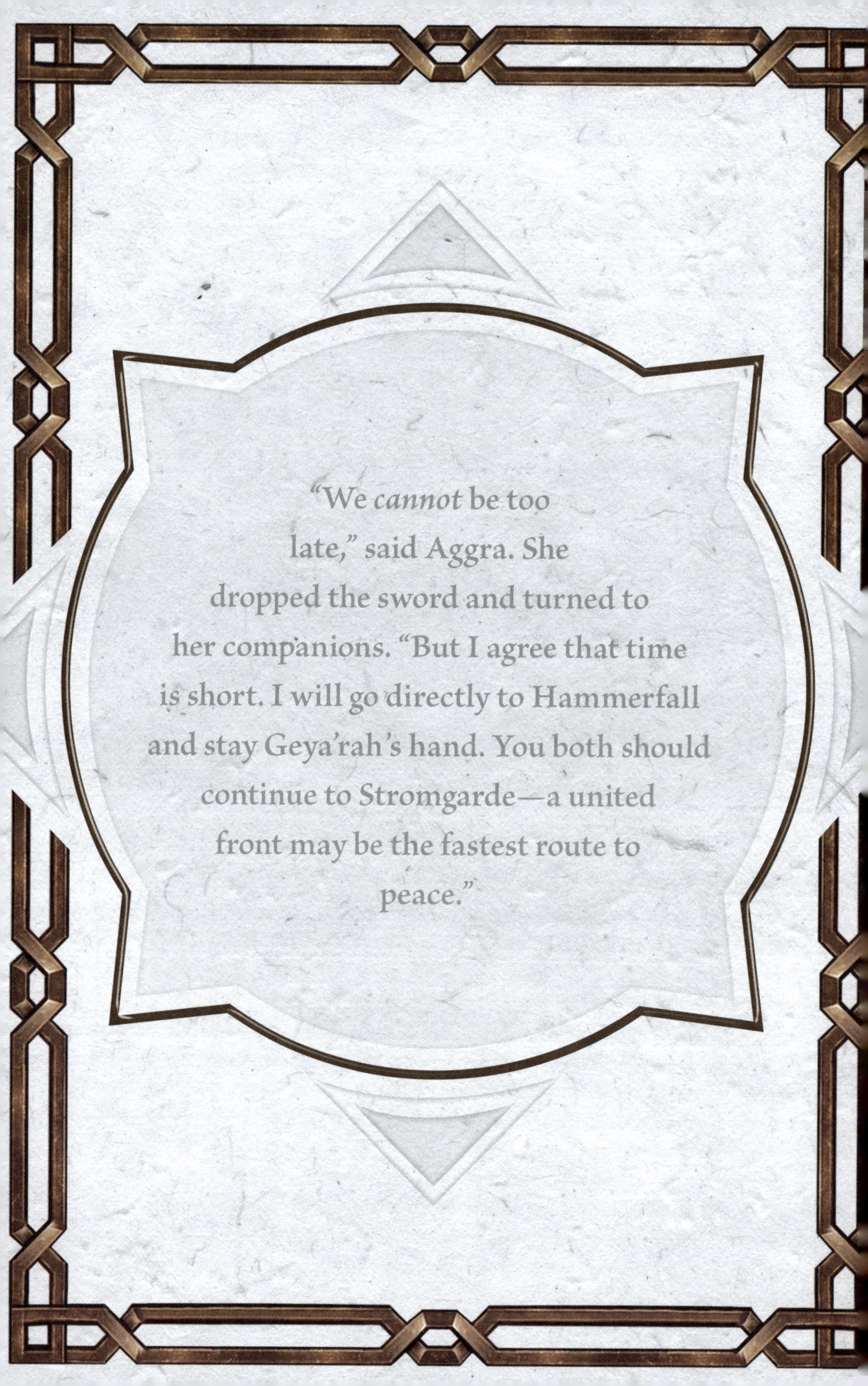

"We *cannot* be too late," said Aggra. She dropped the sword and turned to her companions. "But I agree that time is short. I will go directly to Hammerfall and stay Geya'rah's hand. You both should continue to Stromgarde—a united front may be the fastest route to peace."

continue to Stromgarde—a united front may be the fastest route to peace."

Thrall nodded. "Luck, my love," he said. The two clasped hands, then without another word, Aggra took off, sprinting for the northern hillside, which she deftly scaled before disappearing from view.

Thrall watched her go, then turned to Jaina. "To Stromgarde, then."

But as they left their cover, Jaina heard a high whistling sound. Almost before she registered it, Thrall jerked where he stood and took a stumbling step backward, the feathered shaft of a projectile emerging between his shoulder and chest armor.

Jaina spun, instinctively putting herself between Thrall and the archer. She raised her staff high and cast a protective shield for cover. Another whistle, but this time the arrow glanced off the shield. That moment was all Jaina needed to spot her target. There, by the solitary tree at the top of the hill opposite, came a flash of movement. A cloaked figure broke cover, bow raised, quiver bouncing on their back as they fled.

At once Jaina balled her fist and threw it forward, sending an orb of crackling purple energy flying toward the hillside. A moment later, the tree exploded in a gout of yellow flame and pink light, but of the bowman there was no sign. Cursing, she knelt beside Thrall.

"Leave it`, I will be fine," said Thrall, waving her away. He grabbed the shaft of the arrow, still protruding from his flesh, and pulled it free in a single tug. He held up the arrow to examine it. "I hope, anyway."

Jaina peered at the arrowhead. It was smeared with blood, the liquid near black, but there was something else too—another substance, bright blue, oily. Her eyes widened in horror.

"Poison? Thrall, you—"

Thrall tossed the arrow to one side, then gave his injured shoulder an experimental roll. He winced; the wound was still seeping. "I'll be fine," he said, then paused. "But we do need to get to Stromgarde, and quickly." He gestured to the hillside. "Lead the way."

2
ECHOES of the PAST

"I don't care who you are," said the guard, "you can't enter with *him*."

Jaina and Thrall stood before the gates of Stromgarde. It had been years since she had visited the stronghold, and she didn't remember the entrance being so imposing.

Certainly, it had never been so unwelcoming.

There were six guardsmen at the gate—Stromgarde regulars rather than 7th Legion—and above, on the towers that flanked the entrance, another six armed with crossbows aimed squarely at them.

Jaina tried to keep calm, but it was difficult. The walk to the city had been slow going, and she was very aware that Thrall's strength was being steadily sapped by the arrow's poison. Even now, as they stood before the gates, he was leaning heavily against her, his head bowed, his breathing labored.

"We are here to see Lady Marran Trollbane!" Jaina raised

her voice and looked up at the guards on the towers, hoping that maybe one of them would show more sense. "My name is Jaina Proudmoore, Lord Admiral of the allied kingdom of Kul Tiras. This is Thrall, orc representative to the Horde Council, who is gravely wounded. We are *both* here at the direction of Danath Trollbane on a mission of peace, and we have urgent business with your regent. *I demand you open these gates!*"

The guard in front of them simply shook his head.

"I don't think you understand," Jaina said through gritted teeth, her staff glowing as she channeled the arcane. "I ask permission only as a courtesy—"

She felt Thrall's big yet gentle hand on her forearm. "Danath's message may not yet have arrived, Jaina."

Jaina drew breath to argue, but Thrall pushed himself away from her. "We have a job to do, and I am a hindrance." He nodded at the guard. "Do not make a mistake today. The Lord Admiral is here to meet your regent. I suggest you let her in."

The guard remained steadfast, but there was movement behind him, and as Jaina glanced up, she saw there was one fewer soldier on the wall above. Moments later came the sound of heavy chain and creaking wood.

Jaina sighed with relief and relaxed her grip on her staff. *Somebody* was willing to listen, at least. As the gates began to slowly move, she turned to Thrall, ready to lead him in, but he shook his head.

"You go," he said.

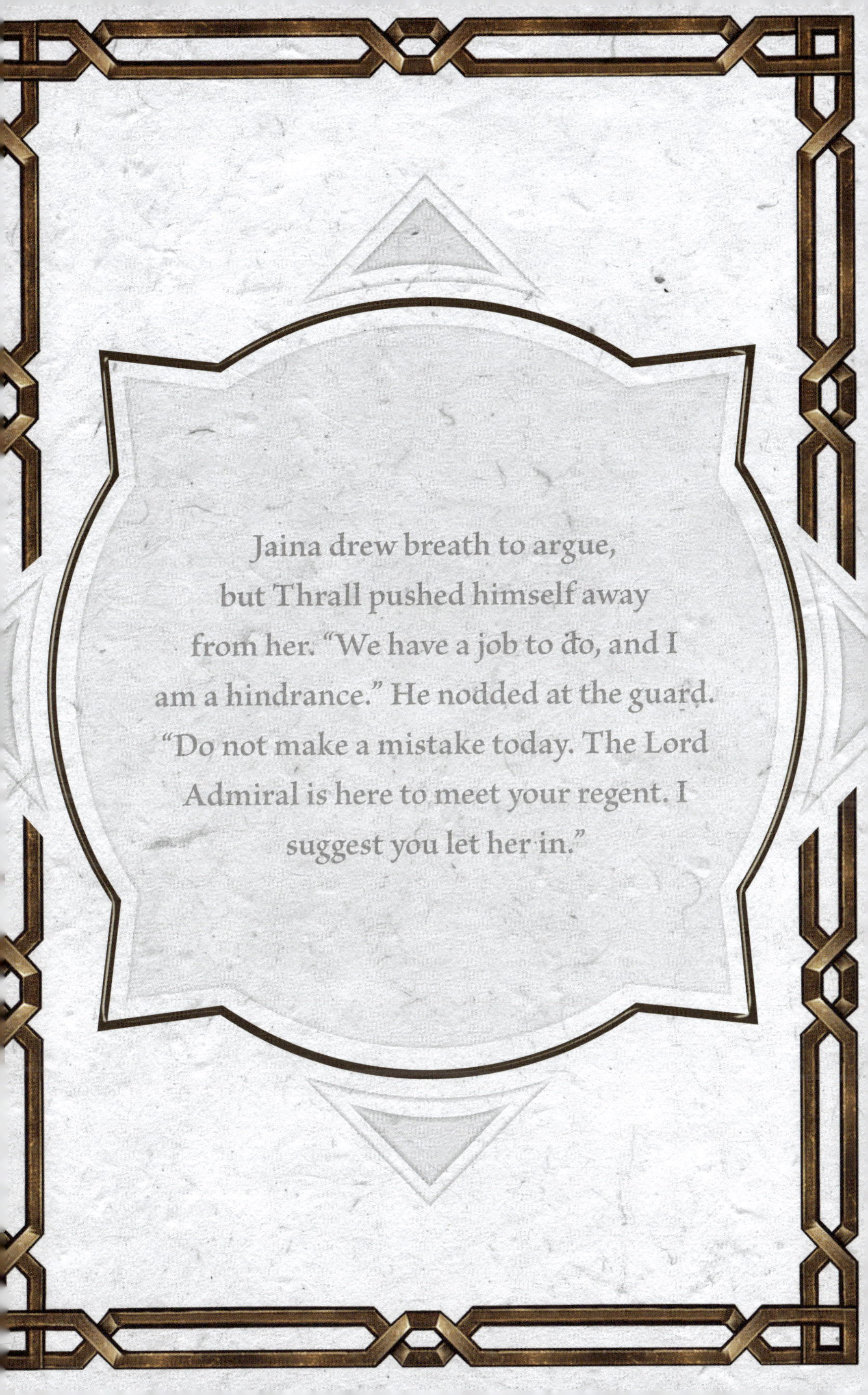

Jaina drew breath to argue, but Thrall pushed himself away from her. "We have a job to do, and I am a hindrance." He nodded at the guard. "Do not make a mistake today. The Lord Admiral is here to meet your regent. I suggest you let her in."

Jaina frowned. "Thrall, you need help. I can't leave you."

"It is *I* who leaves *you*," he said. "And I will get help, but not here. I will go to Hammerfall. Aggra will have spoken to Geya'rah by now." He nodded at the open gates. "Talk to Lady Marran. Remember our mission."

Jaina sighed, then turned as the guard from above—clearly someone with both more rank and sense than his comrade—appeared before her.

"Follow me," he said.

As soon as she stepped through the gates of Stromgarde, Jaina felt the eyes of the entire city on her.

It was busy, certainly—and it wasn't just the 7th Legion Auxiliary here. The main body of the army itself, the liveried soldiers, filled the streets, nearly outnumbering the common folk. Despite the bustle, it seemed the normal business of the city had ground to a halt, with stores, inns, and houses not just closed but boarded up, as though Stromgarde was preparing to weather a great storm. What regular citizens were out stopped and stared as Jaina and her escort passed.

All looked afraid—a common response to a battle happening outside the city walls perhaps, though Jaina couldn't help but sense there was something strange afoot. The people scattered before her, dragging children with them, slamming doors and windows behind as if *she* were the enemy.

Beware the Daughter of the Sea.

The unhappy memory sprang unbidden into Jaina's mind. She dismissed it as quickly as it arrived, but it did nothing to improve her mood.

Soon they reached the keep, the doors of which opened as they approached. Two burly legionnaires emerged, followed by a small woman in more elegant, but far less protective, armor. She was perhaps forty, old enough to know the many perils that had faced Stromgarde in Jaina's lifetime, and she carried those burdens in the sharpness of her eyes, the taut line of her mouth.

"Lord Admiral," Marran Trollbane approached, her arms clasped tightly behind her back. "Thank Thoradin. We are short on allies in this land and welcome your counsel."

Jaina frowned, trying to take measure of the woman. "Yes, my lady," she said. "I've come a long way to talk to you. Danath, said—"

"We've not much to offer in the way of hospitality," said Marran, cutting Jaina off, "but any child of Arathor is always welcome under our gates. Come, please, follow me."

With that, the regent turned and walked through the doors and into the keep.

Adjusting her grip on her staff, Jaina followed her inside.

"I'm quite glad you've come," said Marran as she led Jaina through the keep's wide halls. "Truth be told, I've driven my retainers to distraction, trying to find a solution to this mess."

Jaina heaved a sigh of relief—perhaps the situation could still be salvaged. "I am glad to hear it. Should we convene with your council or meet privately first?"

"Let us talk before summoning the others," said Marran, waving off the guards as they opened the doorway to her study.

"I appreciate your attention on this matter," said Jaina, settling into a plush velvet chair at Marran's invitation. "Most urgently, I came here with an emissary from the Horde, but he was injured in the crossfire of a skirmish between the 7th Legion and the Kor'kron. Your guards would not let him enter, so he left for Hammerfall. I suggest we start there—summoning him back, negotiating a peace he can take to the Mag'har." She paused. "But time is against us. There is much else to discuss. Dalaran—"

"Dalaran?" Marran cut in. She cocked her head at that, as if she hadn't heard right. Then the regent moved around Jaina and sat in a more austere high-backed chair behind her desk before settling her elbows atop a mess of parchments. "I know you've seen a lot of war, Lord Admiral. I know how long you've ruled Kul Tiras." She rifled through the pages on her desk until she found the one she sought. "But do you know how many bushels of grain your kingdom needs for the winter?" She held up another parchment. "How many horses plow the fields of Stormsong Valley?" Another scrap of paper. "The cost per hundredweight of iron ore?" She shook her head. "For years, Stromgarde has lost too many battles and cared too little for its people."

Jaina felt stung—she was losing her. "Of course," said Jaina.

"But there is another fight coming, one that threatens more than just our small kingdoms. It is a fight we must join against, orc and human alike. Fighting each other only diminishes the strength we must show, united. Let the 7th Legion and the Kor'kron fight side by side," she said. "And perhaps in doing so, an understanding—a peace—can be found between your people and the Mag'har."

"A *peace*?" asked Marran quietly. "A *peace*, while my people mourn their kin, lost today to senseless violence?" Jaina could see the woman was actually trembling with rage, but she had to press on. She tightened her grip on her staff and inclined her head in the affirmative.

Marran nodded, but now she looked at her desk. "I see. Now I see." She looked up. "You're not here to reinforce our borders, to help us . . . You're here to lead the Auxiliary off on another grand adventure, aren't you? Another foe to dispatch, another glorious war, the heroes saving us, one and all." Marran's expression hardened. Jaina's heart thudded in her chest as the regent's face flushed, her words almost hissed through clenched teeth.

"And with the Auxiliary gone," said Marran, "the orcs will have their chance. They will put Stromgarde to the sword, and the Highlands will be theirs for the taking."

Jaina shook her head. "How could that—"

Marran spat a laugh. "I shouldn't be surprised that you've come here to ask this of me. This is what the Alliance does, asking us to sacrifice ourselves for the greater good. But I tell you now, we have

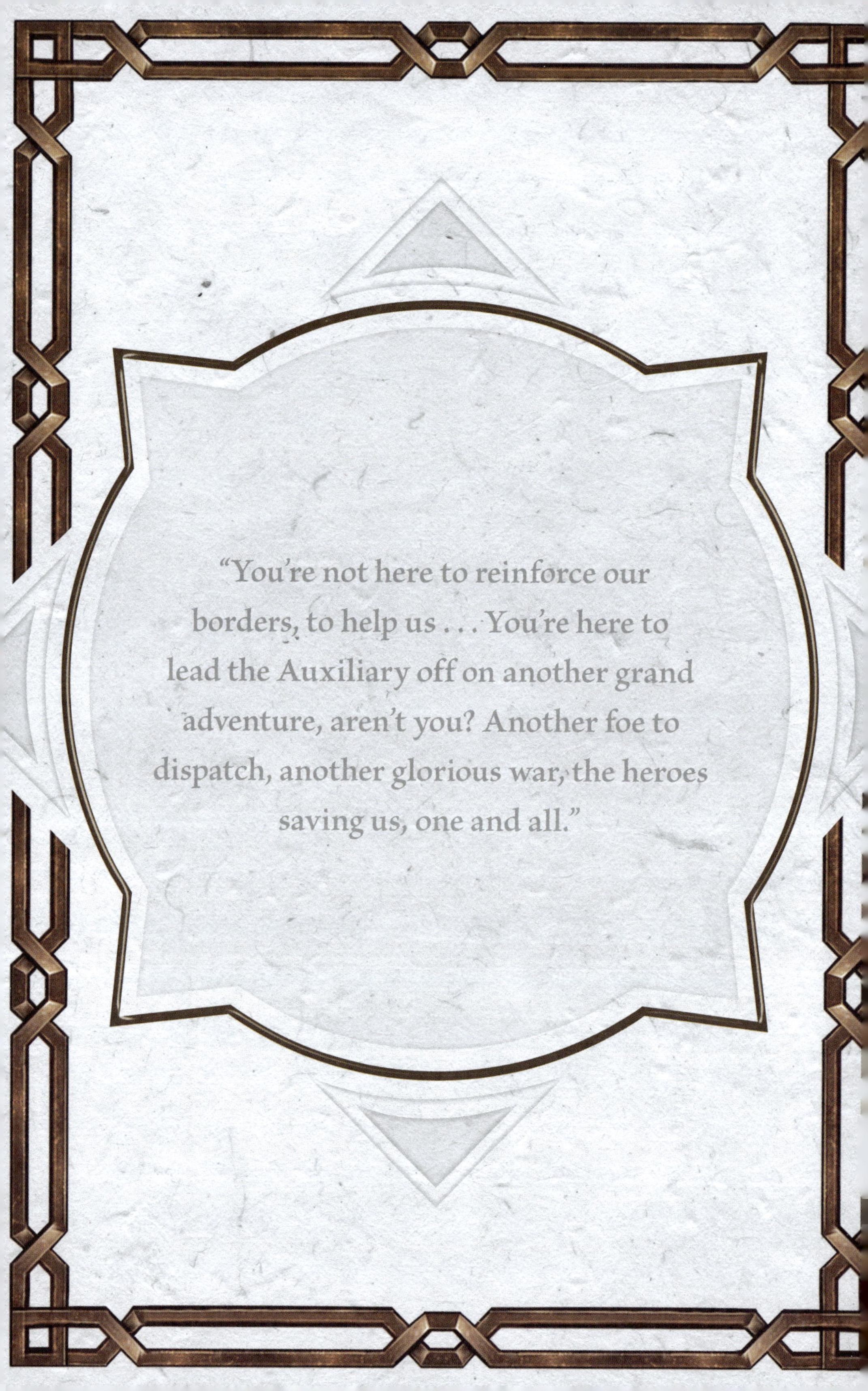

"You're not here to reinforce our borders, to help us . . . You're here to lead the Auxiliary off on another grand adventure, aren't you? Another foe to dispatch, another glorious war, the heroes saving us, one and all."

been cut to the *bone* while the Alliance chases its next battle. I am here for Stromgarde. These are my people. Their lives matter, and I will make sure of it."

"Marran, please—"

"I am the lady regent and will be addressed as such. As an ally of this kingdom, you will be given proper quarter, but I think it best you depart at dawn."

That afternoon, Jaina watched from the window of her guest chambers as the courier mounted a horse and, with a kick of his heels, tore off toward the main gate of Stromgarde, carrying with him a message to Stormwind.

She hoped it was the right decision—she'd felt compelled to write to Danath, outlining her concerns about Marran and asking him to make haste his return. But Jaina was aware that summoning Danath back could well throw fuel on the fire of an already volatile situation.

Following her confrontation with the regent, Jaina had been abruptly dismissed and taken by escort to her guest quarters—and perhaps it was just as well. It had been a long day, and Jaina was happy to let Marran compose herself so they could have a more reasonable discussion later. In the meantime, Jaina decided to walk the city and get a sense of the situation for herself.

As soon as she stepped out onto the streets, she could sense the tension in the air, the citizens and 7th Legion alike keeping their distance with wary looks, if not outright hostile stares. Jaina ignored them. If nothing else, being left alone gave her the space to think.

Despite her concerns, Jaina *could* understand Marran's position, even if it was ill-advised. Stromgarde was ever at the mercy of the hostile forces that surrounded it, and it had been a major battlefront in the Fourth War. Jaina knew all too well what it was like to inherit a kingdom in distress, to have enemies lurking around every corner—to discover that your family's greatest ally had betrayed you. Marran was only doing what she thought best for her people, but she desperately needed guidance. Her uncle's, Jaina hoped, but she feared Danath's return to Stromgarde was more likely to start a power struggle than calm tensions.

In the end, she had opted to be prudent and penned the letter. But as Jaina crossed the city, she became acutely aware of just how little time she had. Danath might come, yes, but he might come too late. Jaina was here, now.

It was up to her to find the right way forward.

One, two. One, two.

Thrall counted his steps, focusing on nothing else as he inched across the Arathi Highlands.

One, two. One, two.

But he was getting slower. He knew that. He also knew that

Hammerfall was a long way away and that the poison was doing fine work, draining his strength with every breath. Already his left arm was completely numb. Already he could feel the ice-cold spread of the poison from the wound, the pain of which pulsed in time with his heartbeat.

At least, he thought with a weak grimace, he knew where he was going. He could reach Hammerfall with his eyes closed. The Arathi Highlands was a country he knew all too well, and as he walked he allowed himself a moment to remember those days past, before the Third War, when he and Orgrim Doomhammer had come to liberate the internment camp—that pit of deprivation, hardship, of pain and sorrow and suffering as the humans put their boot on the very spirit of the orcs—that sat beneath the hills, in the place where Hammerfall now stood.

Yes, Thrall knew the way.

One, two. One . . . two.

One.

Thrall closed his eyes, the blood roaring in his ears. He willed himself to keep walking even as the dark world behind his eyelids began to spin.

And then—a push on his shoulder, a strong, friendly hand guiding him, directing him. His comrades, his warriors, willing him on. *Reach the camp. Free your people.*

Yes, Orgrim. Yes, I hear you!

Thrall opened his eyes—and there, ahead. He was not imagining

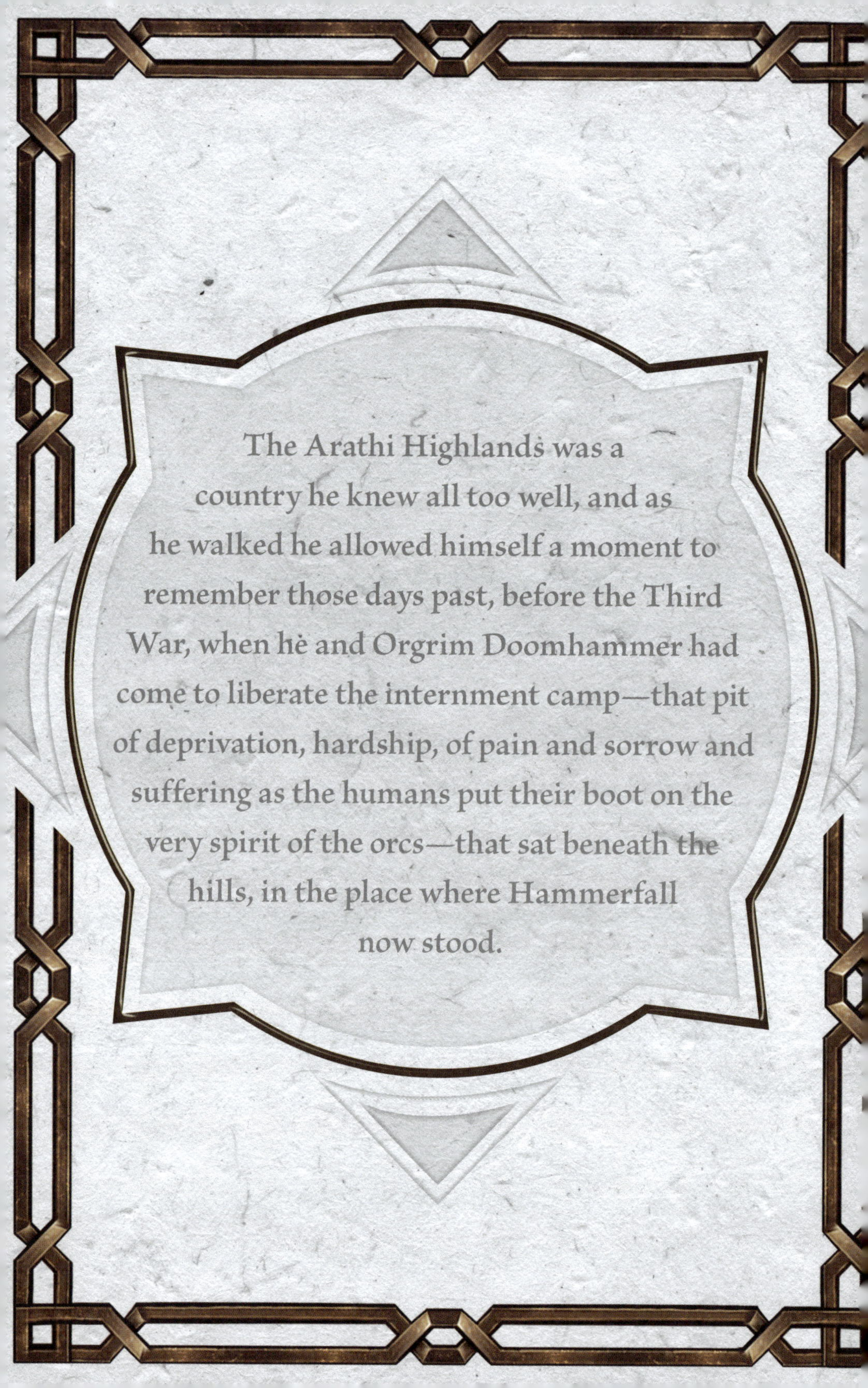

The Arathi Highlands was a country he knew all too well, and as he walked he allowed himself a moment to remember those days past, before the Third War, when he and Orgrim Doomhammer had come to liberate the internment camp—that pit of deprivation, hardship, of pain and sorrow and suffering as the humans put their boot on the very spirit of the orcs—that sat beneath the hills, in the place where Hammerfall now stood.

it, and he was not alone. Was that Orgrim ahead, just disappearing over the next rise? And there, beside Thrall, his men-at-arms, ready to march with him.

If he could just take one more step. Then another, and another.

One, two.

One.

Thrall fell. Was it night already? Surely it couldn't be that dark? He blinked and rubbed his face with the hand that still worked, but his vision was dark and danced with black sparks.

Shapes, moving around him—orcs? No. Humans! Coming in for the kill!

Thrall tried to rise, but he had no strength. He raised his right hand, his fist curling around the handle of an axe that wasn't there. He called out, shouting a warning to Orgrim that they had been ambushed, but somehow he couldn't hear his own voice.

As Thrall's vision faded, the humans rushed toward him, surrounded him. Thrall cried out for his friend, for the Horde. He tried to rise again, but the world around him was now a cold, bottomless ocean, and he felt himself sinking, farther and farther and farther into its depths.

3
BLOODLINES

Thrall woke with a gasp. He went to rise, only for a pair of hands to push him gently back onto the cot.

"Easy, am'osh."

Thrall blinked his vision clear. "Aggra," he whispered. With her help, he sat up slowly; then, suddenly remembering, his fingers found the spot where the arrow had struck him. It was tender, yes, but the wound was healed, the numbness in his arm gone.

"The Lok'osh are skilled," said Aggra. "They say it may take time for your strength to return fully, but I think they underestimate your stamina." She smiled. "I'm not sure they quite believe you walked all the way from Stromgarde in your condition."

Groaning, Thrall said, "How long was I out?"

"A few hours, no more."

Thrall eased his legs off the cot and allowed Aggra to help him to stand. He held her there, running his fingers along the line of

Aggra's jaw. "It is good to see you, my love."

"And I, you," she said. She paused. "I just wish I could wake you with better news."

Thrall sighed. "No luck with Geya'rah?"

Aggra shook her head. "The situation is . . . difficult."

Thrall kneaded his sore shoulder. "So I gathered." He looked around and saw they were in basic military barracks. On the other side of the room was another cot, on which Thrall's armor had been laid—armor that had once belonged to Orgrim Doomhammer.

Thrall's journey across the Highlands came back to him, his fever dream fresh in his mind. As he moved over and began dressing, he thought how strange it was now, to be back here in Doomhammer's armor, as those old hatreds between the orcs and humans rose again.

Just what would it take for Azeroth to move beyond this, to let go of a past that deserved, if not to be forgotten, then consigned to history where it belonged?

He hefted the huge spiked spaulders onto his shoulders and began doing up the straps across his chest. "I must speak with Geya'rah at once."

"Go'el," said Aggra. "That may be harder than you think."

Thrall grunted. "But she knows I am here?"

"Of course. It was fortunate she sent out the patrol that found you. She did not trust Stromgarde to treat with you."

Thrall began pulling his boots on. "Then it is time to talk."

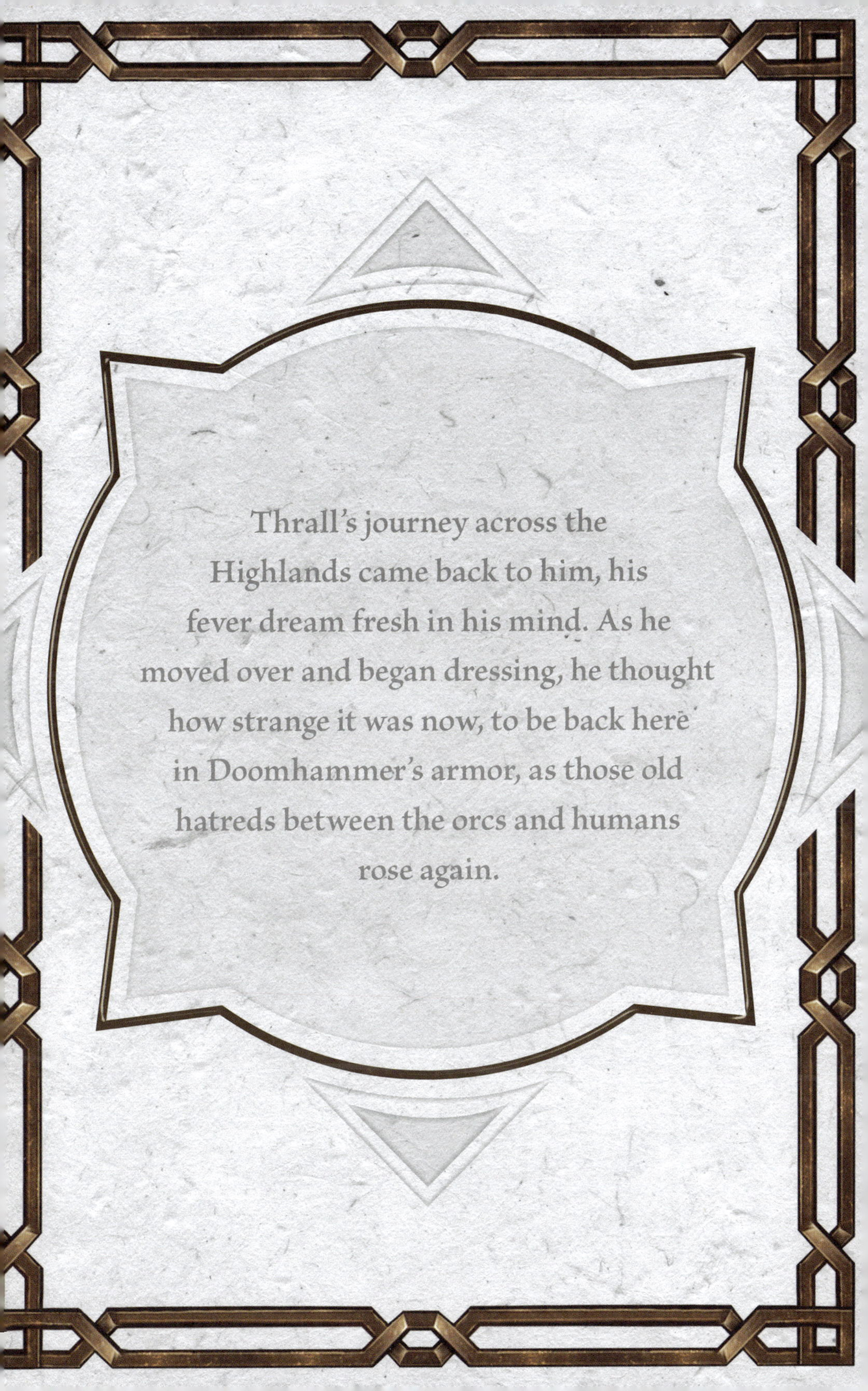

Thrall's journey across the Highlands came back to him, his fever dream fresh in his mind. As he moved over and began dressing, he thought how strange it was now, to be back here in Doomhammer's armor, as those old hatreds between the orcs and humans rose again.

"You don't understand," said Aggra. "She will not grant you an audience."

"We shall see," said Thrall.

Thrall wound his way through the corridors of the base, followed close by Aggra, until he came to a chamber guarded by two Kor'kron, who moved instinctively away from the door to let him pass. It seemed Danath had spoken true in Boralus: though Thrall would never have had reason to test it, the Kor'kron would still defer to him in the absence of a warchief. As he strode into the council chamber, he saw Geya'rah standing over a table covered by maps, with two other orcs—the current Kor'kron general, Talgar, and another green-skinned, gray-bearded warrior he was surprised to see.

"Eitrigg!" Thrall cried, moving around to greet his old friend. "What are the Blackrock doing here?"

Eitrigg clasped Thrall's outstretched arm. "You are not the only one on a mission of diplomacy, Thrall. But I'm glad you are here. We would benefit from your counsel."

Geya'rah met that remark with a scowl. "Eitrigg has advised me to stand down, while the fields of the Highlands are still wet with the blood of our people." Her eyes met Thrall's, and in her fury he could see a fire in her that he had often possessed himself. In many ways, he thought, he and Geya'rah were so alike.

"But *I* command here," said Geya'rah, aiming this comment at Eitrigg before turning back to Thrall. "And if I wanted your counsel, Go'el, I would have called for it."

Thrall held firm. "It seems my hour is very late, and I am sorry for that. I must speak with you, Geya'rah." He gestured to his mate. "I'm sure Aggra has told you everything."

"She told me much I already knew," said Geya'rah, "and you come at the worst possible time, my friend."

"I fear we cannot choose our moment," said Thrall, "but I came here to ask for your help."

Geya'rah sighed. "And you will have it . . . once Stromgarde is dealt with and my people are safe."

Thrall glanced at Eitrigg, but the old orc just shook his head. If Geya'rah had sought the advice of the Blackrock chieftain, then the situation was clearly bad. He needed to take a leaf from Eitrigg's book—he wasn't here to browbeat Geya'rah into cooperation. He was here to negotiate.

"Tell me what is happening," said Thrall, pointing to the map. "And perhaps we can help each other."

Geya'rah didn't move, the muscles at the back of her jaw working as she stared down Thrall. Then she nodded and seemed to calm.

"Fine," she said. "Since coming here, we've existed in peace with Stromgarde." She pointed to their position on the map. "We shared a problem with the area's predators, and all benefitted from culling their numbers. But then Danath Trollbane installed his niece,

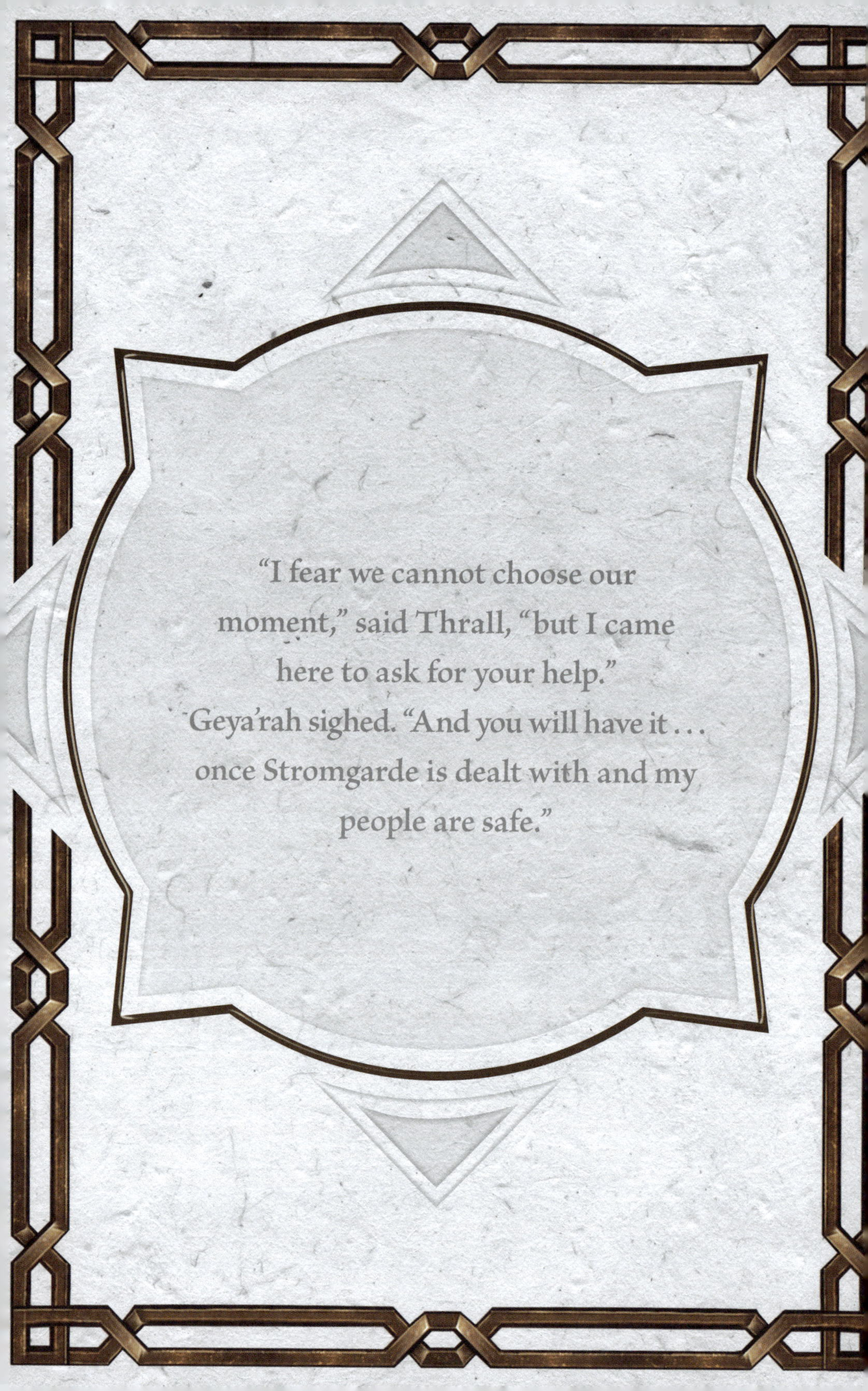

“I fear we cannot choose our moment,” said Thrall, “but I came here to ask for your help.”

Geya’rah sighed. “And you will have it . . . once Stromgarde is dealt with and my people are safe.”

Marran, as regent when his duty drew him to Stormwind City. She gave us only a few months of peace before she began amassing the 7th Legion Auxiliary." She tossed several tokens on the table, representing the Auxiliary. "She said it was to help Stromgarde do their part, protecting farms from predators, but soon their patrols began roaming farther and farther from their base. What had once been amicable encounters between our forces gave way to violence. Today's skirmish marked yet another escalation, and she is far from finished."

"The humans do nothing but provoke," said Talgar. "They make a sport of it."

"They left us no choice," said Geya'rah. "The only way to ensure the safety of our people was to bring the Kor'kron here, to reinforce the base." She placed a different color token on the table, which fell heavily into place beside Hammerfall.

Thrall sighed. "Something that Marran would have seen as a clear act of intimidation too." He gave Talgar a pointed look. "Building two armies only risks one terrible outcome. There is another way."

Geya'rah laughed. "Then please, tell us."

"Talk," said Thrall. He gestured to Eitrigg. "Diplomacy. Negotiation. Even now, Lady Jaina Proudmoore is at Stromgarde, on the same mission as I."

"And good luck to her," said Geya'rah. "Marran Trollbane is not one for conversation. She far prefers to let her archers do the talking.

Besides, as I told you—she isn't finished."

"Explain," said Thrall.

"We know that Stromgarde is planning an attack," said Talgar. "No mere skirmish this time: they intend to capture territory and expand their borders."

Aggra stepped up to the table. "They plan to strike Hammerfall?"

"The cowards wouldn't dare," said Geya'rah. "No, their target is Go'Shek Farm." She indicated on the map. "If Marran thinks to claim an easy victory against our farmers, then she is sorely mistaken." She looked at Thrall. "And trust me, even with the 7th Legion, Stromgarde would fall quickly against the strength of the Mag'har, let alone the Kor'kron. Many will die, and they will not be orcs."

Thrall looked at Geya'rah, at that fire in her eyes. She was so like him, yet so . . . different. True enough, he had been in her position once. But where Thrall had learned, it seemed Geya'rah had hardened. Perhaps because she was from another world, another timeline, a living testament to the older, harsher ways of Draenor.

He shook his head. "Geya'rah, if Stromgarde falls, the full might of the Alliance will answer. There *is* another choice."

"Diplomacy?" Geya'rah spat. "You were shot by *their* archer while on a *diplomatic mission.* We have the enemy preparing to slaughter our civilians in an ambush, and you talk of diplomacy? Marran Trollbane is driven to destroy us. She sees her own victory as the only path to peace."

Thrall felt the heat rise in his face as he took a step to Geya'rah. "Then *show* her! Make the first move to treat. I challenge you! Prove to her that there is *always* a better way."

"What are you afraid of, Go'el?" shouted Geya'rah. "The armistice has made you complacent. Soft. Just like our father!"

Our father?

Thrall felt his jaw go slack. "What did you say?"

But Geya'rah wasn't listening. "I am alive and Durotan is not because I have seen hatred unbridled and dared to stand against it." She slammed a fist on her war table. "Not so long ago the humans kept the orcs as *slaves* on this very ground. Aggra tells me you were here to free them! Or did you forget the legacy of the armor you bear, brother?"

At this, Thrall took a step back. He blinked, his mind racing.

"That's enough!" Aggra silenced Geya'rah. She put a hand on Thrall's arm. He turned to look at her . . . and then he could see. It was plain on her face.

"Brother?" he said.

Aggra's eyes widened. "Go'el, I—"

"You *knew*?" He nodded to himself. "You knew."

Thrall brushed her off and stormed from the council chamber.

After returning to the keep, Jaina brooded in her chambers, knowing she would need to leave on the morrow unless she could convince Danath's kin to see reason. As the hours grew small, she

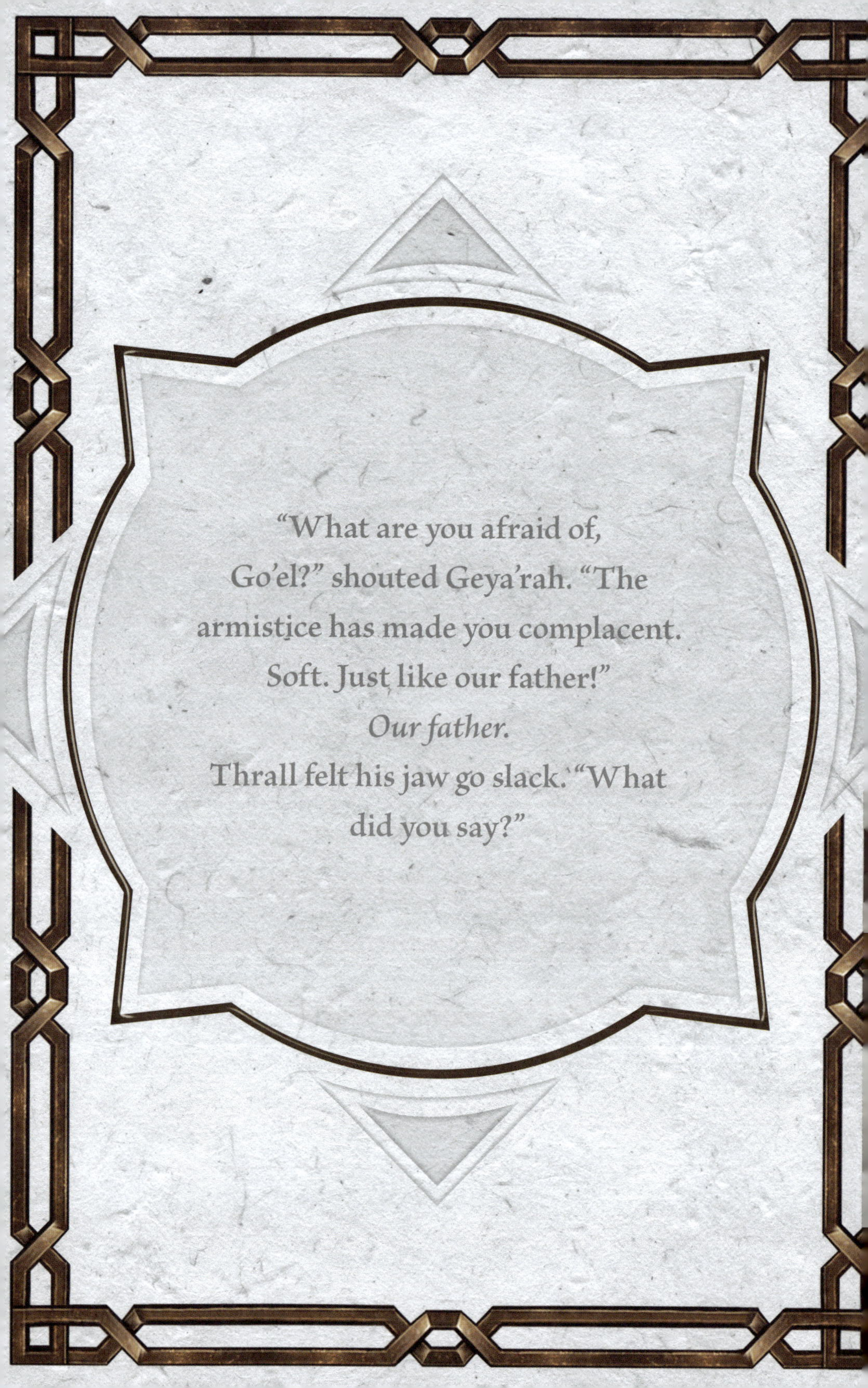

"What are you afraid of, Go'el?" shouted Geya'rah. "The armistice has made you complacent. Soft. Just like our father!"

Our father.

Thrall felt his jaw go slack. "What did you say?"

heaved a sigh and resolved on seeking out Marran herself. Today had been filled with bloodshed for Stromgarde, and Marran's emotions were naturally running high. As the sun sank low on the horizon, Jaina hoped her chance hadn't come and gone.

But as she opened the door to her chambers, she was stunned to see Marran herself, looking exhausted and somewhat embarrassed.

"I . . . apologize for my words, earlier," she said. "They were offered in haste."

"They are forgiven," Jaina said. "But I would speak with you further."

"Let us find somewhere private," Marran offered, "away from the castle's ears."

Marran led Jaina into a long stone chamber, cool and dark, lit only by a flaming torch Marran took from a sconce and the soft glow of Jaina's staff. The chamber was clearly ancient, buried deep beneath Stromgarde's keep. The long spiral stairs that had led them down here had been worn by countless centuries, and the blocks that formed the chamber walls were of a different shape and size to those of the city above.

Marran stopped and held her torch aloft. "We walk in Arathor," she said. "This is all that remains of that ancient place, the last echo of an old world. A fitting place for us to speak freely."

Jaina nodded. "I grew up learning the legend, how Thoradin saw the vision of his father, clad in the pelt of a black wolf, and how he founded the first kingdom of humans."

But Marran shook her head. "Not legend. *History.* One that I have been trusted to uplift and enrich through my own contributions. One that must not be forgotten." She sighed as she turned to the other woman. "I am eager to continue our earlier conversation, but first I wanted to speak with you, about this." She produced a crumpled piece of parchment.

Jaina's eyes widened in the dim light—it was her letter to Danath.

"My spymaster, Zatacia, is a fine shot with a bow, as your orc friend has already discovered. A shame to lose a valuable horse, but in war, sacrifices must be made."

The glow of Jaina's staff flared just a bit brighter. "Marran," she said, "take care with your actions."

Marran ignored the comment. "When I heard you'd come," she said, "I thought you were here to help me. That you might *understand* the position my uncle has put us in."

Her words caught for a moment, and Jaina drew breath to speak.

"Marran, I want to offer you my counsel," she began. "But I must do so in truth and with good intention. Lies will not serve you."

Marran's fist tightened around the parchment. "Then give me your true counsel."

Jaina clenched her jaw as she thought. Every word from now on had to count.

"The Mag'har are a people forged in battle," she said, "and the Kor'kron are the most elite warriors in the Horde. Continue to escalate tensions with the Mag'har and you *will* lose. You say you wish to honor your people, care for them. Forge a pact with Geya'rah and enrich both your peoples, through *friendship*."

Marran took a moment to think. "Yet I stand in the same room as the most powerful mage in all Azeroth, the one who tipped the Battle for Lordaeron to the Alliance. And you tell me still that I will lose?"

At this, Jaina sighed. "I came to offer you my advice, Marran, not my magic."

Marran held Jaina's gaze for a moment, then turned and walked toward the other end of the chamber. She stopped and knelt down, her torch revealing a large, dark mass on the floor.

Jaina followed Marran over, then gasped as she saw what it was.

It was a dead wolf, still wearing the harness of its Kor'kron raider. She'd spoken with Thrall many times about the orcish mounts—for the Frostwolf clan especially, the relationship between orc and wolf was based on respect and friendship, rather than discipline and domestication. The poor creature was huge, its thick black fur shining in the torchlight.

Marran stood and, placing her torch in a wall sconce, pulled a short knife with a curved blade from her belt. She grabbed the wolf's fur at the back of its head and lifted. The creature's jaw hung open, revealing dagger-sharp white teeth.

"Our people are broken," Marran said as she got to work. "I learned that facing every conflict that struck Stromgarde; settling into this castle for a time, only to be spirited away to the country

"Our people are broken," Marran said as she got to work. "I learned that facing every conflict that struck Stromgarde; settling into this castle for a time, only to be spirited away to the country or shuttled about our allies' holdfasts. Through it all, I read nothing but our glorious histories, watching as my parents died and my uncle rode to war again and again. I sat in this keep feeling helpless, realizing what precious little remained of the legacy of Arathor."

or shuttled about our allies' holdfasts. Through it all, I read nothing but our glorious histories, watching as my parents died and my uncle rode to war again and again. I sat in this keep feeling helpless, realizing what precious little remained of the legacy of Arathor."

Jaina could only watch in horrified fascination as Marran began to skin the wolf, sickened by what she knew this ritual represented.

"Dalaran's fall marks the passing of yet another human kingdom, though it had become unrecognizable in recent times. Gilneas succumbed for so long to blight, and we do not speak of what transpired in Alterac . . . or Lordaeron."

There came a terrible ripping sound as Marran separated skin from muscle and bone. "You nearly lost your seat in the Fourth War. And Stormwind . . . what used to be a *backwater* country, now leads us, determines what cut of the Alliance's takings *we* may taste."

The regent of Stromgarde cut the skin carefully from the back now, hefting her prize with a spatter of blood. Sheathing the knife, Marran dragged the pelt clear of the wolf and laid it out over the ancient flagstones of Arathor. "The people look to us for strength, but we sell it time and again to the Alliance. We send their armies our grain while the Stromic starve. We send them our fighters while our children grow up not knowing their storied legacy. As we struggle to repel the ogres, the Syndicate, or worse."

Marran stood back and took the torch once again from the sconce. In its flickering light, Jaina could see Marran's skin was slick with sweat, her chest heaving at the exertion. But she saw something else too. The regent stood in silence before the pelt, staring down at it, entranced, even though she was the one who had just prepared it.

Jaina felt her heart sink as she realized the truth.

Marran was more than just an inexperienced ruler, an idealist.

She was a *believer.* A believer in a glorious past that Jaina also knew to be fantasy. Marran worshipped a misguided, even dangerous nostalgia for a golden age she had never experienced herself.

Marran looked at Jaina. "The Arathi Highlands belong to humanity. They are the heart of a great empire whose blood runs in *our* veins even now, Jaina. We must purge them of all invaders and take back our kingdom. It is our birthright. It is what Thoradin fought for. And we are—*I am*—destined to continue his legacy."

Jaina struggled to contain her disdain as she spoke. "Marran, you are set on a path of annihilation."

"Will you help me, Jaina?"

Jaina shook her head, lost for words.

At this, Marran seemed to tense, bracing for a blow.

"I knew you wouldn't understand," she said. "And I'm sorry."

Jaina felt a sharp sting, and something clattered on the stone-flagged floor. Jaina's hand flew to her neck, and her fingertips came away bloodied. She turned and saw an archer step out of the shadowed corridor behind them. A woman in a long black hooded cloak—the same bowman, Zatacia, who had shot Thrall and intercepted Jaina's letter.

And then Jaina collapsed, hitting the hard floor, her staff rolling out of her grip. She looked up, tried to focus on Marran as the world began to gray around her.

Marran ducked down and picked up a dart from the floor before collecting the wolf pelt. "That won't kill her, right? I can't have the entire Alliance at us too."

The archer smirked. "The Daughter of the Sea will sleep well tonight."

And then Jaina was lost to the darkness.

4
MARRAN'S CHOICE

As twilight fell on the Highlands, Thrall looked out over the dusky landscape from his position atop one of Hammerfall's many watchtowers. In the distance, the vague shadow of Stromgarde's tallest tower was quickly swallowed by the falling night.

Thrall wondered how Jaina's mission was going. It couldn't be any worse than his.

"Go'el!"

He didn't turn as Geya'rah climbed the watchtower. For a moment, he felt the heat of anger rise again, but he quickly quelled it. He had spent hours in solitude and had thought much about what had been revealed—and how he felt about it. He still wasn't sure, but he did know that he wasn't here to fight Geya'rah.

The Mag'har leader leaned on the wall next to him. He could feel the tension between them, and he didn't like it.

He sighed and turned to face her. "I'm sorry."

Geya'rah bowed her head. "It's I who should apologize. I . . . wanted to tell you when the time was right. You should never have found out in the middle of a war council." She looked up and met Thrall's gaze. "I am sorry. Truly. I allowed my anger to take over."

"So did I," said Thrall. "And the truth is, I *am* angry. But I know that feeling will give way to gratitude in time."

She barked a laugh. "Gratitude? Aggra and I should keep secrets from you more often, it seems."

He smiled. "You are a gift, Geya'rah, truly. One I never expected to receive. To know I have a sister, even one from a world—a timeline—different from mine. To know I am not alone. To know that through you I can learn about our parents, even as we learn about ourselves."

"Durotan and Draka—at least, my Durotan and Draka—would have loved you," said Geya'rah softly, "just as they loved me. I should not have spoken ill of our father before. I shamed his memory. It saddens me that you never felt that love."

Thrall shook his head. "I had the good fortune to know them for a time, before you were born, and to meet our mother's spirit in the Shadowlands, to fight alongside her. These encounters alone were enough to fill my cup, but to have a sister too? I hope to know you better, and to hear your memories of Durotan and Draka, if they are not so painful to share. We are nothing but the sum of our memories, all of us. Durotan and Draka live on—through us."

They fell into a more comfortable silence.

"About Aggra," said Geya'rah. "Please, do not be hard on her."

Thrall nodded. "I've thought of little else besides you and Aggra these last few hours. I know the heavy burden a secret can be. And I know it was not hers to share."

Geya'rah inclined her head. They moved to the other side of the watchtower, where Thrall could look down into the muster yard of Hammerfall. Even as night fell, the Kor'kron were busy training.

"You are a fine leader, sister."

"Must run in our bloodline."

Thrall sighed. Even as he did not want to turn to it, there was more urgent business at hand.

"You must hear me, Geya'rah. I have seen enough injustice against our people to fill a lifetime—*several* lifetimes. But I have always tried, at least, to stay true to a single path, to walk toward an ideal that all our people can strive for." He gestured at the activity down in the yard. "Sometimes that ideal must be reached through battle. But more often it can be reached through peace."

Geya'rah shook her head. "Marran will not speak with us, Go'el. She doesn't care about our claim to this territory. She does not believe in our right to exist *at all*. She will not stop until the flag of Stromgarde flies over this very watchtower . . . or it is razed to the ground." She sighed. "At least when the Mag'har faced the Lightbound, they offered us a choice."

Thrall nodded, acutely aware of the history Geya'rah spoke

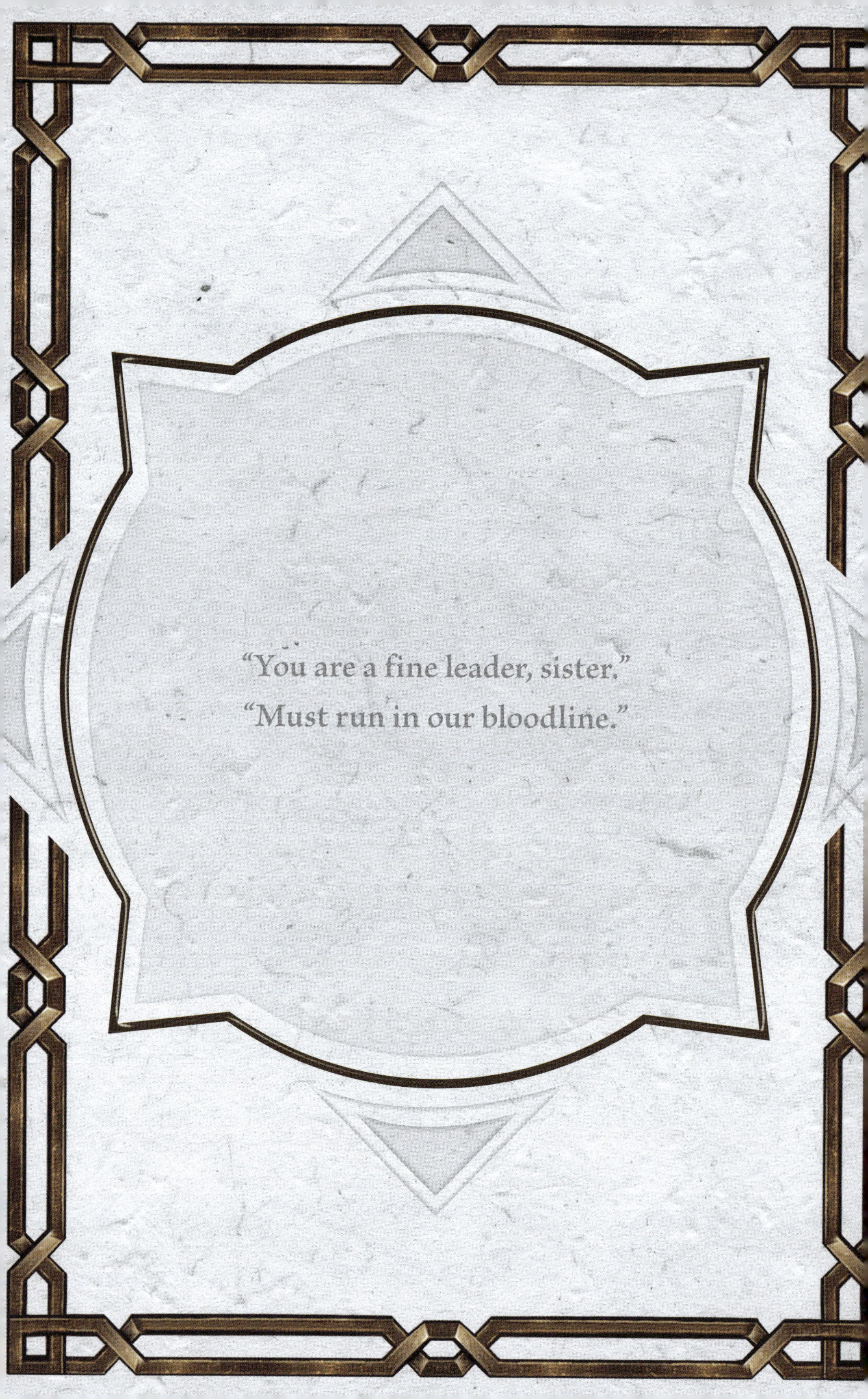

"You are a fine leader, sister."

"Must run in our bloodline."

of. "Your first responsibility is to your people," he said. "I will not deny that. But I will give you this challenge, Geya'rah: Find where Stromgarde is hurting. Seek out the pain that drives them to this path, and you may find that better way. Perhaps Marran will never choose peace over victory, but the people of Stromgarde might." He looked up at the far horizon as the two moons of Azeroth, the White Lady and the Blue Child, began their journey skyward. "It is not just the Arathi Highlands that are in danger—it is all of Azeroth."

"Xal'atath," said Geya'rah. "Aggra tried to explain the situation while you slept. I fear I pushed her away."

"Jaina will make Marran see sense. I know it."

Geya'rah tightened her fist. "I cannot believe that Marran will agree so easily."

Thrall raised an eyebrow. "But will *you*?"

"I will help, Go'el. You know I will. But we must fight one battle at a—"

A horn sounded, distant. Geya'rah froze, then ran to the opposite wall. Thrall followed and soon spotted a raider tearing up the road to the main gates. The orc blew his horn again, this time answered by the same from within Hammerfall itself.

"Raider!" yelled Geya'rah, leaning over the parapet. "What news?"

"The 7th Legion, the Stromic army!" The raider's wolf mount rose up on its hind legs and howled at the rising moons. "They march! We are under attack!"

The yard below jolted into frantic activity. No sooner had the war horns sounded than the Kor'kron and Mag'har assembled, quickly organizing themselves into companies of raiders. Thrall turned to where Geya'rah had stood just a moment before, but quickly realized she was already gone. Thrall could only despair as the Kor'kron headed out through the opened gates, ready for battle.

"Thrall!"

As the last of the mounted warriors rode out of the muster yard, Thrall saw Eitrigg and Aggra waving at him. He hastened over to join them, the trio clasping hands in greeting.

"Eitrigg is with us," said Aggra. "The Kor'kron will stand down if you command it."

Eitrigg cursed under his breath. "This could very well start a new war," he said. "I will not let the armistice that Varok Saurfang fought for die so easily." He laid a heavy hand on Thrall's shoulder. "Say the word, my friend, and I will deliver your orders to Talgar."

"No," Thrall cut in. "Not yet. Countering Geya'rah's command would only sow chaos on the field. I may be able to sway her, but I must reach her."

"Luck, then, my friend," said Eitrigg. As the old chieftain rushed off, Thrall surveyed the muster yard, spotting the wolf stables on the other side.

"Come," he called to his mate. "We may yet have a chance."

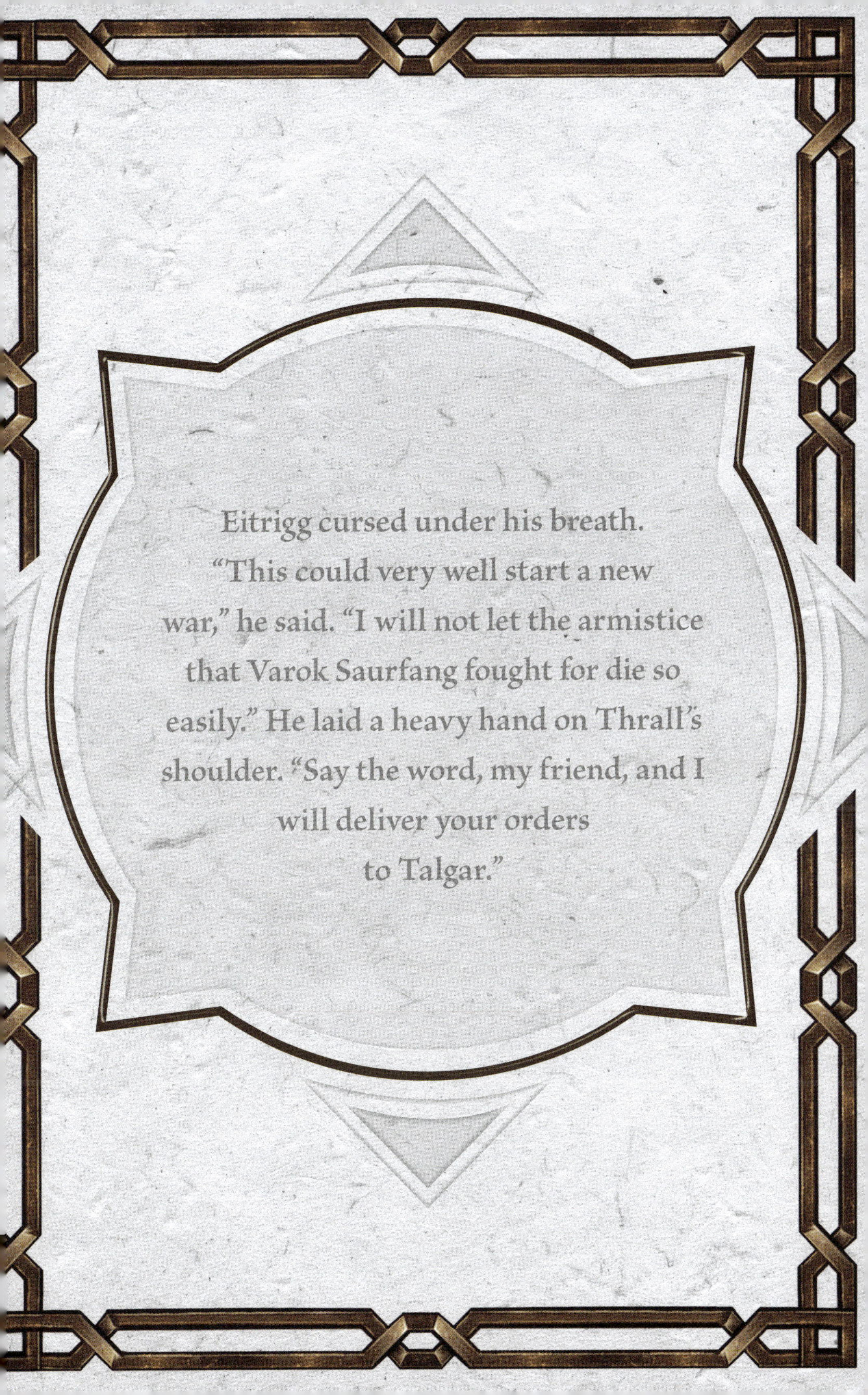

Eitrigg cursed under his breath. "This could very well start a new war," he said. "I will not let the armistice that Varok Saurfang fought for die so easily." He laid a heavy hand on Thrall's shoulder. "Say the word, my friend, and I will deliver your orders to Talgar."

Jaina woke with a start. The room was dark and eerily quiet. She sat up, only for the thundering pain in her head to almost send her back to oblivion. Closing her eyes, she counted to ten, then tried again—slower this time.

This seemed to work. She saw she was back in her quarters, but it was now night. She gingerly felt her neck. Zatacia's dart had only just grazed her, but it had been enough to deliver a knockout dose of sleeping poison.

Or had it? Because now Jaina was awake, and while it was night, she realized that the effects of the poison had worn off far sooner than Marran had planned. She moved to the window and opened the drapes, revealing a city brightly lit by two moons high in the night. A city that was quiet and still—far too still. While it was reasonable to expect the citizens of Stromgarde had retired for the night, there was also no sign of the 7th Legion or Stromic army below.

It didn't take Jaina long to realize why. She could hear it—distant, but clear. The shouted commands, loud over the clank of plate armor; the thunder of many steel boots marching beside the trot of heavy horses. And there, coming out from behind the far city wall, ordered rows of flaming torches, carried by troops as they advanced in the night toward the orcish holdings.

Jaina wasted no time. She had to stop Marran before it was too late.

Picking up her staff from the floor, Jaina focused her power and teleported out of the room.

Atop a crest a few miles from Hammerfall, Thrall swiftly dismounted, ducking down into the shadowed cover of the tall rocks to get a view of the battlefield. He turned at the sound of Aggra's mount following up the slope, waving a hand for her to join him in the shelter.

On their journey from Hammerfall they hadn't sighted Geya'rah at all, though their search had been impeded both by the darkness and the battle itself. Even now, as he and Aggra watched the fighting below them, it was all Thrall wished to be able to somehow stop the bloodshed. It wasn't just the warriors who would die needlessly this night—there were civilians too, common folk on both sides who had made the Highlands their home and who now found themselves in the middle of a pointless, bloody fight.

"Go'el, there!"

Thrall followed Aggra's outstretched hand—and yes, there was Geya'rah. The Mag'har leader, still on her mount, was perhaps half a mile distant, her axe swinging as she fought off one hapless Stromic soldier who dared get too close. As the man fell, Geya'rah reined in her mount, then disappeared down a hillside.

"Come," Thrall said. "We must get to her."

But Aggra did not move. "You have your mission," she said. "But there is more I might do." She pointed down at the battle. "I can feel the elements would lend their aid to stopping this violence—even if it means tearing the very earth of the Highlands apart. It is there I must go."

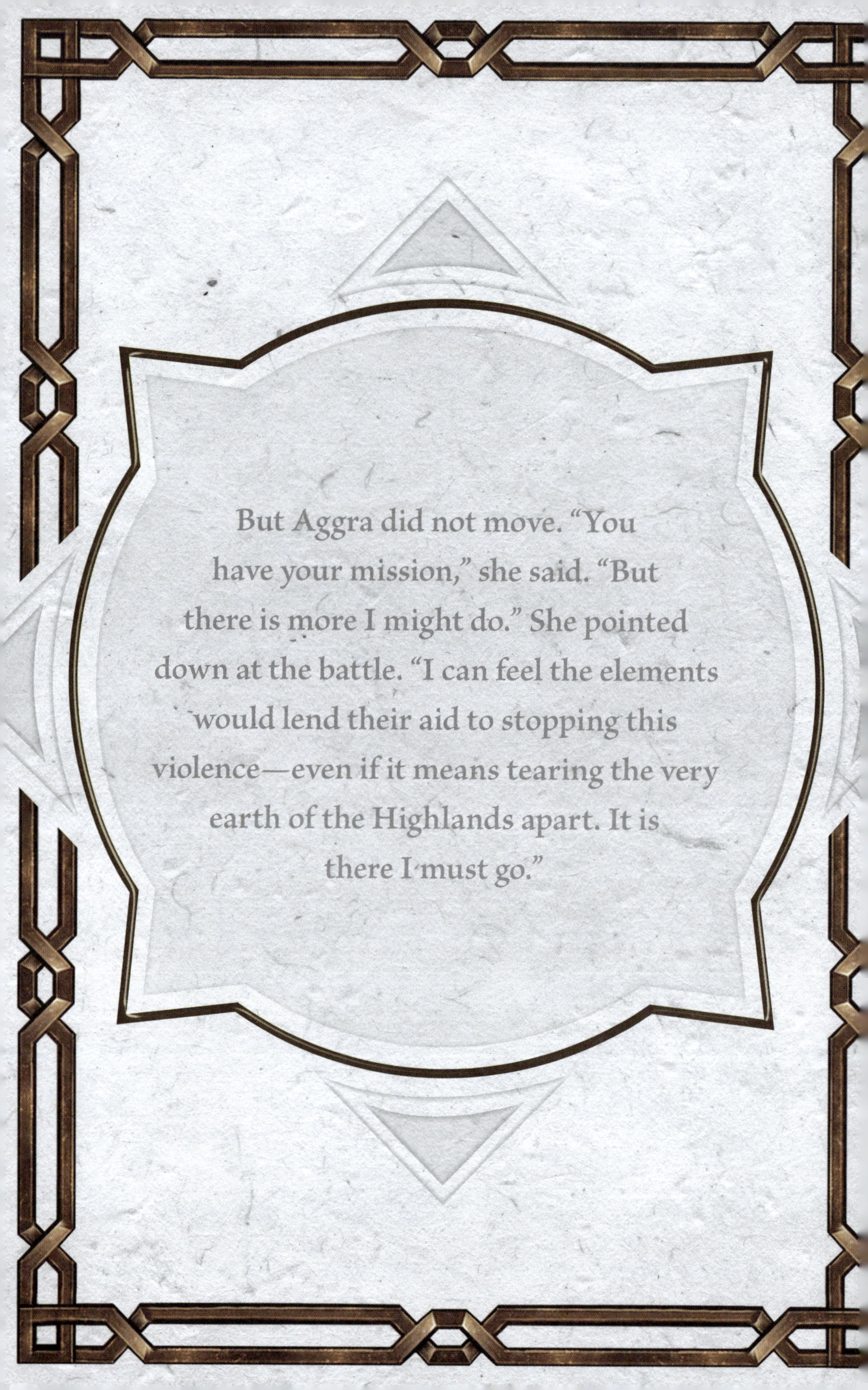

But Aggra did not move. "You have your mission," she said. "But there is more I might do." She pointed down at the battle. "I can feel the elements would lend their aid to stopping this violence—even if it means tearing the very earth of the Highlands apart. It is there I must go."

Thrall looked wary. Though he would never doubt Aggra's skill, he knew well the chaos of battle and the many friends he'd lost on the field. "You're certain?"

Aggra nodded as she mounted her wolf. He registered only a moment of shock on her face before she cried, "Go'el, down!"

Thrall did exactly as Aggra commanded, ducking as somewhere over his head came the roar and heat of flame. Risking a glance at the hillside, Thrall saw a fire elemental careening toward a squad of 7th Legion soldiers who were advancing toward them. At Aggra's command, the fire elemental exploded before it reached its target, the resulting shockwave knocking the humans back.

Immediate danger over, Thrall stood. The dazed humans rolled on the ground, groaning, as he went back to Aggra.

"I suppose I have no reason to worry," he said, and to his surprise he found the compliment sticking just a little in his throat. Aggra's command of the elements was indeed masterful, and he was . . .

He cleared his throat. At this, Aggra smiled.

"They will come back to you, am'osh. As will I."

Thrall smiled as he watched Aggra disappear into the fray. Then he returned to his wolf and took the reins.

Jaina materialized back in the same hollow she and Thrall had first arrived in.

She reeled, senses alive to the battle already raging around her.

At her back, a squad of 7th Legion—recovering from the surprise of her sudden arrival—lifted their weapons as warriors of the Kor'kron appeared on two sides from behind the ridgeline. The orcs, their battle cry loud enough to make Jaina's ears ring, charged down the slope. The humans, answering, braced themselves for combat.

Jaina was caught right in the middle. Spinning on her toes, she swept her staff in a great horizontal arc, the crystal lighting the hollow with its magic, her hands radiating frost and snow. Around her, a water elemental spawned with a great splash, the apple-size globe of blue-and-pink light growing instantly into a towering giant of energy. It surged out, rolling like a wave as it pushed both humans and orcs out of the hollow.

Racing up the slope, already conjuring another elemental, Jaina saw a troop of warriors engaged in a fierce melee.

Staff alight, Jaina channeled the arcane. She might not be able to stop the battle single-handedly, but she could do her best to keep the combatants apart and casualties low.

Geya'rah raced across the battlefield, cutting through the wheat fields of Go'Shek Farm on her mount, axe high to rally the Kor'kron as the army spilled out behind her. Already the 7th Legion was close to their holdings, already she could hear the din of battle as advance riders from both sides clashed in the shadowed foothills of the Arathi Highlands. To attack at night was madness, Geya'rah knew, but she expected nothing less from Marran Trollbane.

She did not expect to see flashes of vibrant color in the distance, however. As her warriors surged around her and met their enemies in bloody combat, Geya'rah commanded her mount to a nearby hilltop so that she might survey the scene.

She glimpsed a mage, aiding the battle for the humans.

Jaina Proudmoore.

Geya'rah felt the fury burn within her. It seemed the Alliance treachery ran deeper than her brother knew. She would put a stop to this interference.

With a battle cry, Geya'rah kicked her heels into her mount and rode off toward the mage, but as she crested the next hill, she realized all too late that she had charged straight into an attack.

She saw the flash of light, bright as the morning sun's first shard, and then the water elemental, summoned by Jaina, barreling toward her, growing in size until it filled her entire vision. Geya'rah knew it was too late to even try to outrun it, but she still pulled the reins of her mount, turning the beast, which howled in protest in a last-ditch attempt to avoid contact.

The elemental struck her like a runaway kodo, and as the magical creature vanished in a splash of purple light, Geya'rah found herself thrown from her mount.

5
The BATTLE of GO'SHEK FARM

Geya'rah blinked the spots from her vision and pushed herself to her feet, shaking her head as she regained her senses. Tumbling down a steep hillside, she'd been fortunate enough to hit something soft—a haystack?—at the bottom. She looked around to get her bearings.

She was in a farmstead—a human one. It seemed she'd been swept some distance from Go'Shek, to Stromic holdings. The place was deserted, but Geya'rah took no chances. She skirted the rocky hillside and headed back toward the sound of fighting, aiming for a large barn that would provide good cover.

"Stop!"

She skidded to a halt as a tiny form leapt out of the structure, right in her path. It was a human—a *child*, she realized, no more than a dozen years of age, holding a sword that was longer than he was tall, and clearly far more than he could handle.

Geya'rah hissed in disgust. Was Marran so desperate she would conscript *children* to fight for her?

"You will not take our crops!" the boy yelled, lifting the unwieldy weapon as best he could. "Mother and Father worked hard all season, and the castle collected most of the harvest as tax. We'll starve! I won't let you take them!"

Geya'rah took a breath. This child was no soldier. He was protecting the farm—his home. "Little one, I will not hurt you," she said gently. "And I am not here to steal—none of the Mag'har are." She walked slowly toward him.

The boy stumbled and fell backward. Abandoning his weapon, he crabbed toward the barn, only to be quickly yanked backward by a pair of hands.

"You stay away from us!"

Geya'rah stopped and peered into the barn. There, huddled in the darkness, were people—many people, older men and women, children, and even babes in arms. Geya'rah took a step forward, and almost as one the humans shrieked in fear and shrank back before her.

There was not a soldier among them. These were regular people, people who had settled the Highlands to find peace and good work, following a dream or a promise or perhaps just a chance, trying to make lives for themselves and their families. And now war had come, a fight they hadn't asked for and didn't want.

All they wanted to do was *live.*

At the front stood two men. One was older than the other; both were lean from a lifetime of hard labor. They held makeshift weapons—a hoe for the older man, a bent pitchfork for the younger—that made Geya'rah cringe in pity.

The older man lifted his chin in defiance, although when he spoke, the trembling fear in his voice was plain.

"Marran's told us all about you orcs!" he said. "Bloodthirsty and cruel, you are!"

"And starving!" said the younger man. "Desperate for what we have, right? You'd put us all to the sword and take what is ours for yourself!"

Geya'rah felt the energy leave her. She knew just how big she was compared to them, how terrifying she must look, fitted for war. They were afraid of her. Desperately so. And, Geya'rah knew, it was the same for her people. Right now, in Go'Shek Farm, she knew the same scene could unfold so easily. Orc families and farmers, confronting a terrible, faceless enemy, one determined to *kill* and *take* and *conquer.*

She took a step back, but her movement made the whole group flinch.

"We came here seeking peace," she said. "To escape war in *our* world. We did not come here to fight."

But it was no use. The humans weren't even listening. All they saw was an enemy—big, strong, frightening. *Different.*

The 7th Legion were mighty, but even before the battle Geya'rah knew the Stromic were fewer in number. The Kor'kron, backed by the Mag'har forces, outnumbered them three to one, if not more. Marran Trollbane's relentless hatred had led her to attack despite the odds. It was going to be a massacre. After the legionnaires were finished, the farmers—these people—would be next to fight. The humans would be wiped out, and that very thought sickened Geya'rah. The children in this barn would learn hatred, something they would pass to another generation. Here was battle without honor, feeding an unending cycle of animosity. All their victory would do was cement this feeling as fact.

But maybe it was a cycle she could still break. Marran may hate her—Geya'rah *knew* she did—but Geya'rah couldn't let Marran's hatred change who she was, or who the Mag'har were.

She remembered Thrall's words—*Find where Stromgarde is hurting. Seek another way.*

Well, here it was. Stromgarde and Hammerfall had more in common than not.

"Geya'rah!"

The humans screamed as Thrall rode in on wolf-back. Geya'rah held up a hand, motioning him to stay where he was.

"We can stop this," Geya'rah said to Thrall. "We *must* stop this."

Thrall looked at the humans and nodded. "There are many battles to fight, but this is not one of them. You can save these people, and yours. That power is in your hands."

Geya'rah nodded. "I understand." She swung herself onto

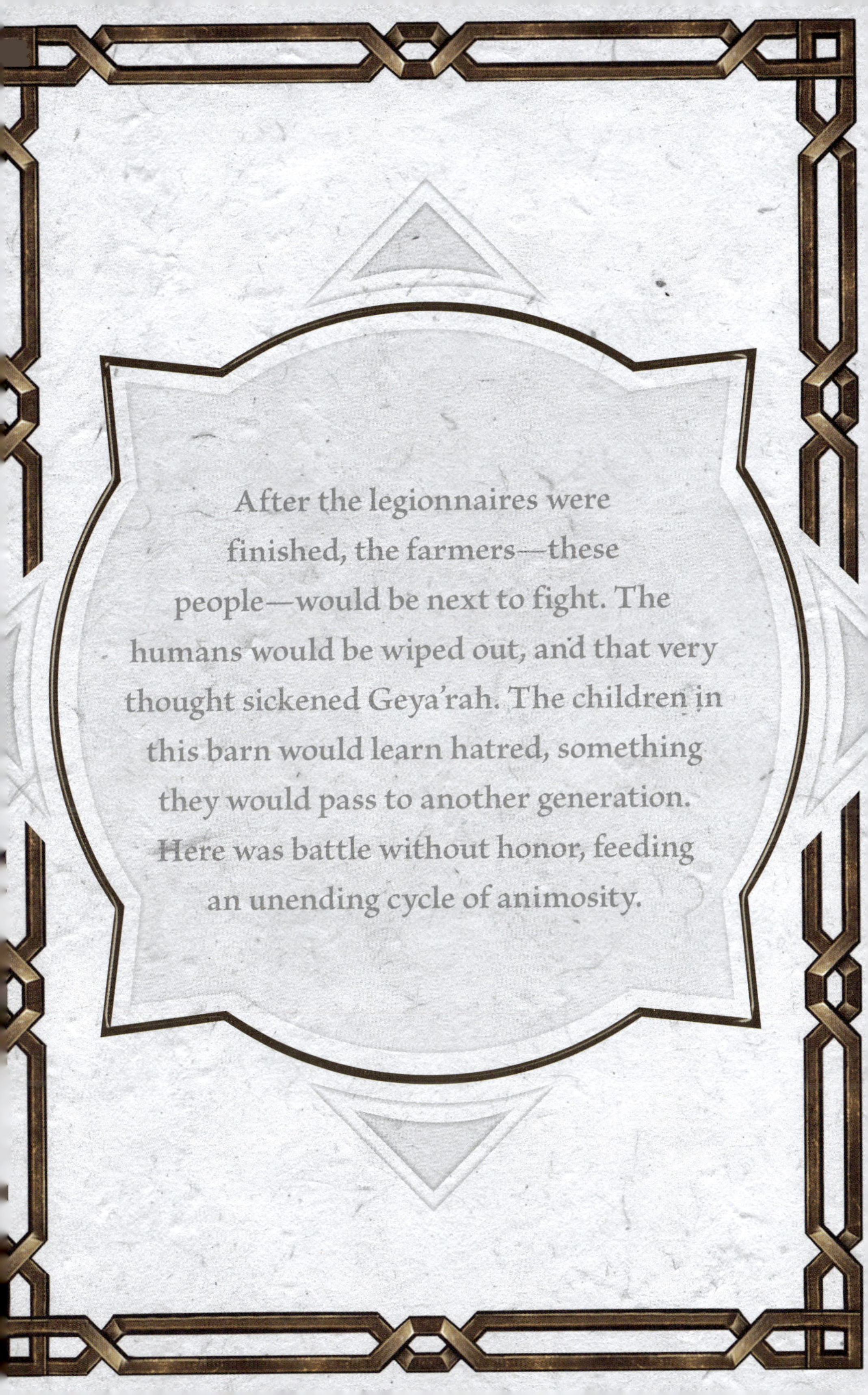

After the legionnaires were finished, the farmers—these people—would be next to fight. The humans would be wiped out, and that very thought sickened Geya'rah. The children in this barn would learn hatred, something they would pass to another generation. Here was battle without honor, feeding an unending cycle of animosity.

Thrall's mount behind him. "But how?"

Thrall flicked the reins. "I think I know. But we must find Aggra—she and Jaina are doing what they can to stop the fighting."

With a yell, Thrall encouraged his mount, and they headed up the hillside.

This is hopeless, thought Jaina as she raced across the battlefield. While she was doing her best to keep fighters away from each other with arcane magic, she knew she couldn't be everywhere at once, and she had seen enough fighting to know which side was going to win.

Marran had gambled, and she had lost. Now Jaina had to find her before it was too late.

Summoning an arcane familiar beneath her boots, Jaina allowed herself to be lifted high into the air in an attempt to spot Marran—and she quickly saw that she was very close. Marran was just ahead, urging her troops forward, clad in the wolf pelt she'd thought symbolic of her right to rule.

Jaina dismissed her servant, which dissolved beneath her. Using that momentum, she sprinted forward and landed next to Marran. Jaina summoned a portal and, tackling Marran around the waist, dived through it. The pair fell out onto a clear patch of ground, some distance away, the portal snapping shut behind them.

Marran got to her feet, but Jaina was faster, aiming her staff squarely at the regent.

"Is this how the Alliance treats its own, Lord Admiral? Compliance by force?"

Jaina approached, ready to subdue the regent if necessary. "Open your eyes, Marran! For all your talk of the Alliance chasing meaningless battles, you've started the most meaningless one of all." Arcane energy crackled down her staff. "You've lost. I won't let you inflict further damage on your kingdom or the Alliance."

Above them, the sky flared red, blinding in the failing night. Jaina gasped in surprise and stepped back, turning her focus from Marran as she shielded her eyes. The two women looked to the north. There, from a nearby hilltop, a column of roiling flame shot into the night sky, bright enough to light the entire landscape where the Kor'kron and the 7th Legion stood, frozen in battle, all eyes on the figure Jaina could now see illuminated by the rising sun.

Geya'rah.

Atop her mount, the Mag'har leader raised a war horn to her lips. As she blew, the sound reverberating across the battlefield, Jaina could now see two other figures with her—Aggra and Thrall.

The sound of the war horn faded, and Geya'rah spoke, her powerful voice echoing against every hill, in every hollow, the undulating landscape of the Arathi Highlands acting as the perfect natural amplifier. "There will be no battle here! There is no honor in this slaughter! The Kor'kron and Mag'har will hold. I call upon the 7th Legion and Stromic army to do the same!"

Jaina turned to survey the battlefield from her new vantage point. The light of the rising sun stretched its tendrils almost from Hammerfall behind them to Stromgarde on the far horizon. It also illuminated the terrible cost of the fight. She could see bodies strewn across the Highlands, many fallen on both sides—Stromic, Mag'har, 7th Legion, and Kor'kron.

"Stromgarde, hear me!" Geya'rah continued. "This land is yours. But Mag'har, hear me also, for this land is *ours* too. There is room and riches enough for both our peoples to share, and much to be gained in partnership. This battle is unwarranted, but your strength is still *needed.* There is a new land waiting, and a new enemy too—not just of the orcs, or of the humans, but of all the peoples of Azeroth. We sail for Khaz Algar. I challenge the 7th Legion to have the strength to sail with us!"

There was silence across the battlefield. And then, as Jaina watched, a powerful-looking Kor'kron general stepped out of the ranks, watching from beneath the flame-lit hill. From the nearby line of the 7th Legion, a knight-commander emerged and walked up to the orcish general.

Jaina held her breath . . . and then the Kor'kron leader held out his hand. The knight-commander paused, then clasped the outstretched hand in his own.

"This isn't over," Marran hissed through clenched teeth, snapping Jaina's attention away from the others. "I follow the will of the people. So long as the blood of Arathor runs in my veins—"

"Stromgarde, hear me!" Geya'rah continued. "This land is yours. But Mag'har, hear me also, for this land is *ours* too. There is room and riches enough for both our peoples to share, and much to be gained in partnership. This battle is unwarranted, but your strength is still *needed*. There is a new land waiting, and a new enemy too—not just of the orcs, or of the humans, but of all the peoples of Azeroth."

That was when another voice cut in.

"If you would permit me a word with my regent, Lord Admiral?"

Jaina stepped to one side as Danath Trollbane walked out onto the field, leaders of the Stromic army following close behind.

Marran's eyes thinned to slits, locking with Jaina's as her uncle approached. "I showed you mercy beneath the keep. I don't make the same mistake twice."

Jaina joined Danath's side. "Neither do I. I didn't trust the situation in Stromgarde from the moment I passed under its gates. For all I knew, that courier would deliver the letter straight to you anyway."

"So she sent a raven too," continued Danath. "And what a very prescient decision that was."

Marran took a step toward Jaina, but was restrained by a Stromic captain.

"Captain Brewston, timely as always."

"My lord," the captain inclined his head. "What are your orders?"

"Marran Trollbane is hereby relieved of her official duties. Escort her to her chambers, where she will remain under arrest until I decide what to do with her." Danath turned to another in his party. "Captain Wren, organize search parties and bring in her supporters. I suspect there will be many still afield."

"Take care," said Jaina. "Marran has a spymaster—a hunter called Zatacia. She will be the most loyal of them and is an expert shot, adept with poisons."

Wren gave a salute, then began organizing his men. Jaina looked back at the hilltop, where she saw in the dying light of Aggra's fire the trio of orcs marching down the hillside toward them.

"Thrall!" she cried. "You are well!"

Thrall gestured to Geya'rah. "I've much to thank the Mag'har for," he said, before moving to Danath. The pair clasped forearms in greeting, and Danath bowed to the group.

"Thrall, my friend," he said. "Aggra. And Geya'rah, I am honored to meet you. I must apologize for my regent. She painted a different picture of her intentions than what culminated here. Stromgarde will offer reparations—"

"They are unnecessary," Geya'rah cut in. "I do not wish to punish your people for Marran's actions. Their losses here were great. I would like to quash this animosity between our peoples before it can grow further."

"You have my eager support in that," Danath said.

He turned to Jaina. "Kurdran and Turalyon wait for us at Stromgarde. I suggest we join them."

Dawn broke as the party, now joined by Talgar, Eitrigg, the Kor'kron, and the 7th Legion, arrived at Stromgarde.

Kurdran Wildhammer and Turalyon were waiting in the square outside the main keep. Turalyon shook Jaina's hand.

"Lord Admiral, the Sons of Lothar will answer your call."

Kurdran coughed. "Little dramatic, Turalyon? We've not gone by that name in . . . What? Two decades? More?"

The paladin grinned. "Maybe it's time we reclaim it." He turned to Jaina. "Once Danath gave me his report on the summit at Boralus, I realized the gravity of the situation. You'll have to forgive my absence at your council."

"Of course," Jaina said. "But tell me, what of the Radiant Song? How does Stormwind fare?"

Turalyon pursed his lips. "The troubles still weigh on my mind, but I've left Genn to rule—he'll keep a tight rein on things in my absence."

"We bring good news as well," said Danath. "The Kul Tiran fleet will dock here within the week."

"Excellent," said Geya'rah. "Time enough to prepare." She turned to indicate her orcish companions. "My general, Talgar," she said as the warrior inclined his head, "and my advisor, Eitrigg."

Eitrigg stood tall while Danath and Turalyon exchanged an uncomfortable glance. It was Danath who broke the silence, clearing his throat as he bowed stiffly to the Blackrock chieftain.

"It is good to see you again," he said. He looked up at his friend. "Isn't it, Turalyon?"

"Quite," said Turalyon, his expression tight. He and Eitrigg held each other's gazes for a moment, before Eitrigg turned to Jaina.

"Are we sure we want *these two* for champions?" Eitrigg smiled sharply. "Having faced both of them in the Fourth War, I can't say

I was impressed. Surely the Alliance can offer someone a bit . . . younger?"

Kurdran snorted a laugh before Jaina stepped between the trio.

"We should . . . hasten to make our plans," she said, turning a diplomatic smile on Eitrigg.

"An excellent suggestion," said Danath, letting out a long-held breath. "Please, if you will all follow me."

The group headed toward Stromgarde Keep, Thrall and Aggra at the rear. Now that the current crisis had been contained, the weight of their mission once again took precedence.

Aggra took Thrall's hand in hers. "It would seem you have your strike force."

Thrall nodded. "We must not fail," he said. "The fate of the world depends on it."

"And we won't," said Aggra. "We have won this battle. We will win the next. What is it that troubles you?"

Thrall looked up at the gates of Stromgarde. He would not soon forget standing before them, closed against him in hatred as he knelt, dying on the cobbles. Yes, they had succeeded in the end, but at what cost? As they turned their attention to Xal'atath and her machinations, what seeds of hatred grew their roots ever deeper in the Arathi soil? What bitter crop remained for Geya'rah and the Mag'har to later reap?

And this . . . bothered him. Marran was under arrest, yes, but she had supporters—including her spymaster who, according to Jaina, had shot *both* of them and remained at large. A dangerous loose end to leave, but Thrall had to trust that Danath's loyalists would be successful in their hunt. That they could stamp out what had started fomenting here.

These old hatreds, thought Thrall. *With every victory, they still remain. Perhaps they can one day be solved.*

Perhaps.

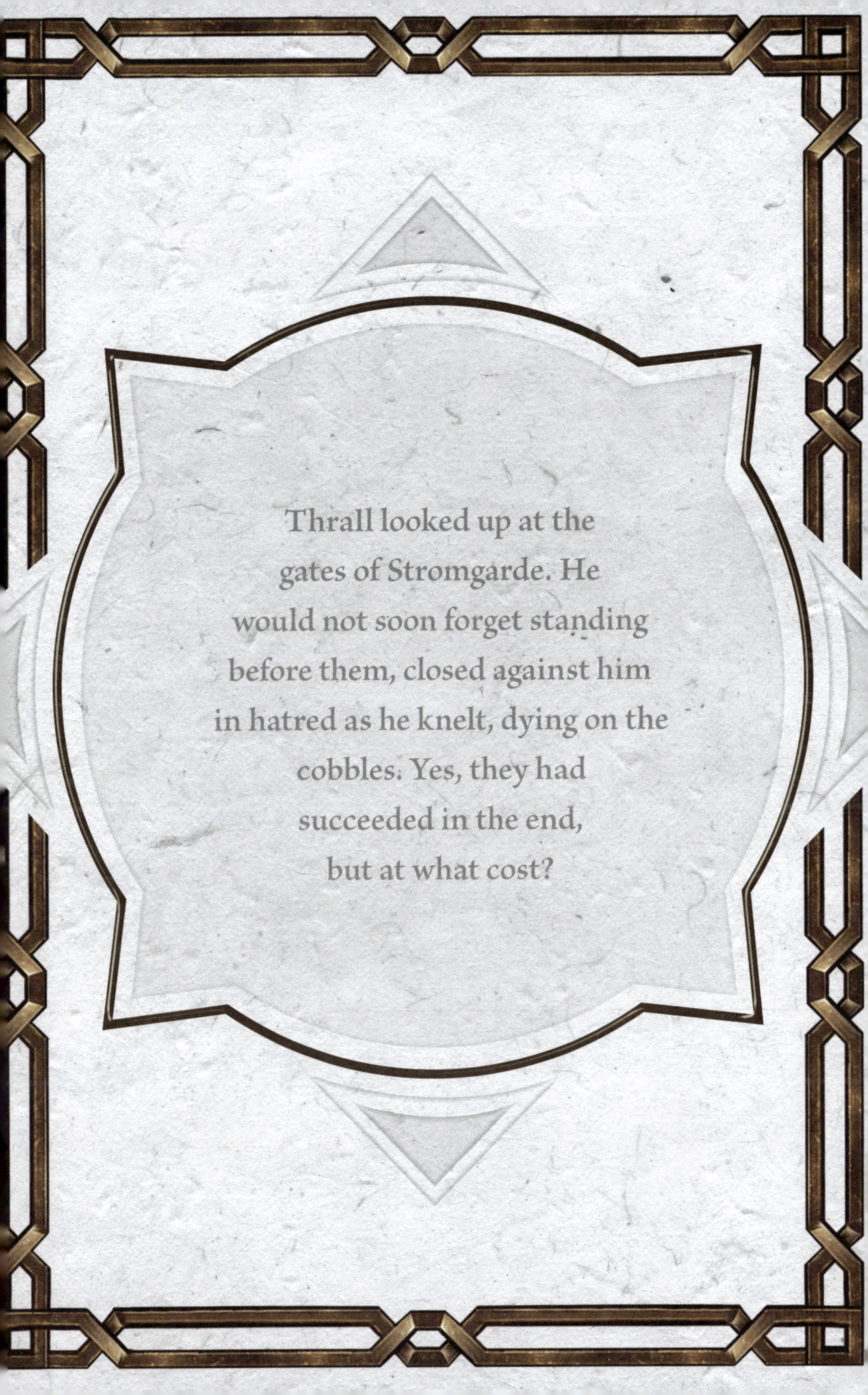

Thrall looked up at the gates of Stromgarde. He would not soon forget standing before them, closed against him in hatred as he knelt, dying on the cobbles. Yes, they had succeeded in the end, but at what cost?

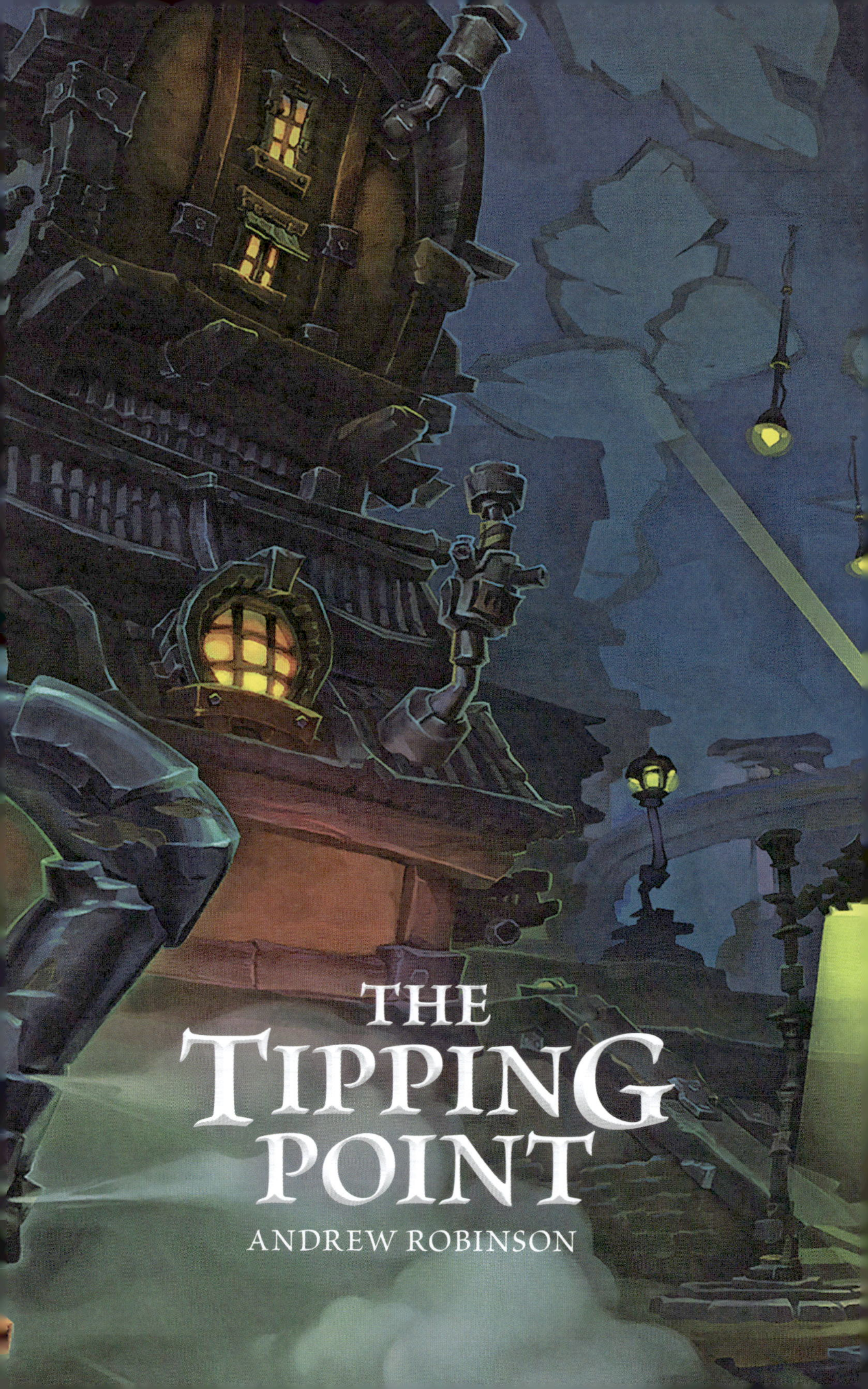
THE
TIPPING
POINT
ANDREW ROBINSON

THE TIPPING POINT

Vivi Vendklaxxon dug in as her ramshackle trike groaned beneath her. Getting through this pass was always the hardest part of the run. She downshifted, grinding gears, and—not for the first time, or even the twentieth—cursed the mechanics, the bosses who refused to pay for proper repairs (let alone new parts!), and the world in general. She *hated* driving cargo on the graveyard shift. The *pop* of a tire blowing was the last straw; she eased the limping vehicle over to the side of the road.

Vivi climbed down the trike, using rungs she'd installed herself, then hopped lightly to the ground. She examined the flat and was dismayed to find a large metal caltrop embedded in the tire.

"Ah, blast it," Vivi muttered. She spun around, only to find herself face-to-face with three tall figures, their faces hidden by black masks.

"Ooh, a flat tire," said the apparent leader. "Most regrettable, on a desolate stretch of road like this."

"No kidding," Vivi spat. "What luck you're here to put the spare on for me." She sensed the smile behind the mask.

"I don't suppose we will," he admitted. "What's your name?"

Vivi goggled for a moment, reaching for her wrench. What were they playing at? "Grizelda," she grunted. "And if you're not gonna help me, it's probably best you get on your way. Dangerous out here for travelers."

"That it is," he said, not unkindly.

She looked up at him. This could end very badly for her, but she'd worked her way out of tough situations before, even with pirates and highwaymen. "Do I get to know *your* name?"

"Not tonight, I think," he replied.

"Well, 'Not Tonight,' if you'll kindly shove off, I'll fix this *myself* and be on my way."

The masked figure laughed merrily, waving one hand, shaking his head. "I think not." Then he stopped, suddenly serious. "What's that you're towing, *Grizelda*?"

"Pickled peppers," Vivi snarled.

The other two figures climbed into the back of the cargo tow and wrestled a barrel to the ground. One used a crowbar to open it, revealing row upon row of small explosives packed neatly in straw.

The leader looked over the contents, then back at Vivi. "These peppers must pack quite a punch." He produced a long dagger. "Hold out your hand, please."

Vivi paled. "I-I didn't know," she stammered. "Please don't kill me!"

"*Kill* you? I'd prefer to avoid that if possible. Grizelda—if that *is* your name—I like you. That said . . ." He almost gently pricked her palm with the point of the blade; she looked at the tiny drop of blood it produced and suddenly felt woozy. The leader caught her as she lost consciousness and laid her gently in the seat of her trike. "We can't have you following us."

The bandits removed their masks and set about the task of hauling the shipment of explosives—each earmarked "V.C."—to their own nearby cart.

"Info was spot-on," his first companion remarked. "Nice work, Shaw. Good to have informants you can trust."

"Didn't think that was possible in the Undermine," the second said with a laugh.

Mathias Shaw smiled thinly. "We'll certainly put this to good use. And anything that puts a wrench into the Venture Company's operations is a good thing for Stormwind. With any luck, this will help destabilize the trade princes' hold on the Undermine too. Infighting will disrupt their supply chain."

The second agent shook his head. "If one trade prince falls, someone else will take their place," he said. "There's always another shark."

Shaw hefted another barrel. "We'll see."

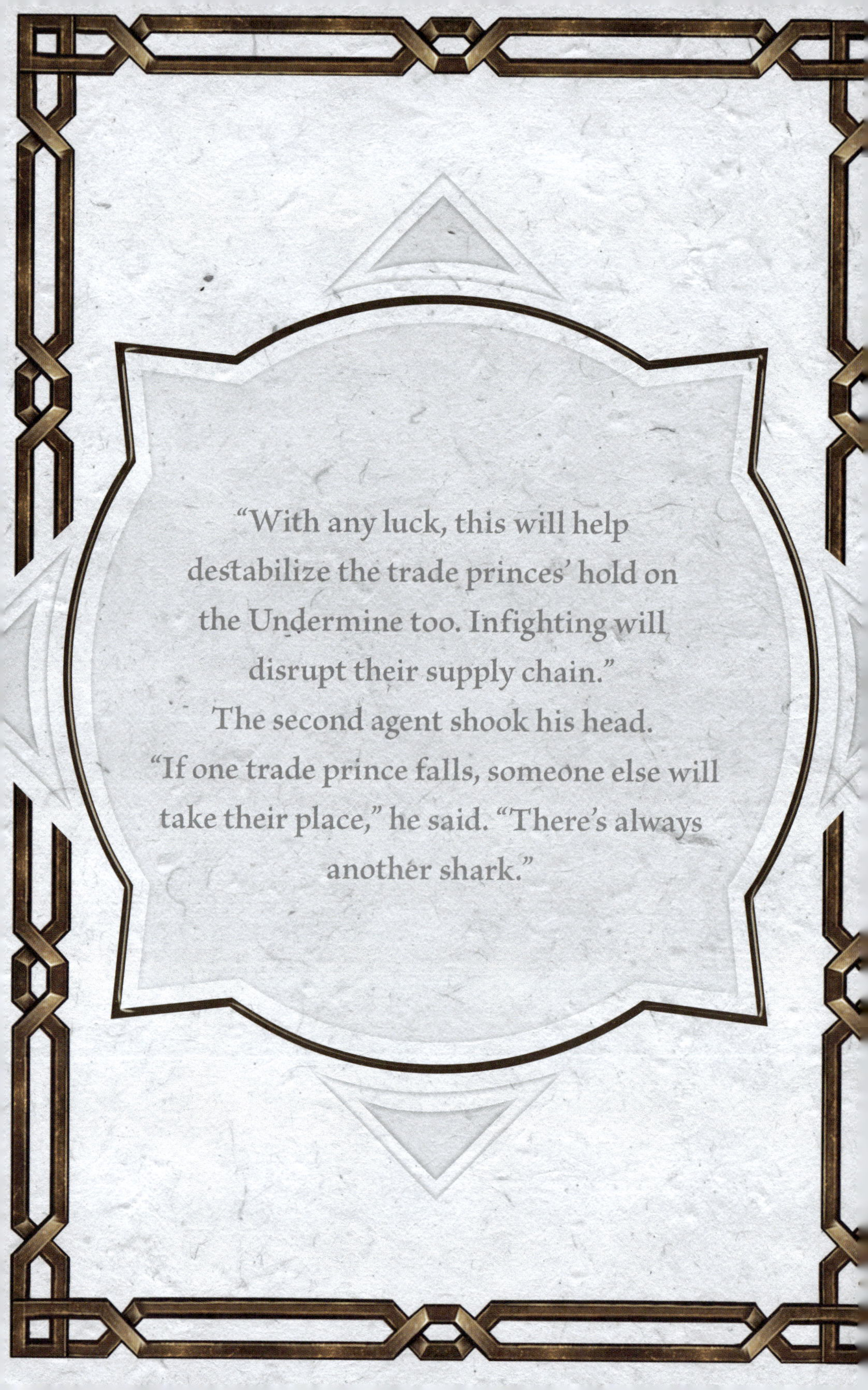

"With any luck, this will help destabilize the trade princes' hold on the Undermine too. Infighting will disrupt their supply chain."

The second agent shook his head. "If one trade prince falls, someone else will take their place," he said. "There's always another shark."

THE TIPPING POINT

The Undermine was always a little too cold, and usually a little too dank, for Renzik's comfort. He cricked his neck to one side, adjusting his long coat that was stiff with blades. Was it the most comfortable thing to wear? Honestly, no, but experience had taught him that the more weapons you had on your person, the more likely you were to live another day down here. He took a bite from his sandwich.

Renzik grunted at one of the two street urchins who stood looking up at him. The young goblins were both a little too skinny, but he knew the hunger in their eyes wasn't just for food; he'd lived in their shoes for years. "So whatcha got?"

"Heard Skunkie Splitflange was tossin' dice with the Slackhouse boys today."

"Did he win?"

"Does he ever?"

Renzik frowned. "He owes Trade Prince Gloxscorn five large."

"Yeah, we know." The second kid—a scrawny little girl, couldn't've been more than nine—jutted out her jaw. "That's why we ran to tell ya."

Renzik nodded. "Good job, Spatter, Jinzi." He divided the remains of his sandwich and handed both halves to the kids. As they stuffed their faces, Renzik dropped a few coins into their outstretched hands. "Go find out where he'll be tonight, but keep a low profile."

They nodded and moved quickly down the street, ducking into an alley, no doubt to count their take. Renzik allowed himself a faint smile.

"Aw, ain't that adorable," came a gravelly voice. Renzik had noticed the two midlevel brutes from the Krackslagger Cartel—Bask Topscrew and Gizgank Brokebolt—approaching, but he didn't want to pay them more attention than they deserved. "Shivvie's playin' with kids. What's wrong, Renzik, you miss your mommy? You goin' soft on us?"

Renzik's eyes narrowed as the two buffoons shared a laugh at his expense. His fist flashed out, meeting Bask's crooked nose with a *crunch*, and the bigger goblin fell to the greasy pavement, groaning in pain. Gizgank turned on Renzik but pulled up short at the shiv that had almost magically appeared in Renzik's other hand, now pressed hard against Gizgank's cheek. Renzik smiled unpleasantly.

"I seem *soft* to you?"

Gizgank gulped and shook his head.

"Because if I'm getting that reputation, I can think of two actions I could take right now to correct it."

"Okay, okay," Bask groaned as he staggered to his feet. "Don't gotta take it so personal. Just came to deliver a message. Boss is callin' in all the captains."

Renzik wondered what could be so important, but he knew it couldn't be good. "Okay, you delivered your message. Scram."

The brutes scowled but left, Bask holding a dirty kerchief to his bloodied face. "Ya broke my nose again," he grunted.

"Did you a favor," Renzik shot back. "*Again*."

He watched them turn the corner before sheathing his makeshift weapon. Dummies like that you could see coming a mile away, but nobody seemed to understand the value of street kids. As far as the Undermine was concerned, they were either a minor nuisance or completely invisible, which made them useful.

Renzik knew that truth from harsh experience. He'd spent most of his childhood as an orphan on the streets of the Undermine. He remembered the day his parents had been murdered for what little they had. The monsters who did it barely offered a word of consolation. *Nothin' personal, pipsqueak. This is just how it goes. It's a dog-eat-dog world out there, so ya better learn to eat.*

He spent the next few years of his life begging, stealing, and worse. He learned to give no mercy and to expect none in return. And he started to carry a shiv—his last line of protection on the mean streets. His "activities" caught the eye of a local captain who, catching him pilfering from a cashbox one night, was impressed with the kid's "moxie." Rather than ending Renzik, the captain put him to work.

As Renzik grew, older goblins would send him on increasingly dangerous errands: stealing, running contraband, sometimes knocking out a guard. When he succeeded, he ate. He earned a reputation as a strong fist and a reliable knife in the dark. Eventually, though, he got caught filching from one of the trade princes and was sent to work in the mines. The brutal conditions toughened him and made him even stronger.

Eventually, Renzik was recruited into the cartel of a local trade prince, Mozzy Gloxscorn. His childhood had taught him everything he needed to survive in the Undermine; few knew the back alleys and sewers better than he did. They called him "the Shiv"—for both his use of the improvised weapon and his ability to improvise himself—and he quickly rose through the ranks from lookout to runner, to brute, to enforcer. Eventually, he caught Mozzy's eye personally, and the trade prince named him a captain, part of his inner circle—a "made goblin," so to speak, the bloody fist of the Krackslagger Cartel.

To hear Mozzy tell it, Renzik had broken the nose of every goblin in the Undermine at least once, and broken noses was the least of it. His shiv had carved out the cartel's territory, its business, its enemies, but he had few regrets. Like he'd learned as a kid, it was dog-eat-dog down here, and he was happy enough to be alive with coin to burn.

That said, he had to admit he'd gotten a little tired of it all. Never a moment's peace; never knew who he could trust. He took some measure of pride in his skills—they were the reason he was still suckin' air on a daily basis—but lately the work was just . . . *stale.* Somewhere deep down, he knew this life was ugly, and he wished he'd walked a different road to get here. And the thing he almost

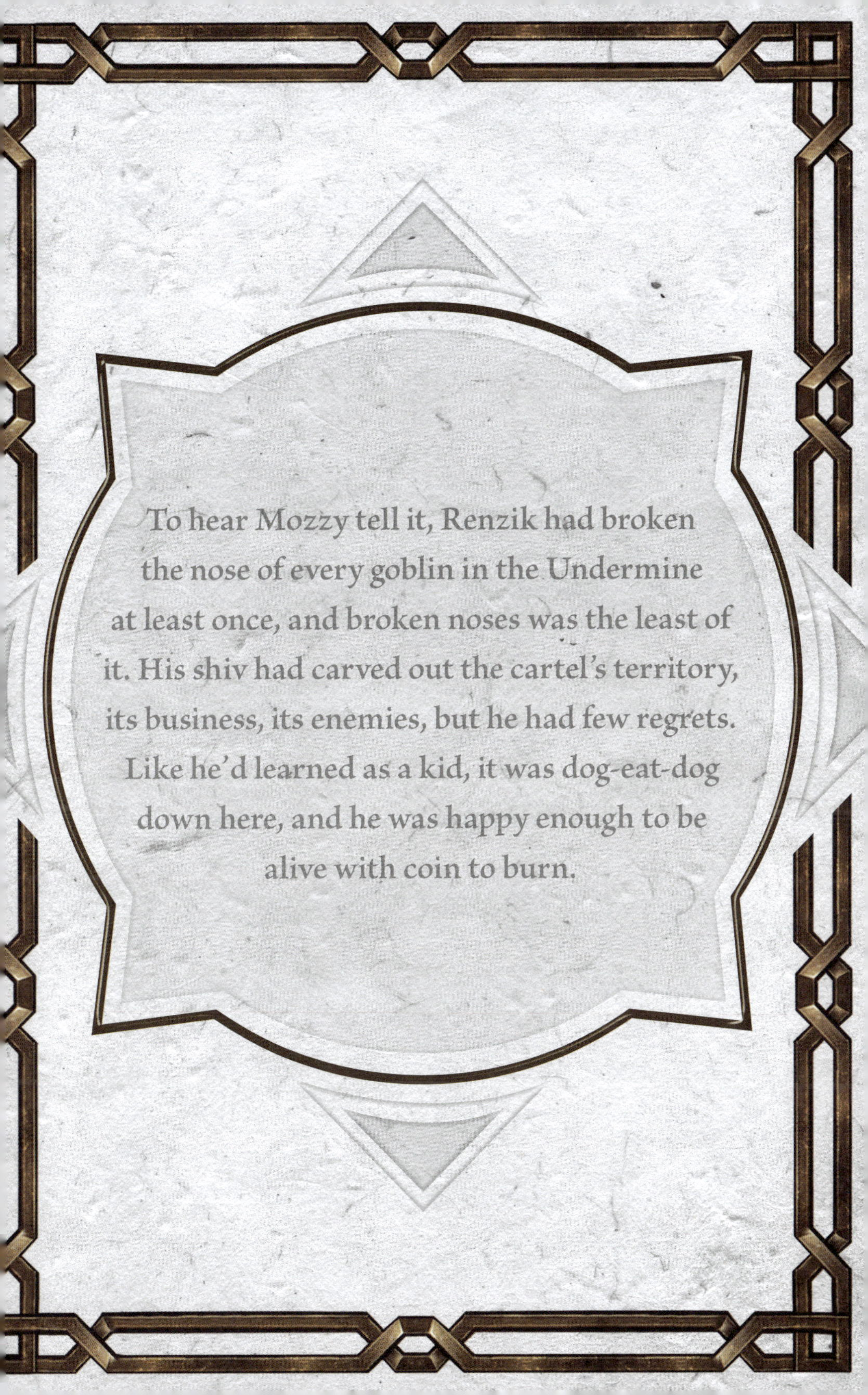

To hear Mozzy tell it, Renzik had broken the nose of every goblin in the Undermine at least once, and broken noses was the least of it. His shiv had carved out the cartel's territory, its business, its enemies, but he had few regrets. Like he'd learned as a kid, it was dog-eat-dog down here, and he was happy enough to be alive with coin to burn.

never dared admit to himself: he did indeed miss his mother. He'd never known a tender moment since the day she was murdered. He paused for a moment. *Did* he have a soft spot for those street kids? All he knew was, no kid deserved this life. And that little flame of injustice that had kept his heart beating all these years had never quite gone out.

He shook himself out of his reverie. It was being the best and most ruthless that had gotten him where he was. And he recognized that—albeit through force of will and violence—the trade princes had managed to create some stability in the Undermine, where there used to be only chaos. This was how things were done down here, and they would likely never change.

He started toward headquarters, wondering what Trade Prince Gloxscorn wanted.

Renzik sat uncomfortably at a long table with a dozen other high-level goblins. He hated meetings like this, partly because he hated not knowing what he was going into, but also because he didn't much care for people—particularly this group, none of whom he could trust as far as he could throw 'em.

Trade Prince Mozzy Gloxscorn, dressed in his trademark silks, stalked around the table, holding a rough club. "*Another* shipment got disrupted," Mozzy seethed, slamming the club on the table.

Several of the captains flinched. Renzik actually relaxed a little—this had nothing to do with him. The trade prince's shipping business was none of his concern—unless he got sent to strong-arm a customer who hadn't paid on time.

"This time it was mithril frag bombs!" Mozzy snarled as he dragged the spiked club across the carved wooden surface. "And the whole shipment was stolen!"

"Who'd be dumb enough to steal explosives from you, boss?" wondered one of the captains.

"Maybe *YOU*, Flumbuck," growled Mozzy, shoving the end of the club into Flumbuck's brand-new green leather jerkin. The spikes penetrated the shiny leather—and Flumbuck's chest.

"No, sir," came the gasped response. "Never!" Blood dripped down the leather, and Flumbuck's eyes bulged.

Renzik scowled. There were two kinds of people in the Undermine, the smart and the stupid, and Flumbuck . . . was not smart. Renzik had seen it coming, had known the boss was going to lash out, partly because he had to keep control of his people, but also partly because the trade prince was just violent and vindictive. It wasn't like Renzik had any affection for Flumbuck, but whatever his faults, the captain was as loyal as a dog.

Renzik cricked his neck to one side to cover his discomfort just as the door opened and a brute ushered in a diminutive female goblin.

"Trade Prince Gloxscorn, sir? This driver's got somethin' ta tell ya."

Mozzy turned to the driver. "What?"

Vivi Vendklaxxon nodded. "I was drivin' the trike that got bushwacked. It was three humans, sir. Men. Tall, all dressed in black. They knew what I was carrying—even though I didn't!"

"Why didn't you fight back?" Mozzy demanded.

She looked at him. "Against three armed robbers? Why weren't there guards along?"

"IT WAS SUPPOSED TO BE A SECRET!" he screamed. He calmed himself. "I want every pirate in the area rounded up. Mozzy Gloxscorn can't look soft. Make an example out of 'em."

Vivi coughed. "Beg your pardon, sir, but . . . I don't think it was pirates."

"Oh, really?" the trade prince sneered.

"Too . . . polite. Well spoken. And frankly? Pirates in these parts tend to smell rank—sea rot and dead fish. These guys smelled clean."

Mozzy paused to take this in as the captains rushed to redirect the trade prince's attention.

"Could be a competitor horning in on your affairs, sir."

"Could be the buyer, runnin' an end around!"

Mozzy turned a vicious eye on his captains.

"Or . . . it *could* be one of *you*, lookin' to line your pockets."

Furious denials ensued. Renzik looked around carefully at them all.

Mozzy barked with a harsh laugh. "Who knows—it could even

be someone from the Alliance lookin' to score some freebies. One thing I know for sure: some snitch in my organization is passing information to someone who's robbing me!"

The captains looked around uneasily, casting suspicious glares at one another. *Could* it be one of them?

"And *that* can't happen. Who. Knows. Why?" Mozzy looked at Flumbuck, who was trying to stanch his wounded chest. "Flumbuck?"

The wounded goblin looked up, pale. "It's b-bad for business?"

"IT'S BAD FOR BUSINESS!" Mozzy roared, swinging the club and taking splinters out of the table. "Explosives is our most lucrative operation! If any other trade princes think I'm weak, they might try to take me down. And if I go down, you mooks go down with me! Everything we've built is at risk!"

The captains assured Mozzy that they were innocent of treachery, wrongdoing, or incompetence, and promised to help him get to the bottom of this horrible malfeasance. "No," Mozzy growled. "Mind your businesses. Until we got more explosives ready to roll, you all are gonna have to pick up the slack. Now get out!"

The table cleared with astonishing speed, a brute hauling Vivi out of the room just in front of Renzik. As Renzik approached the door, Mozzy stuck the club out in front of him.

"Have a seat, Renzik."

Renzik looked at the club blocking his path, then up at Mozzy. "Sure, Mozzy. What can I do for you?"

Mozzy laid the club gently on the table. "*You're* gonna root out the snitch."

Renzik was surprised. "Me? I'm an enforcer. This is a job for a brains guy."

"You don't need brains for this." Mozzy grimaced. "And frankly, you're about the only goblin here I can trust."

Renzik nodded.

"Plus, y'know. You got a talent for pounding heads and getting things I need—money, information . . . *confessions*."

Renzik shrugged. "Whatever you say, Mozzy."

Mozzy smirked. "When you catch 'em, let 'em know their usefulness to this organization is terminated."

In the cellar beneath Trias' Cheese shop, Mathias Shaw pored over a complex map, frowning.

"What's this, then?" asked Elling Trias, setting down a stein of ale and a plate of aged cheddar.

"Working on how to get my informants out of the Undermine."

Trias cocked an eyebrow. "Why would you do that? An informant is only useful if they're in a position to gather information."

"Yes, but they're also of no use to me *dead*."

"Ah. Things took a nasty turn after your raid?"

"Indeed," Shaw replied. "Trade Prince Gloxscorn has his entire

Mozzy laid the club gently on the table. "You're gonna root out the snitch."

Renzik was surprised. "Me? I'm an enforcer. This is a job for a brains guy."

"You don't need brains for this." Mozzy grimaced. "And frankly, you're about the only goblin here I can trust."

territory on lockdown, looking for the traitor in his midst. My informants are pretty sure someone's going to find out about them."

"Not sure why that's your problem," the Master of Cheese offered. "All good things must end."

"That's awfully cynical." Shaw fixed Trias with a steady gaze. "They've put themselves at risk, they've given me good information, and Light help me, I can't just let them perish. If you had any idea how rare it is for a goblin to be willing to risk everything for an uncertain shot at a better world . . ."

"Vanishingly so, I imagine."

Shaw turned his gaze to the floor. "I've spilled plenty of blood in my career—or allowed it to be spilled while I stood aside. I find that doesn't sit well with me here."

"Why, Mathias, you sound almost . . . idealistic." Trias smirked.

Shaw scowled. "These people aren't criminals. They're just looking to break the cycle."

He studied the map, then looked up at Trias. "Besides, it'd be far better for the Alliance if they're not caught and forced to confess to helping Stormwind steal their best armaments. The less anyone knows about our dealings, the better. Wouldn't you say?"

Trias sipped his ale. "You make a compelling point. So. Given that SI:7 doesn't exactly have anyone who can . . . enter the region unnoticed, as it were, how do you plan to extract them?"

Shaw knitted his brow, plotting his mission on the map. "Isn't that the question."

THE TIPPING POINT

Renzik was getting a little frustrated. This assignment wasn't exactly playing to his unique set of skills, and his reputation tended to precede him. Outside the kids he used, he didn't have informants so much as folks he threatened. But at least he had made progress. He'd started with an overseer in a nearby sulfur mine, who had quailed at Renzik's threat to put him *in* the mine and had immediately named a mine worker who had been "stirring things up."

In her ramshackle hut, Fritzi Strifetalker looked defiantly up at Renzik. "Are you nuts? I wouldn't know anything about that!"

Renzik gazed down at her. "Overseer said you're a troublemaker."

She sighed. "If organizin' miners for better working conditions and a living wage is *makin' trouble*, then sure."

"So you *didn't* tell the mine bosses that you could make things difficult for them?"

"I meant I'd call for a work stoppage." She gave Renzik a plaintive look. "I don't wanna die, but there are too many workers down here who *are* dying, whether they're getting hurt or sick, kept poor. The bosses just want you to make an example of me to stop us working together."

That gave Renzik pause. His own time in the mines was not something he remembered fondly, and there was no reason to think workers' situations had improved since then.

"Besides," Fritzi continued, "even if I *wanted* to do it, explosives gotta be chemically blended, refined, packaged; the shipments would be charted and timed. All that's way above my pay grade; try someone who knows about schedules."

She made good points. He nodded his thanks and turned to go, then paused and tipped a lamp off a table, breaking it.

"Hey! What was that for?" Fritzi demanded.

"Sorry," Renzik sighed. "I got a reputation to keep."

Renzik stopped outside a surprisingly well-kept cottage on the lower east side. He'd strong-armed the cartel's dispatcher into naming a driver who he'd said had complained about low pay and long hours. Deep down, Renzik thought it sounded like management was using him to get rid of another potential rabble-rouser, but he had to check it out.

He knocked on the door; moments later, a young female goblin opened it, looking up at him nervously. "Yes?"

"Beezle Gnarflux?" he asked.

A young man joined her. "I'm Beezle," he said, putting himself between her and Renzik.

Renzik appreciated his bravery, protecting her like that. "Name's Renzik," he said. He didn't even notice the blood drain out of their faces. "Mind if I come in?"

The couple silently moved aside, and he stepped heavily into the small house.

The room Renzik found himself in was . . . honestly, pretty nice—not luxurious by any means, but clean and neat—and what they had was better quality than most working goblins he'd dealt with. There was even a decorative plate on the wall, nicer than he'd expected they could afford. The couple stood there, the wife wringing her hands anxiously. He examined the plate—definitely not goblin work. He turned back to them. "That's beautiful. You buy that in the Undermine? On a driver's salary?"

"It was a . . . gift," the wife offered.

"Uh-huh. What's your name?" he asked her.

"S-Seersa," she stammered.

Renzik cocked his head at her. "You seem nervous, Seersa. Why's that?"

She looked at him as if he'd said she was stupid. "You're . . . Renzik. The Shiv. No one wants you knocking on their door."

Beezle put his arm around her shoulder. "Seersa, don't—"

Renzik waved him off. "That's actually pretty reasonable. A little *hurtful*, but reasonable." He squared off to them. "So. Beezle. You know why I'm here."

Beezle looked more nervous. "I do?"

"You're a driver for the cartel."

"Yeah . . ."

"So being a driver, you must have heard that some shipments have gotten hijacked lately."

"No, I hadn't. Who's stupid enough to steal from Mozzy?"

"Funny—that's what I thought when they told me."

Renzik produced the shiv, and the couple took an involuntary step backward, the wife flickering a quick look to the back room.

"Here's the thing," Renzik said. "Someone on the inside's been selling information to pirates—or rival merchants, or heck, maybe even the Alliance—about those shipments. There's evidence that points to you. All of this will go easier for you if you confess."

"Easier . . . or *faster*?" Beezle asked.

The shiv flashed out and nicked Beezle's ear; the goblin put a hand up, trying to stop the blood flowing.

Renzik shrugged. "Both, I guess."

Now Seersa stepped between Renzik and her husband. "He *couldn't* know anything. They don't even tell him when his gigs are coming up until the last minute."

Renzik paused. This was giving him a headache. "Okay, let's say that's so. Let's say hubby's not involved. Who do *you* think's behind it?"

At this point, he realized, any lead could help, no matter who it came from.

The couple offered ideas, speaking over each other in their haste. "Who else wants it?"

"Who's the buyer? Maybe *they're* telling pirates about it—pirates split the take with the buyer, who doesn't have to pay for it."

"Maybe it's someone in the refinery, trying to establish their own connections."

Beezle finished: "They always say, 'Follow the money,' right? So who handles the money?"

Renzik considered all this, then carefully sheathed his blade. "Huh. This was more useful than I thought. Thanks. You're both smart. Anything pans out, I'll even tell the boss how helpful you were."

"Not necessary." Seersa smiled uncomfortably. "We're just happy to help."

Renzik smiled back, pointing a finger at her. "See? Smart."

The couple maintained their grimaces as he walked out the door, then looked at each other, dread in their eyes.

Renzik led off with a punch to the nose. It was hardly original, but it sparked cooperation nine times out of ten.

"Are you *kidding*, Renzik?" wheezed Specs Clinkstack from the thick crocolisk hide that covered the floor of the bookkeeper's lavish office. Renzik stood over the aging goblin, cracking his knuckles.

"You're the one behind the explosives going missing, Specs. All the shipments. Admit it."

The bookkeeper snarled as he climbed shakily to his feet, fumbling for his spectacles, which had miraculously not been broken

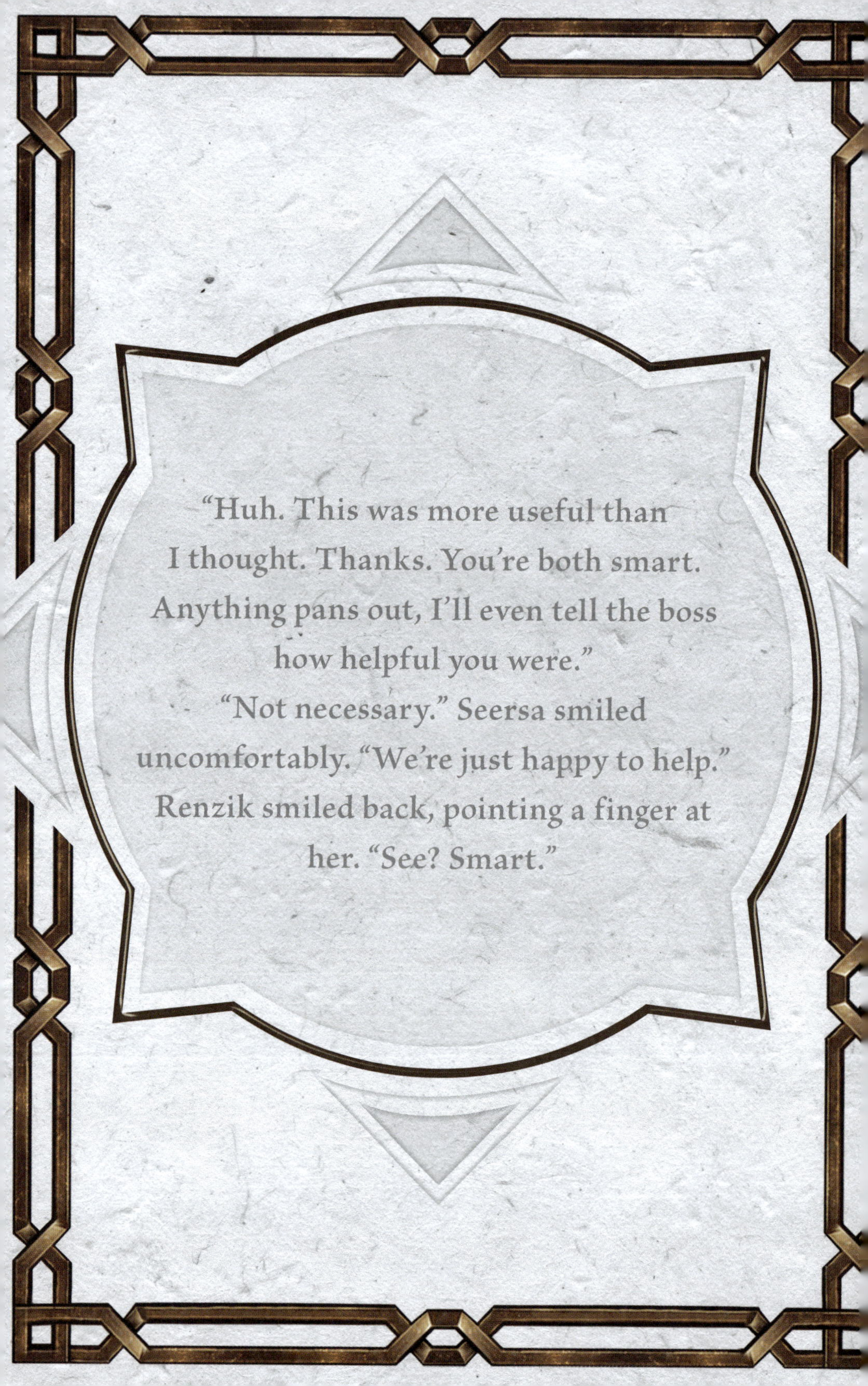

"Huh. This was more useful than I thought. Thanks. You're both smart. Anything pans out, I'll even tell the boss how helpful you were."

"Not necessary." Seersa smiled uncomfortably. "We're just happy to help."

Renzik smiled back, pointing a finger at her. "See? Smart."

by Renzik's punch. "What proof do you have of that spurious accusation?"

"What's spurious?"

"It means 'worthless,' you ignorant ox!"

Renzik decided to ignore that insult for the moment. He'd have plenty of time for retaliation. "You control the books, Specs. You're the one who runs all the operations for the boss. You know about the mining, the assembly, the shipping schedules, everything. And look at this place. I've never seen an office so fancy—except maybe the boss's own house." He leaned over the frail older man. "Where's all the money *come* from, Specs? It's gotta be you."

"You . . . idiot."

Renzik didn't care for that one bit, but the bookkeeper continued, actually advanced on *him*. He could see why that made people uncomfortable.

"Of course I have nice things! Mozzy pays me handsomely. He *values* me." Specs turned to a table that displayed photographs of him with various higher-ups in the organization—either working or enjoying celebrations—and picked up an accounting ledger. He opened it on his desk and thrust it at Renzik. "I keep *impeccable* records of exactly where everything came from. I know I would be the first logical suspect: I live with my head in the bookworm's mouth! How stupid would I have to be to give up *all this* just to steal from Mozzy? I'm the one who suggested he use *you* to find the snitch!" he almost screamed.

Renzik looked at the ledger; what little he knew of numbers seemed to indicate that the bookkeeper's outrage was justified. He sighed. He had hit yet another dead end, and truth be told, he didn't know where to go from here. He was tired of this game. Tired of it all, actually. Defeated, he closed the ledger and put it back on the table. He glanced at the photos—photos were uncommon around here—and paused. He picked one up, taken in this very office, of Specs toasting with Mozzy and several of his captains. In the background was a female goblin, slightly out of focus.

Renzik got a small tickle in the back of his brain. He held up the photo to the bookkeeper and pointed at the figure. "Who's that?"

Specs squinted at the photo, pulled his eyeglasses on, then turned away dismissively. "That's just one of my secretaries, Seersa."

Renzik placed the photo carefully back on the table and left.

Renzik was in a bad mood as he headed back toward the lower east side. He'd kinda actually liked that young couple, and they'd played him. In fact, he realized he hadn't even broken anything when he'd left their house. Was he losing his touch? As he approached the neighborhood, however, he saw Spatter and Jinzi running toward him. That in itself was unusual; he'd trained them better than that. But he was so intent on his goal that he paid them no heed until Spatter tugged on his coat.

"Somethin's up, Mister R," Jinzi gasped. "We been lookin' all over for ya."

Renzik nearly thundered right past them but thought better of it. "Well?"

The kids exchanged glances. "Follow us."

The urchins led him through a couple of alleys to an intersection, where they pointed out one of Mozzy's lower-level lookouts sitting down, back to a building, asleep on the job. Mozzy would blow his top about this.

"He ain't the only one," Spatter whispered, and the little spies guided him to two more corners, where two more guards were passed out at their usual stations. Worse, they were now not far from the house where that Gnarflux couple lived.

Renzik's bad mood now included a growing unease. When he examined the third guard, the dart in her neck told him that she'd been drugged. He pulled a second dart from the collar of her coat and sniffed it, pulling back a bit from the slightly sour tang. He recognized the nonlethal but potent herb they called purple lotus on the streets. Before he fully knew what he was doing, he started running toward the Gnarfluxes' cottage.

The couple were just about done packing their rucksacks, taking only what they could carry with them, when the front door burst off its hinges. Renzik stepped into the house, and Seersa and Beezle froze in fear.

"Y'know, I may not like all the things I gotta do for a living . . .

but I *really* don't like bein' made a fool of. If you'd just confessed,"—Renzik glowered at Beezle—"it woulda been quick and painless. As for you"—he pointed at Seersa—"you'll answer to the boss now."

Seersa backed away. "You don't understand," she said tightly. "We had to. They wouldn't give us—"

"I don't care," Renzik said. "Everyone's got a story, a reason. But you knew the rules, and you broke 'em anyway."

Before he could say another word, Renzik heard a whizzing sound. As he dodged the round of poison darts, a human stepped into the room from the back of the house. He was tall and built pretty good, and he'd put himself between Renzik and his targets.

"I'll take care of him," the man told the couple. "Get to the escape tunnel. I've cleared out any likely interference. My people will meet you on the other side."

Seersa disappeared into a side room for a moment, then emerged carrying another bundle. "Be careful, Shaw. He's dangerous," she warned, then followed her husband out the back of the house.

The taller man winced at the sound of his name; his cover had been blown.

Renzik made a move toward the back door, but the tall man—Shaw—intervened with a smile. "I don't think so, friend."

Renzik's shiv appeared in his right hand, and he assumed a fighting stance. He had to end this quick. "No one has friends down here, *Shaw*."

"Well, the night is young." Shaw's grin annoyed Renzik, and he

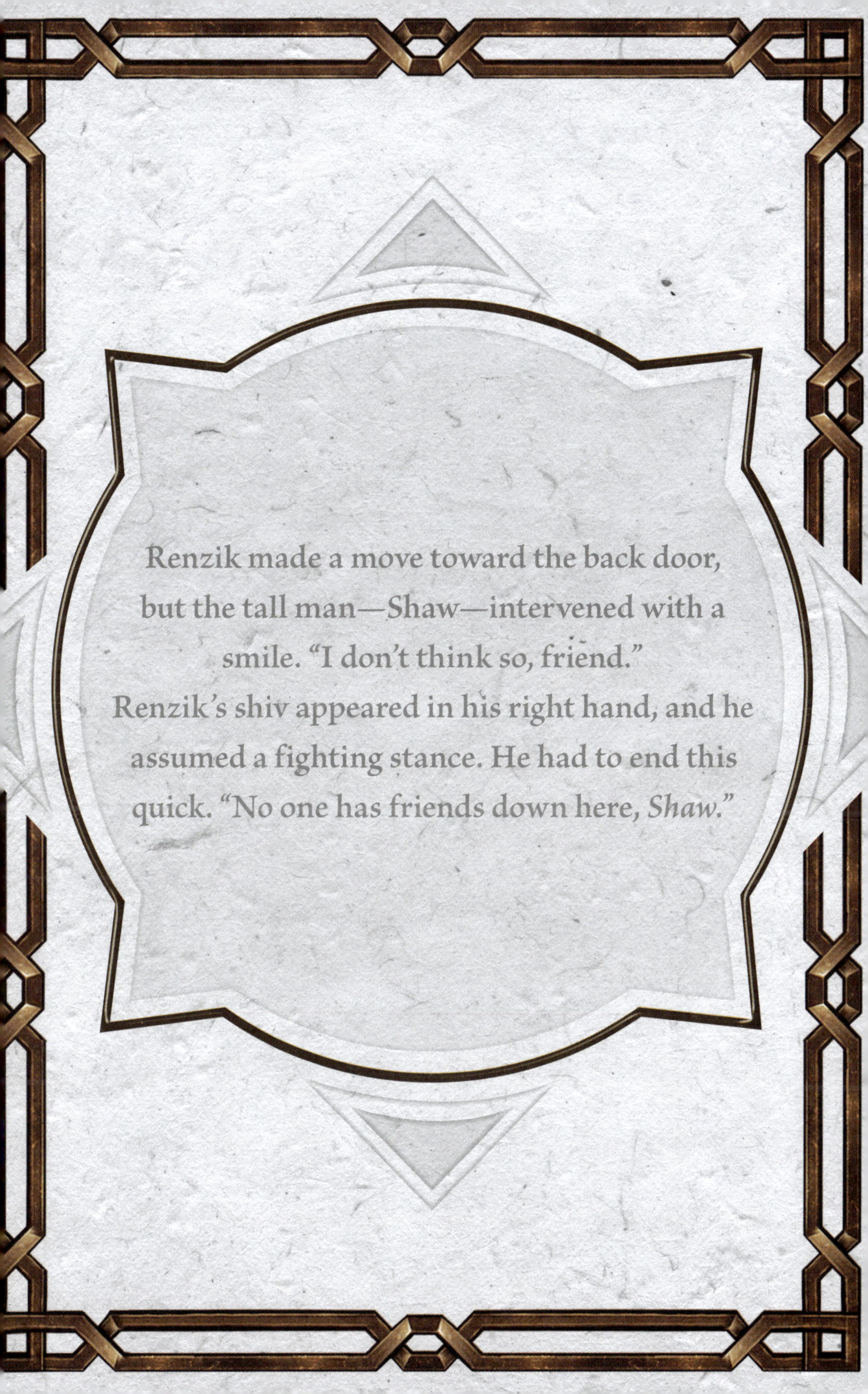

Renzik made a move toward the back door, but the tall man—Shaw—intervened with a smile. "I don't think so, friend."

Renzik's shiv appeared in his right hand, and he assumed a fighting stance. He had to end this quick. "No one has friends down here, *Shaw*."

started forward, but Shaw suddenly had his own wicked-looking dagger in one hand . . . and a second in the other. Whoever this Shaw was, he was clearly no easy mark. The two fighters feinted and circled each other, seeking an opening, swiping and jabbing.

"You're excellent with a blade," Shaw said, stabbing in.

Renzik deflected Shaw's dagger with his shiv. "Not so bad yourself," he admitted as Shaw blocked his riposte and nearly sliced him open with the second dagger.

Renzik looked around and remembered the Gnarfluxes' fancy plate; there would be a wire loop on the other side to hang it on the wall. He backed up, holding Shaw at bay, and fitted the plate around his off hand, fashioning a makeshift buckler.

Shaw appraised him. "Clever. Resourceful. Raised on the street, I'm guessing. Grew up struggling for every morsel."

Renzik tried to tune him out.

"So how, if I may ask, can you stand by your trade prince, seeing the brutality, the violence, the oppression he inflicts on good people like these?"

"Vivi was right. No way you're a pirate," Renzik growled as he grabbed a chair and rushed at Shaw, who kicked out and splintered the chair, bringing Renzik up short. "Gotta be Alliance, bringing morals like that to a place like this."

"It shows," Shaw shot back. "Selfish trade princes siphoning profits, preventing their people from getting medicine? Keeping everyone dependent on *their* good will—which I hear is in short supply at best."

Renzik grimaced; the splinters stung, even if the words were nothing new. "Before the trade princes, it was every goblin for themselves, nobody was safe. Ever. At least now there's order." Renzik tossed the remainder of the chair at Shaw, who threw up a hand to block it, giving Renzik an opening. "Are they brutal? Sure. But there's two kinds of people in the Undermine: the smart and the stupid. And I know what happens to the stupid." He lunged at Shaw.

Shaw leapt onto a low table, which broke under his weight, and he stumbled back but regained his footing. "I suspect *you* are what happens to the stupid. Is this really all you want for yourself . . . for your family?"

Renzik laughed bitterly as he advanced. "I've got no family."

"You must care about someone down here," Shaw insisted as he swiped and twirled his blades, stymying Renzik's charge. "I noticed your little lookouts on my way in—all those children, relying on you for their next meal . . ."

Renzik thought about the street kids—what their futures looked like without him—then snarled; this guy was trying to get into his head. "Down here we live for ourselves, and I've seen it much worse."

"Yes, but you could *create* better. Like we have."

Renzik scoffed. "Right. Getting back to that—what's the Alliance doin' here, spyin' on us? Stealin' from us? If you're so high and mighty?"

Shaw shook his head. "Goblins . . . there is much to admire about your people. You're creative. Inspired. You build brilliantly. And yet you seem satisfied to live in a system engineered to exploit you. Your boss sells bombs to line *his* pockets. He keeps your people down here, sick, poor, starving, doing *his* work. But those bombs also harm good people everywhere—including my people. I stole them to get them away from bad actors."

Renzik stabbed forward, but Shaw dodged him. "The Alliance has committed its share of ugliness."

"Absolutely," Shaw admitted. "I've had a hand in some of it. The Alliance isn't perfect, nothing is. But they do want peace. They are trying to be better."

"By undercutting our system? And using those sick, starvin' goblins to do your dirty work? You just like makin' traitors."

"Oh, come on," Shaw countered as the two continued to dart and feint. "Traitors to what? A corrupt crime lord? The Gnarfluxes just wanted medicine, and maybe to do a little more than just exist."

Renzik slashed at Shaw. "I survived well enough without bein' a fink."

"You're so focused on going it alone, on your *strength*, how you *survived* this place," Shaw snapped as he parried. "But you must understand that's what Mozzy wants—for you all to feel alone, on guard, keeping each other in line. You're doing the hard work for him. Tell me, friend, what happens when the trade prince realizes your little lookouts are more loyal to *you* than they are to *him*? When you're less a tool than a *threat*?"

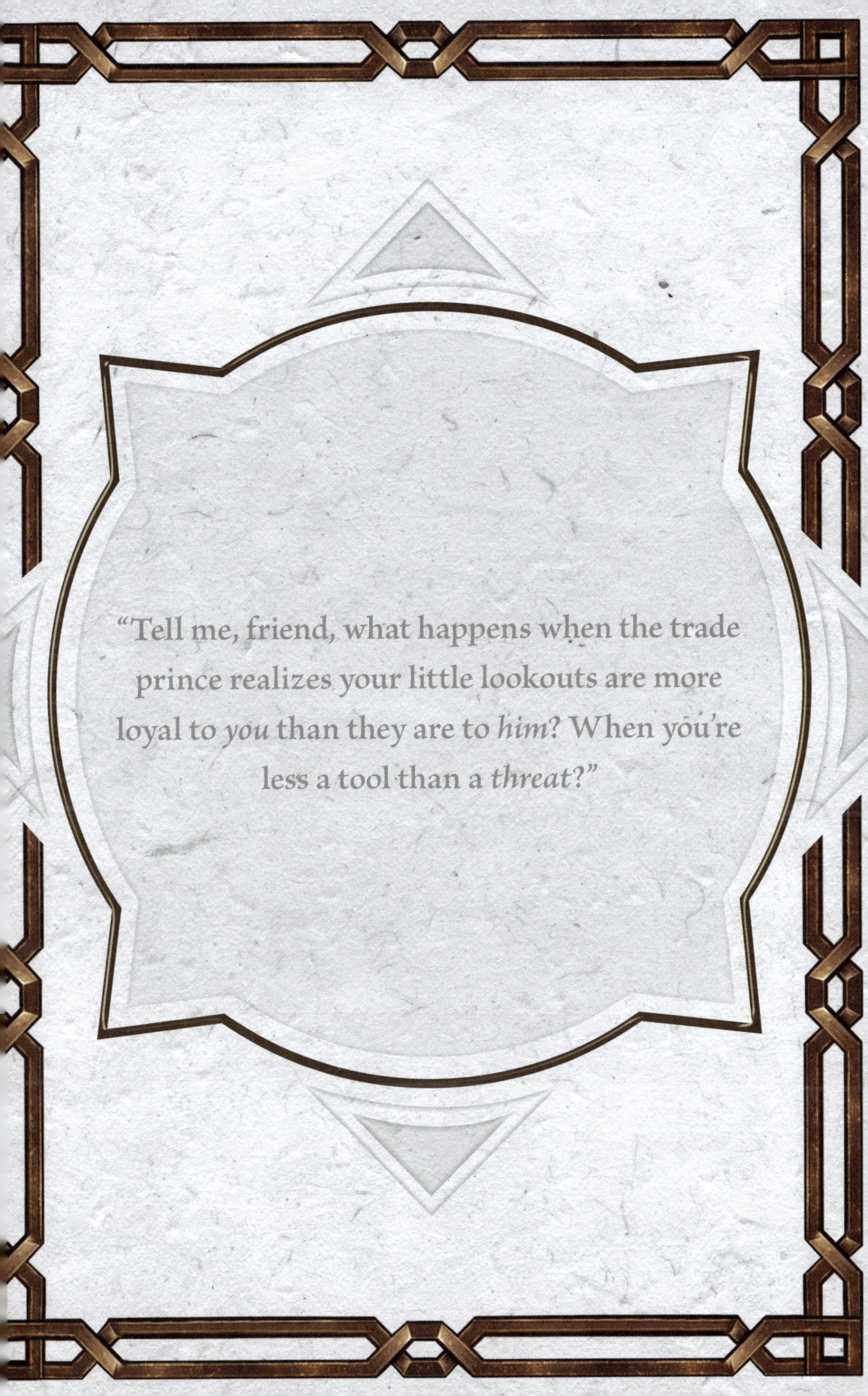

"Tell me, friend, what happens when the trade prince realizes your little lookouts are more loyal to *you* than they are to *him*? When you're less a tool than a *threat*?"

Renzik sagged just for a moment under the weight of the thought—which gave Shaw his own opening. The spy flicked one of his daggers at Renzik, who barely deflected it with the broken plate; it stuck into the floor at his feet. Renzik grabbed it and launched himself at Shaw. The taller man would normally have had the advantage, but Renzik dove for the legs, slicing through Shaw's pants; the larger man's gasp of surprise and pain told him he'd scored a hit.

Rolling to his feet, ready to continue, Renzik prepared to attack, but Shaw began to stagger, gave him a strange smile.

"Well played, *friend*." Without another word he collapsed, out cold.

Renzik was confused for a moment. He hadn't scored anything like a fatal wound; heck, it wasn't more than a deep scratch. Then he realized, ran a finger over the blade and sniffed it. It was coated with purple lotus. He'd gotten the tall human with his own strategy.

What gave Renzik pause was that he knew purple lotus was almost never fatal; it just put you to sleep. So even if Renzik'd lost—he realized as he trussed up Shaw securely—the tall one wasn't looking to kill him or any of those lookouts. He examined the dagger, a very nice blade, and dropped it into his coat pocket. He had his prize for Mozzy, a far better outcome than he could possibly have imagined, but he felt a little twinge of . . . regret for what would almost certainly happen to the guy. Still, he was just doing his job.

Renzik dashed out the back of the house and looked around. To his surprise, Jinzi and Spatter were in the alley, a block apart.

He called to Jinzi, "You see where they went?"

She nodded. "This way."

Renzik felt a glow of pride in the kids, tinged as it was with the weight of Shaw's words. At least they'd all eat well tonight.

Seersa and Beezle made their way down the sewer tunnel toward the grate. They were tired, and Seersa stumbled under the load she was carrying.

"Let me," Beezle said, taking it from her. "We're almost free. Tomorrow at this time, we'll be living another life."

"Don't bet on it," came Renzik's cold voice.

The couple stopped and turned to him, misery on their faces; they were *so close* to getting away.

Renzik was too angry—and frankly too tired—to care.

"You . . . you don't have to do this," Seersa pleaded.

"No, no. I do," Renzik said flatly. "It's you or me." He raised Shaw's dagger overhead and grabbed Beezle, who cringed, hunching over the bundle he was holding.

Just before he brought the weapon down, Renzik saw what Beezle was protecting: a little girl, maybe four years old, sick and sweating with fever.

"No!" she cried. "Don't hurt Daddy!"

Renzik froze, and the world seemed to spin. Unthinking, he

released Beezle and took a step back.

Seersa saw him falter. "We did what we had to, to save our little one," she quavered. "What would you have done in our shoes? When Squeex got sick, there was no way we could pay for the medicine she needs. You've seen Specs Clinkstack's office. Do you know what that's *like*, to go to work there every day and be so powerless, so poor you can't save your own kid?"

Renzik stared. "It's a dog-eat-dog world," he muttered, a thousand leagues away.

"But does it always have to be?" she asked tearfully, placing a hand on his arm.

Renzik stared down at her. This was where *his* life had started. And he'd become the monster that created him.

He sagged and swore . . . quite a lot.

Seersa and Beezle looked on, terrified as he punched the slimy wall of the tunnel. What would he do? Finally, Renzik stopped, breathing heavily, and glared at them.

"Go."

They looked back, daring to hope.

Renzik squeezed his eyes shut, didn't watch as the little family disappeared into the dark.

Shaw woke slowly, groggily. His ear itched. He tried to scratch it, only to realize he was bound hand and foot. He looked around; he was still in the Gnarfluxes' house. He rolled over with a groan—and stopped short. Sitting in the lone unbroken chair was Renzik, flipping the dagger he'd taken from Shaw, glaring at him.

"Well," Shaw ventured, "I suppose the fact that I'm still alive is . . . hopeful?"

"We got us an optimist," Renzik grunted. "Nah, Mozzy is gonna want to meet you."

"Fair enough," sighed Shaw. "What did you do to the family?"

Renzik paused. "They're fine. I assume they're with whoever you had waiting for 'em."

"Interesting," Shaw mused. "That was a good deed you did."

"Yeah, well, it won't be good for *me* if the boss finds out," Renzik muttered.

"Then why did you let them escape?"

Renzik stared at his captive for a moment, then shrugged. "Scars are a funny thing. They . . . hurt at first, especially the deep ones. But after a while, you lose all feeling there, they look less ugly. You stop thinkin' about them as painful, see them as a point of pride. You talk about them with anyone who'll ask, because they show that you're strong for having survived something nasty."

Renzik sighed deeply. "But that . . . doesn't mean you wanted to get hurt in the first place. I've been survivin' down here for a long time—like you said, a pretty miserable long time—and I do better than most, but that's because I do my job better than most. You're

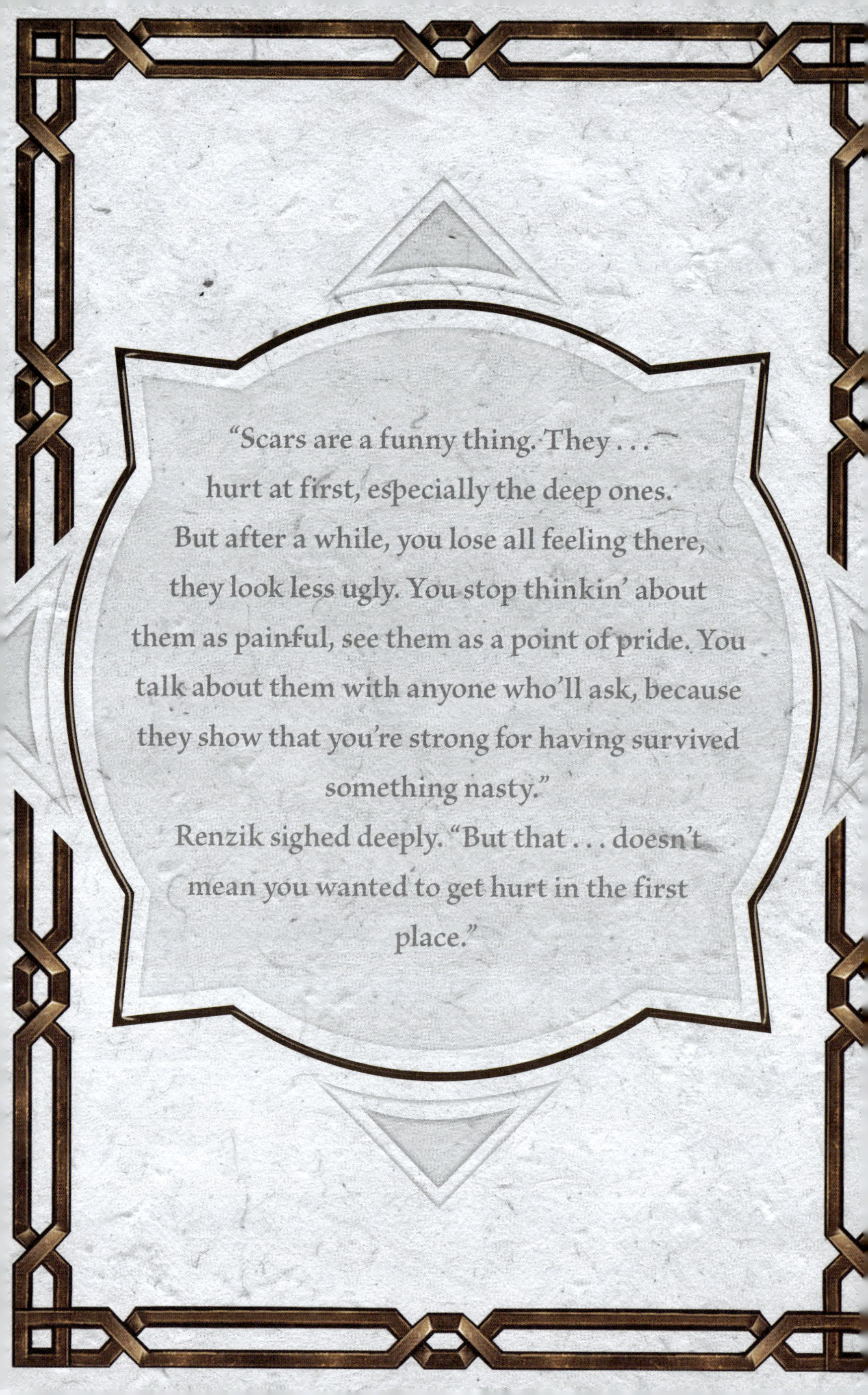

"Scars are a funny thing. They . . . hurt at first, especially the deep ones. But after a while, you lose all feeling there, they look less ugly. You stop thinkin' about them as painful, see them as a point of pride. You talk about them with anyone who'll ask, because they show that you're strong for having survived something nasty."

Renzik sighed deeply. "But that . . . doesn't mean you wanted to get hurt in the first place."

the first one who's ever challenged that this is how things should be. That this is how things'll *always* be."

Shaw sat up slowly. "And . . . ?"

"I don't really like to think about my life . . . but what you said kinda made me. I've only ever done anything to survive or to get ahead, only ever worked for more and more powerful criminals. I make a living breaking things—or worse. Most folks I deal with don't have a pot to piss in. I never really considered that things could be different . . . better. That things could be *fair*."

Shaw nodded. "I know, from experience . . . when something is all you've ever known, then you think that's just the way it is. And you wonder how one person can ever hope to change it."

"At least I'm respected here," Renzik protested weakly.

"There is a difference, my friend," Shaw offered, "between respect and fear."

Renzik scowled at the bound man, held up the dagger, crossed to him . . . and cut the rope binding the spy. "Ain't that the truth. You think there's another way to go about"—he waved the blade around, indicating everything—"this?"

Shaw rubbed his wrists, then slowly rose to his feet. "Honestly, I don't have many answers, and I can't promise that I ever will. But I see something in you that gives me, well . . . hope."

"You're dumber than you look."

Shaw shrugged. "Probably true." He looked at his dagger. "I don't suppose . . ."

Renzik snorted. "Nope. Souvenir."

Shaw nodded. "What made you decide to release me?"

Renzik cocked his head. "Don't look a gift kodo in the mouth, dummy. But while we're asking, why would *you* risk everything to save some nobody goblins who already got you what you wanted?"

Shaw sighed. "Because they deserved it. Because I said I would. And if my word is worth nothing, then maybe . . . I'm worth even less. Light knows I can't pretend I'm a good man . . . but I can serve a good cause."

Renzik stared at him.

Shaw smiled wanly and started toward the rear entrance of the house, then paused. He tossed a coin onto the table.

Renzik picked it up. It bore a strange insignia.

"If you can find a way into Stormwind City, take this coin to the Master of Cheese," Shaw told Renzik. "Maybe we can help you find what you're looking for. Or at least something . . . more worthy."

Renzik sheathed his new knife. "Just so you know. I don't know that I can ever be a good guy—already done too many bad things—but maybe . . . maybe I can see being a bad guy in service of a good cause too."

Shaw nodded his approval. "If I may abuse the cliché, we're not so different, you and I." He slipped into the night. Renzik sat there for a few long minutes before pocketing the coin.

The little house burned quickly enough. Renzik wanted to make sure it wouldn't go out accidentally, then walked away. He hadn't gone more than a couple of blocks when he realized that Jinzi was following him.

Renzik stopped and sighed. "Figured you'd have already found a place to sleep for the night, Jinzi."

She said nothing.

"So . . . what's up?" he asked.

She side-eyed him suspiciously. "Who was that human? Was he the guy who tranqed Trade Prince Gloxscorn's lookouts?"

Renzik's eyes narrowed a little. "Don't you worry about that. And don't you talk about that neither."

He reached into a pocket and handed her several more coins.

She counted them in a split second and jutted her jaw at him defiantly. "It's gonna take a *whole* lot more than that to buy me off."

He cocked his head. "You want more money?"

She shook her head. "I want a promotion."

Renzik grinned. "Let's talk. I'll buy dinner."

"So?" Mozzy demanded from Renzik the next day.

"I found the culprits, Trade Prince Gloxscorn. Young couple short on cash. A driver and one of Specs's secretaries."

"Specs! You think he was involved?"

Renzik considered. He certainly didn't like the old jerk, but it wasn't worth the trouble. "No, sir."

"I assume you took care of them?" Mozzy said. "I need to send a message to anyone who might get ideas about crossing me."

"Let me put it this way," Renzik assured him. "They ain't never gonna make trouble for you again."

Mozzy smiled and nodded. "Knew I could count on you. Now, get back out there and crack some heads."

Leaving Mozzy's HQ and stepping into the streets, Renzik pulled his coat a little tighter against the dank and reflected on the events of the last week. Maybe it had been stupid to lie to Mozzy—so if he was smart, he'd have to figure out how to evade the trade prince's inevitable fury. He still felt the weight of the spy's coin in his pocket.

Perhaps there were warmer days ahead.

FAITH & FLAME
L. L. MCKINNEY

Faerin Lothar sat in her favorite of the three leather chairs situated outside Great Kyron's office. She was familiar with this one, especially the slight grooves in its right arm where plenty of Lamplighters and hopefuls alike had picked and scratched nervously at the finish. Herself included.

Beledar's light poured through the high windows on the far wall, shafts of aureate radiance carving the corridor into slanted fragments. The setting should have been tranquil, a place of shelter and peace. Instead, Faerin felt the unease that had been churning in her gut for the better part of an hour begin to slowly spread through the rest of her body. It took hold of her legs, which started to bounce, and her arm, until her fingers drummed uselessly on her knee.

Closing her eyes, she tried to focus on anything but her swirling thoughts as Anduin Wrynn's words danced through her mind. *You should come with us. See the world. Let it get a good look at you . . .* The invitation stuck between her ears nearly as much as the stories he told. They painted a picture in her mind's eye of the old world born anew: outlander tales of heroes and legends, myths like the very one borne by her bloodline. The Lothar name was an inheritance she'd all but renounced the day she stole away on *Ariah's Ascent*, believing she was avoiding a destiny stuck amidst dusty histories and decrepit parchments. Plenty of legends had lodged themselves in Faerin's heart like splinters, all of them kindling for a single, burning truth: A life tending the past was not one she endeavored to live.

But what Anduin had shared about her family—how the Lothar name belonged to a great champion of the people . . . What if that past could reveal her way forward? Not in tomes but in trials faced and victories won. Those stories about heroes drawn to a calling they couldn't explain—a cause greater than they understood except they knew it was bigger than themselves—struck at something deep in Faerin. A familiar feeling that hummed at the base of her skull, similar to what had drawn her to the docks that fateful day. A duty. A charge. This was the difference between her and the rest of her family. She'd heard such a call in the depths of her very being, while they believed it to be the whims of a child.

Now, she heard it again.

Unable to contain her disquiet, Faerin found her feet to pace the length of the upper hall. The rest of the building remained blessedly silent, abandoned while her fellow Lamplighters saw to the start of their daily duties. That's why she'd picked this time: early enough that she would go unnoticed, at least for a little while. She didn't want to explain to anyone what she was planning, to face their disappointment or sadness. Most of all, she didn't want anyone to try to change her mind. Not that they could. The only ones who stood even a flicker of a chance were . . . gone.

Sadness welled in Faerin's chest, but she tamped it down, pushed it deeper with each footfall. "Calm yourself," she murmured into the silence.

For so long she'd believed the Sacred Flame had summoned her to Hallowfall. That she, blessed as she was by the Flame to fight, was *supposed* to be here. But deep down she'd always given refuge to something . . . hungrier.

A smile pulled at Faerin's face as different memories rose in the quiet. She let these fold over her mind, anything to keep from thinking too much about her plans, how wrong it could all go, and what she would have to do if it did.

Memories of the orphanage enveloped her. How empty it lay in the beginning, save for Faerin, the only child in the entire expedition for some time. Barely a flicker of a candle in an awfully large tinderbox. The building had seemed massive then, imposing. Who knew having so much space to yourself could feel suffocating?

The only thing that made those early days bearable was Sygfraed Siegepyr. He'd been selected as caretaker of the orphanage in Mereldar. The old man had been less worn and weary then. *Signs of a life well lived,* he'd often say. He said a lot, actually—most of it calling after her not to run there, slide down this, or climb that. While General Vaelisia Steelstrike was Faerin's official guardian, it was Sygfraed who saw to her daily needs at the orphanage. It was Sygfraed who made sure Steelstrike's rules were studied and committed to memory—which still did not prevent Faerin from often breaking them.

It was also Sygfraed who tucked Faerin in at night and told her the stories—tales from glory days past, the legendary champions who'd spurred the Arathi Empire to greatness—that formed the foundation of who Faerin would become.

"I want to hear one about a battle!" Faerin had demanded one night, freshly washed and dressed in a cotton nightgown perfect for the temperate evening. The copper-tinged winds blowing in from the north crawled through open windows to stir the curtains and loose parchment covered in scribbles from her lessons that day. Seeing as she'd given a sketch of General Steelstrike a lynx's head in place of her own, it was safe to say the day's teachings hadn't fully taken.

"Oh ho," Sygfraed had laughed while fluffing Faerin's abandoned pillows, his dark-brown face alight with amusement. "Stories are for *after* we curl up under our blankets. Otherwise, how will the Dreamers catch your wandering thoughts?"

With a huff, Faerin flopped back onto the bed, kicking her way beneath the blanket, though she didn't lie down just yet. She adjusted the covering on her head that kept her braids in place and fixed the man with narrowed eyes. "*Dreamers* aren't real."

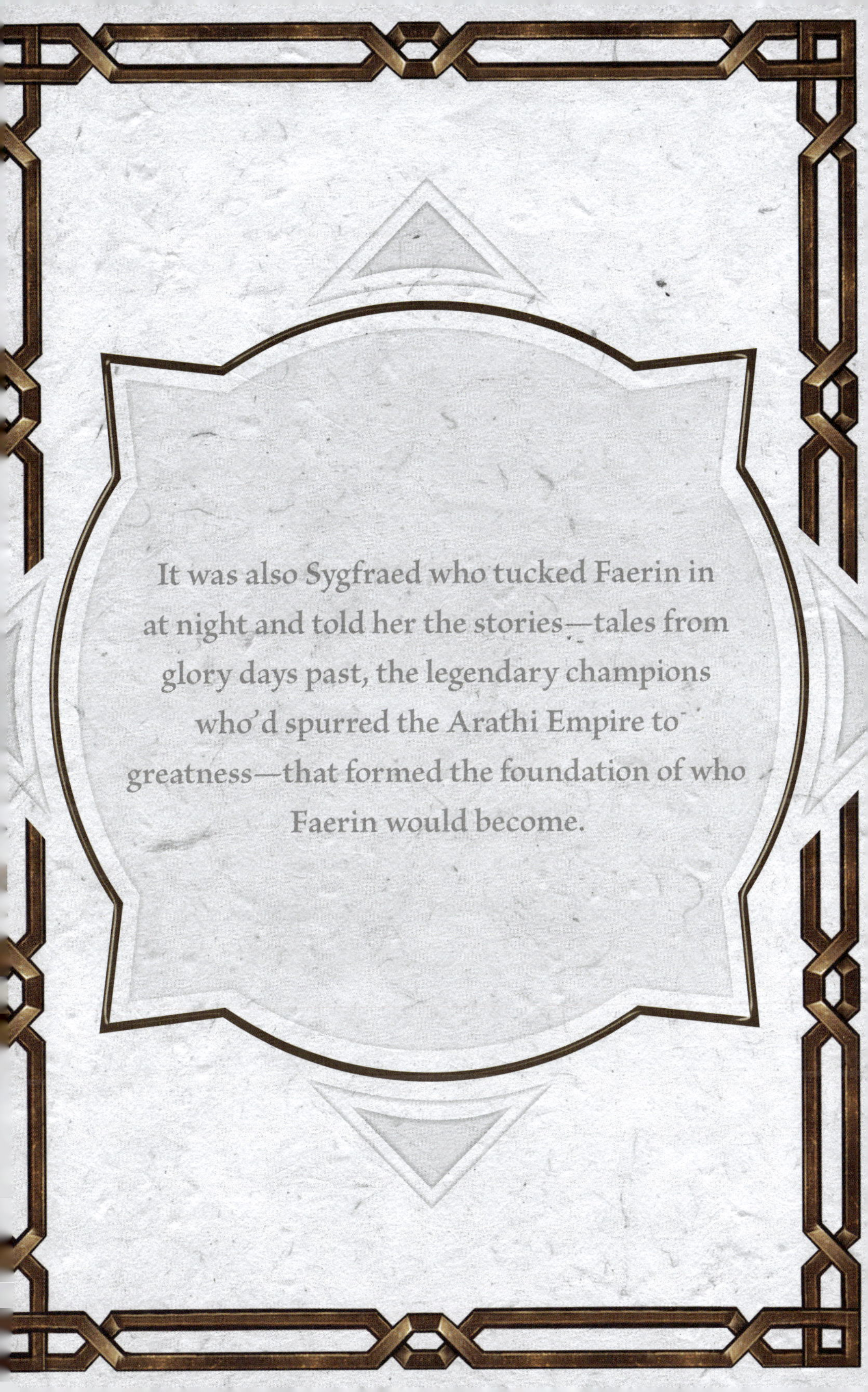

It was also Sygfraed who tucked Faerin in at night and told her the stories—tales from glory days past, the legendary champions who'd spurred the Arathi Empire to greatness—that formed the foundation of who Faerin would become.

"Of course they are," Sygfraed said with an affronted sniff. "Who else brings you visions while you sleep? Certainly not pixies." He patted the newly fluffed pillow and reached to lay a hand atop the heavy tome settled on a nearby table.

Faerin watched with bated breath as his fingers brushed the cover but did nothing else. They tapped, waiting. With a giggle, she finally flung the blanket over herself and tugged it to her chin. She couldn't help but smile as Sygfraed winked and plucked the book free, his hands dipping slightly with the weight of it.

"Now then," the old man said while balancing the book on his knees to open it. "Why don't we try one a little less stimulating?"

"Aww," Faerin whined with practiced petulance. "But fighting is the best!"

"Oh?"

"Yes! If you're strong, you fight! Everything else is *boring*."

Sygfraed hummed in that way of his that wasn't exactly judgmental but still suggested you reconsider whatever you were doing. "You think so? Well, that gives me the perfect idea for tonight's tale." The old man opened the book and traced the vine detail framing the page. A gentle golden glow bled outward from the ink, enveloping the tome and flipping the pages in succession until they settled somewhere deep in the text.

"Whoa!" Faerin exclaimed, eyes now wide and wonder-filled. She'd never seen the book do that before. "You know magic?"

"I'm afraid not," Sygfraed chuckled, then bowed his head and whispered conspiratorially, "but the book does."

Faerin settled further into her spot, enraptured.

"*This* story," Sygfraed began while patting the open page, "is a special one, hidden amidst all the fighting and all the battles, nearly forgotten due to the oath that was sworn by the Secret Keepers, guardians of our most secret-y secrets."

Eight-year-old Faerin hung on every silly word, but then, that was the magic of storytelling.

Sygfraed cleared his throat a bit theatrically, then began to read. "*The Ballad of Craishae the First Flame: Tale of the Lost Queen of Arathor.* According to legend, Craishae was a daughter of kings, descended from the line of Thoradin.

"She was your ancestor," Sygfraed exclaimed with a wave toward Faerin.

She all but gasped aloud. "I never heard of her!"

"Few have," her caretaker continued. "This is but one of many myths about the lost queen." He read on.

"Craishae was a rambunctious child full of fire and spirit. She was bright and intelligent but often neglected her studies or chores in favor of playing games or venturing into the wilds.

"Sounds like someone I know," Sygfraed chided.

"Craishae was the oldest of her father's children, born to a noblewoman from Quel'Thalas. She adored nature and spent much of her time coming to know the forests and rivers that marked the land, making friends with creatures and all manner of folk. Despite her station, Craishae cherished her time among the people. She was afforded much respect but spurned any and all special treatment. She had a knack for fighting, and wielding the arcane was among her natural talents.

"As Craishae came of age, a terrible curse struck the land, tainting anything and anyone it touched, mutating them into vicious beasts. People turned on their loved ones, ripping their homes and villages apart. The kingdom was besieged both from without and within.

"At the height of the conflict, an army of contorted creatures breached Thoradin's wall, which had stood a stalwart sentinel over the land for generations. Witnessing the devastation firsthand, Craishae pledged her skills and power to the protection of her kingdom. She would hunt down and eradicate the source of this magical malediction.

"In the following months she fought battle after battle, winning great victories and helping others survive grave losses. It was during one such encounter—as monsters closed in around the princess and her wounded allies—that she unleashed a torrent of flame and Light the likes of which had never been seen. The smoke and dust cleared, revealing the princess now wielded her fire as a sword and shield. With her gleaming armor and blazing weapons, it was as if Craishae commanded the power of the sun itself."

Faerin had pictured this shining warrior—her foremother—with rich, dark skin like her own and radiating power.

"Though the princess emerged triumphant, time remained against her. The curse spread, and the war took a terrible turn. Some unseen force strengthened the dreadful enchantment, hastening its spread. Defenses began to crumble. All hope seemed lost.

"But one night, while asleep in her tent near the front, Princess Craishae was visited by an entity of light. It gave her a vision, spoke of a place hidden deep in the wilds. A temple where the heart of the world and the eye of the heavens met. But only she was strong enough to find it, possessing a soul true enough to wield its power.

"So Craishae set off on her own and combed the continent, facing foe and fiend alike, all the while praying her people would survive another day. When she eventually found the hidden temple, she climbed the stairs while battered and exhausted, prepared to fight whatever guardian stood in her way. Instead, in the central chamber, she discovered the being of light from her dream, whom she could now see was a woman dressed in stardust robes, standing vigil over a pool of swirling light and fire. The woman looked up, and her face changed. From elf to human to troll and back again, every time she moved her appearance shifted.

"The woman called herself the Scion and explained that she had sensed something in Craishae. Something willing to fight in defense of others. The world would need such strength in the coming age, just as Craishae's kingdom depended on it now. 'It is why I summoned you to this sacred place,' the Scion declared. 'To offer you the means to defeat this nightmare.'

"Relief nearly overcame the princess. She confessed that she had journeyed far to find the power to save her people, and at last her quest was at an end.

"Upon hearing these words, however, the Scion appeared disappointed. If power was truly all Craishae sought, then she and her people would be lost to the evil overtaking the world.

"Yet the princess corrected the woman. 'I did not come here for power,' Princess Craishae declared. 'But for purpose. Help me deliver my kingdom from this malevolence, and I will live in defense of *all* lands.'

"Pleased with this answer, the woman bid Craishae to bathe in the fiery waters of the temple. When she did, her old life and essence were burned away and made new. With eyes blazing and hair of flame, the princess emerged wielding an ember that could never go out: the First Flame.

"For you see, there were no paladins then," Sygfraed explained. "There were many mages, yes, but when Craishae returned with the ember, she wielded both the Light and fire to drive back the evil that had tried to take the land. The queen even cleansed those who'd fallen to the curse, returning them to their previous form.

"After she had won many battles and ruled for many years as queen, Craishae left the kingdom to her children, who had inherited a portion of the ember that blazed within her. In time, they began to spread her lessons amongst the people so as to light the path forward. Craishae then took what remained of her power into the

"Pleased with this answer, the woman bid Craishae to bathe in the fiery waters of the temple. When she did, her old life and essence were burned away and made new. With eyes blazing and hair of flame, the princess emerged wielding an ember that could never go out: the First Flame."

world, trying to trace the curse back to its source so it could be purged and her kingdom, the world, could be safe forever.

"Time between sightings of the former queen grew further and further between, until none could say where she'd gone. Eventually, she passed into legend, and those legends were handed down. One being this tale," Sygfraed murmured as he closed the book, its glow brightening briefly and then dimming once more.

Faerin was not able to sleep that night. She waited until the wee hours of the morning to sneak out of bed and try to find the story herself, but she was never able to glimpse those pages again.

Still, Queen Craishae and her legend lived in Faerin's heart and bolstered her spirit. Perhaps it was her foremother from whom Faerin inherited her need to go where she felt led, to do what she could for her people. For her faith.

A faith that had carried Faerin across the world, and perhaps, farther still.

"Faerin?"

The sound of a voice so near drew her out of her reminiscing with a jolt. She turned to find a familiar face in fellow Lamplighter Meradyth Lacke.

"Meradyth," Faerin sighed.

"Have you been up here this entire time?" Meradyth asked as she approached.

"Not for long. There is a matter I wish to discuss with Great Kyron." Faerin leaned casually against the wall as if she hadn't been trying to walk off her nerves mere moments before.

"I just left them." Meradyth turned to glance over her shoulder but stopped herself. "They have gone to speak with Anduin. I hear he is leaving soon, along with the oth—"

"I know," Faerin cut in.

Meradyth paused, her nose scrunched. It was an expression Faerin recognized easily.

"Is everything all right? You seem . . . nervous."

Faerin felt the frown pull at her face before she could stop it. "Do I?"

Meradyth only smiled. It was small and genuine. "Yes. Or perhaps a better word would be *uneasy*?"

It was a way out, of sorts. Taking it would be an admission, but it would mean Meradyth would spare her further questioning, allowing Faerin to come to her in time.

Training, rising through the ranks, and being sparked together had made the two women unlikely friends. Where once there was mistrust, now there was true camaraderie. Faerin's only annoyance with Meradyth was how well the former reservist *knew* her.

"With what we have faced of late, anyone would be uneasy," Faerin deflected.

"True, anyone but *you*." Meradyth folded her arms. She arched a brow, her silvering blonde hair drawn back enough to make the expression pinched. "Your faith is unshakeable."

"And that remains true." Faerin made her way back to the row of chairs, retaking the one in the center. "I simply wish to discuss something that happened during the confrontation with the Harbinger."

The faint but smug smile that had started to play across Meradyth's face faded. "Out with it. What's the matter?"

Faerin dipped her head in a deep nod, hiding her face so Meradyth couldn't glean the truth. "All is well, I promise. No cause for concern."

Meradyth looked Faerin over once more as if deciding whether to believe her. She seemed to make up her mind, her shoulders sagging with a faint wounded sound. "If you insist. After you finish speaking with Kyron, you should join us later at the inn."

"Us?"

"Regald wants to tell of some mishap or another, and Nalina promised us a round after recent events. You would be most welcome."

"I'm not sure I'll have time . . ." Faerin murmured, mostly to herself.

A beat passed between them before Meradyth folded her arms. "You're not . . . leaving us, are you?"

Faerin's head snapped up from where she had been inspecting the grooves in the chair. "W-what?"

"Flames help me." Meradyth pinched the bridge of her nose. "You have that look on your face. The same one you wore when you went chasing after Ry—hmm."

The comment caught Faerin by surprise. She could do little more than stare, unsure of what to say.

Meradyth continued before she lost her nerve or could be interrupted. "Your faith and zeal are unparalleled. To the point where some might even call it foolhardy. But it is clear that whatever force guides you does so because you are *worthy*. You have been since the beginning, when the shadow first found us. And while I cannot trust in unknown entities, I can trust you. It was you who kindled the Sacred Flame in me after I spent years cowering in darkness. If something spurs you on, I've no doubt it's the right path. But at least . . . at least spare us any more sudden losses."

With that and a curt nod, Meradyth tromped swiftly back the way she'd come, leaving Faerin gazing after her.

Because you are worthy. You have been since the beginning, when the shadow first found us.

Faerin remembered that night, when the Sacred Flame first burst to life within her, just as life in Hallowfall changed forever. The orphanage was less empty in those days. People had done as they were wont to do—seek companionship, make vows, have children.

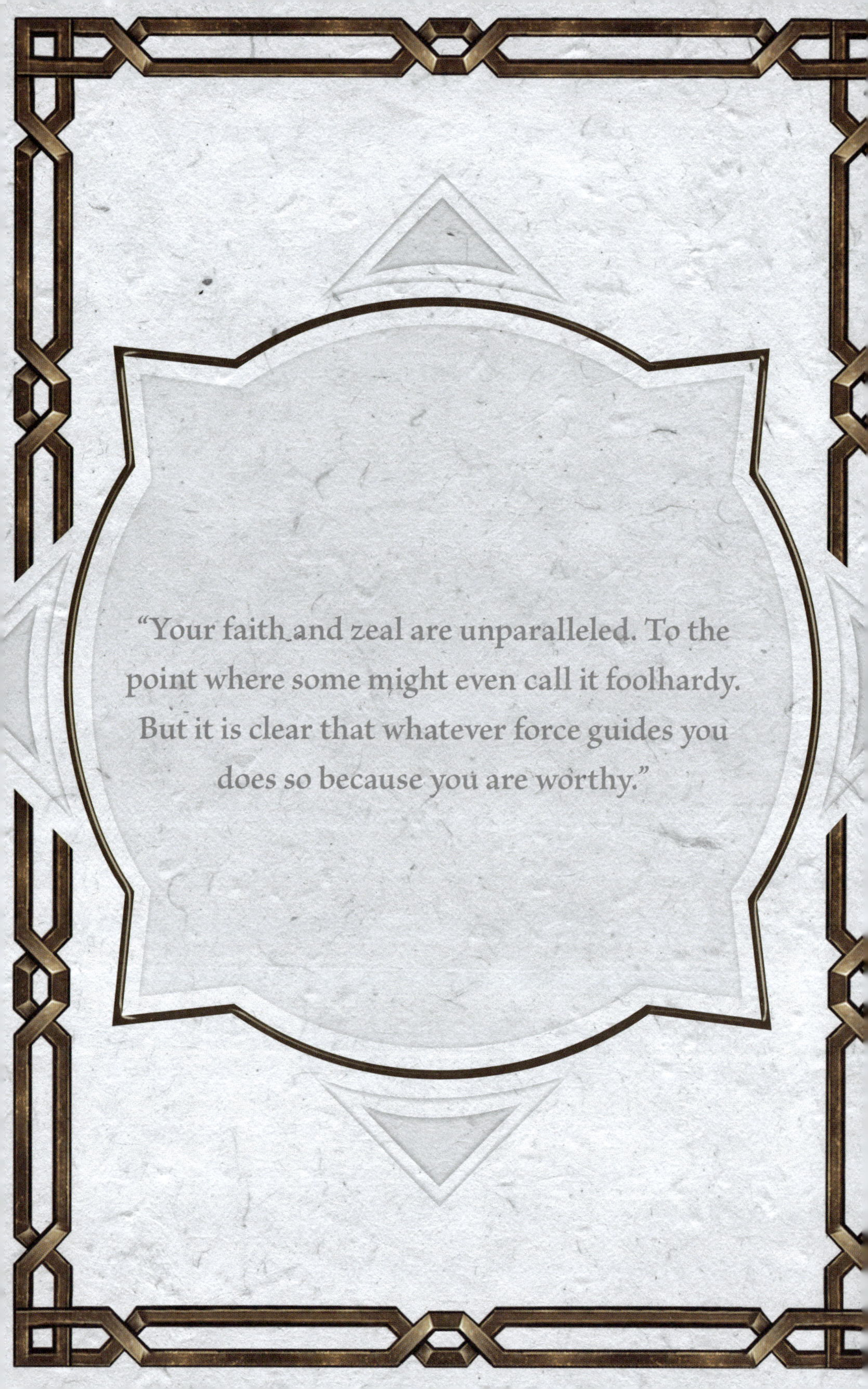
"Your faith and zeal are unparalleled. To the point where some might even call it foolhardy. But it is clear that whatever force guides you does so because you are worthy."

But there was still a war to fight. The nerubians and kobyss did not relent simply because the Arathi decided to build lives here. Lives that were still cut short in too many instances.

While the circumstances that brought new children to the orphanage's doorstep were always poor, Faerin had learned that this place was still a blessing, a home for them to go to. And she would do her best to make it as welcoming and warm as she could manage.

That particular evening she had decided to do story time while Sygfraed saw to other business. More and more the man's duties involved administerial work—managing supplies, food, the education and training of young ones. Turned out it took a lot to run an orphanage beneath the world. At least, that's what Sygfraed complained of more oft than not in those days.

And it was during those days that Faerin's arc of rebellion seemed to peak. Adolescence brought forth an entirely new fire, one that balked at the thought of being seen as or treated like a child. Tending the children was some small relief in this—a new responsibility, a duty to protect the little ones—but it was exhausting. Besides, she knew she could do *more*, that her abilities stretched beyond reading stories.

Fortunately, she *liked* reading stories.

"This is a good one," Faerin said triumphantly after flipping through the book for perhaps the thousandth time, hoping to stumble upon the pages about the lost queen. Alas.

Instead, she'd landed on a story about a prince who learned magic from a dragon. Stories with spells and mythic creatures usually went over well, but tonight her audience was searching for something else—*dinner.* None of Faerin's lessons had prepared her for the task of wrangling a pack of hungry toddlers.

She settled the book in her lap, her back straight, so the tome could rest open against her chest, leaving her hand free to turn pages, playact sword fights, and claw at the air like a magical monster. Today, she was an azure dragon with glistening scales and glimmering wings. The story didn't include all that, but she imagined that if she had wings, they would shine.

Faerin lilted her voice as she recited the tale from memory. "The prince took one look at the dragon and knew he had found his teacher. 'Great and powerful one!' the prince said—Molly! Molly, don't put that in your—augh. One moment!"

Setting the book on the chair, she made her way over to the little brown-skinned girl who had turned three this past spring—Faerin remembered all their names and their birthdays. Someone had to. It made a difference.

"Moliana, come now, I'm sure dinner will be much more delicious than a block!" She knelt on the floor and proceeded to wrangle the toy from the little girl, who fought valiantly, tears pricking the corners of her eyes.

That look shot straight to Faerin's heart. "Aw, fine," she relented, smiling as the child squealed in victory. Thankfully, she played with her spoils rather than trying to eat them.

Faerin rose to return to her chair and continue reading, but movement outside the large window at the front of the building caught her eye. Soldiers from Steelstrike's army raced by. Probably a drill. Or maybe the reservists had stayed at the inn a touch too long and were now late for training.

"Someone's in trouble," Faerin sang under her breath before reaching to wriggle the block out of Molly's mouth once more. She winced as the child let out a wail before hurriedly reaching into the pocket of her trousers and pulling out a bundle.

Wiping at her brown eyes and sniffling, Molly peered at the hunk of honeyloaf bread resting on Faerin's palm. It was a few days old but still good. She'd stashed her helping away instead of eating it the second night in a row Sygfraed looked grim during dinner.

The other children noticed and gathered round; Faerin set down the cloth for all of them to share. Warmth blossomed in her chest as the children's faces brightened while they snacked. She didn't even care about the crumbs falling from their faces, knowing she would soon be sweeping the entire first floor. It was more than worth it.

"This is our secret, okay?" she said with a soft laugh, putting a finger to her lips.

The children mirrored her action while giggling, as they often did.

But as the mood brightened, the room began to grow dark. It happened slowly. The light fading as if the sun had slipped behind the clouds. After all these years, Faerin still remembered the sun.

Barely. Remembered its rising and setting. The falling of night.

The shadows in the room seemed to notice first, lengthening as if stretching after coming awake. They danced and twitched as the only source of light became the fire in the stove. And as the light faded, so did the chatter. All the children fell silent at once. That never happened unless they were asleep.

Sygfraed moved from the stove, ladle in hand. The sound of his steps was like thunder in the shivering quiet. "Everyone just stay where you are," he called as he went to open the door and peer outside.

Faerin gestured for the children to remain still while she made her way over to the large window that faced the square.

People stood in the lane, paused in their comings and goings, some with baskets or bags in their hands. There was even a wagon being drawn by an imperial lynx. Everyone stared in the same direction—*Beledar's* direction—their faces drawn in shock, disbelief, or terror.

Faerin squinted and pressed forward against the glass, trying to see what they were all looking at.

"Faerin Lothar, get away from that window!" Sygfraed bellowed as he stormed across the room and started ushering children toward the cellar.

Surprise jolted through Faerin. Even when scolding her, he didn't usually raise his voice.

A protest parted her lips. *I was only looking!* But before the words

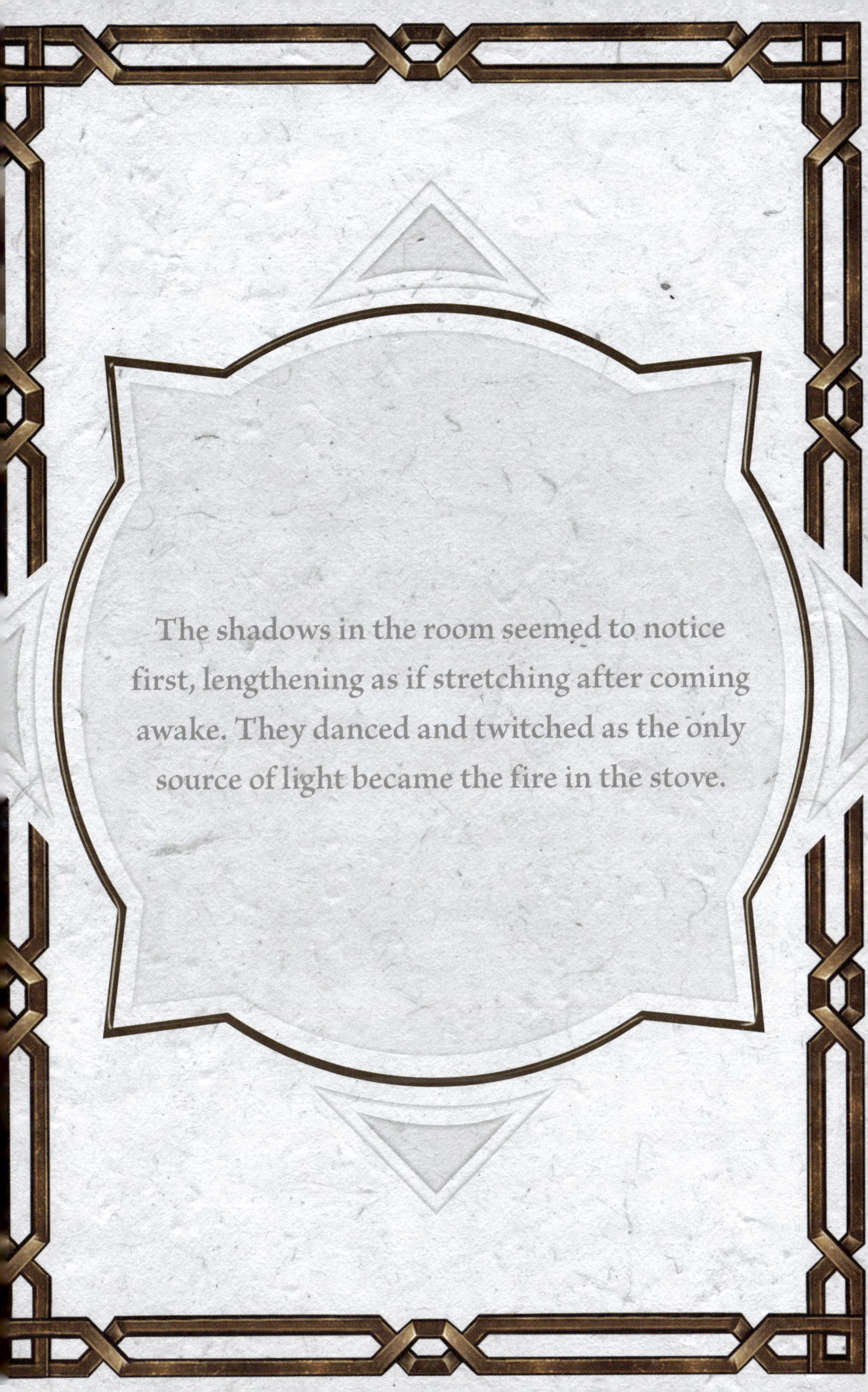

The shadows in the room seemed to notice first, lengthening as if stretching after coming awake. They danced and twitched as the only source of light became the fire in the stove.

left her, the window exploded in a shower of glass and wood and the shriek of metal. Screams filled the air as a paladin came crashing into the room.

He hit the far wall, then crumpled to the ground in a heap, spear and shield falling uselessly from still hands. Massive grooves in his armor were coated red and slicked black with blood. Outside, a shriek—keening and inhuman—rose in victory, and Faerin's entire body went cold.

Nerubians.

"Faerin!" Sygfraed shouted, hurrying the orphans below. They could hide in the cellar until the attack was over. Bolt the entry and wait.

But before Faerin could get to safety, a shadow fell across the room. A multilimbed monstrosity loomed in the space where the window used to be. It reared up on its legs, bulbous body a thing of nightmares, its mandibles clacking, its many eyes glinting with malice in the flickering light of the dying fire.

Secure all entrances. Find a weapon, locate a defensible position, and take cover. Faerin could hear Steelstrike's instructions for an attack driven into all the residents of Hallowfall. She ducked behind a table toppled onto its side, a hand pressed over her mouth to trap the whimper that threatened to escape. At the other end of the room, she could see a scramble of movement as Sygfraed closed the door to the cellar, saving the children he could.

There was no one else here but her, the monster, and the limp paladin.

As the nerubian stalked forward, Faerin shrank back, her heart pounding in her ears, fear surfing her nerves.

"Death draws near," groused a low voice, clicking with a rumbling hiss.

The terror sinking into Faerin's stomach threatened to pull her to the floor. She could run. Make a dash for the back stairway that would take her up to the bedrooms. Find a cupboard or wardrobe to hide in, pray the door held until help came.

A soft whimper snatched at Faerin's attention, her eyes wide. She wasn't the only one who noticed, the nerubian turning toward the sound. There, crawling from beneath an overturned chair, was little Molly. The girl whined with the start of tears. Faerin *knew* that cry, had lamented hearing it more times than she could count. Poor girl didn't know to stay quiet, that she was drawing danger toward her.

Faerin's mind raced as her heart wailed in her ears. There was no one else here. If the monsters had breached this far into Mereldar, the soldiers would be busy fighting. There was no one she could call. And Beledar's light no longer shone bright enough to shield them from the perils in the dark.

Nothing.

No one.

I'm here, something inside Faerin protested angrily. She had promised Molly and the others she would look after them. Had insisted that the Sacred Flame would always show up for those who needed it most, like it did for the heroes in their stories. Like Craishae had shown up for her people, in the midst of war, in the midst of carnage.

As long as there is someone to carry it forward . . .

. . . a torch will always burn in the night.

Clenching her eyes shut, Faerin took a hard breath. The heat in her center intensified, burning away the fear that had frozen her. She pushed to her feet just as the nerubian loomed over Molly, who finally lifted her little face. Her dark eyes went wide with dread. A sudden resolve rose in Faerin like an inferno overtaking the night.

The nerubian reached for the girl.

Faerin rushed forward.

The howl in her throat burst forth. Her vision went bright as she flung herself between those outstretched claws and the child. The creature shrieked. She braced for pain.

Nothing happened.

She blinked her eyes open, and shock lodged itself in her throat. A dome of radiance shimmered around both her and Molly, the source—her raised palm—now glowing gold. The nerubian beat against the shield uselessly, but the Light prevented the attack from landing.

The monster screeched its frustration of a meal denied, its warbling cut short by the bladed end of a spear erupting from its chest. Thick ichor splattered across the floor and sizzled against the dome, the monster sending more tendrils flying as it scrabbled at the

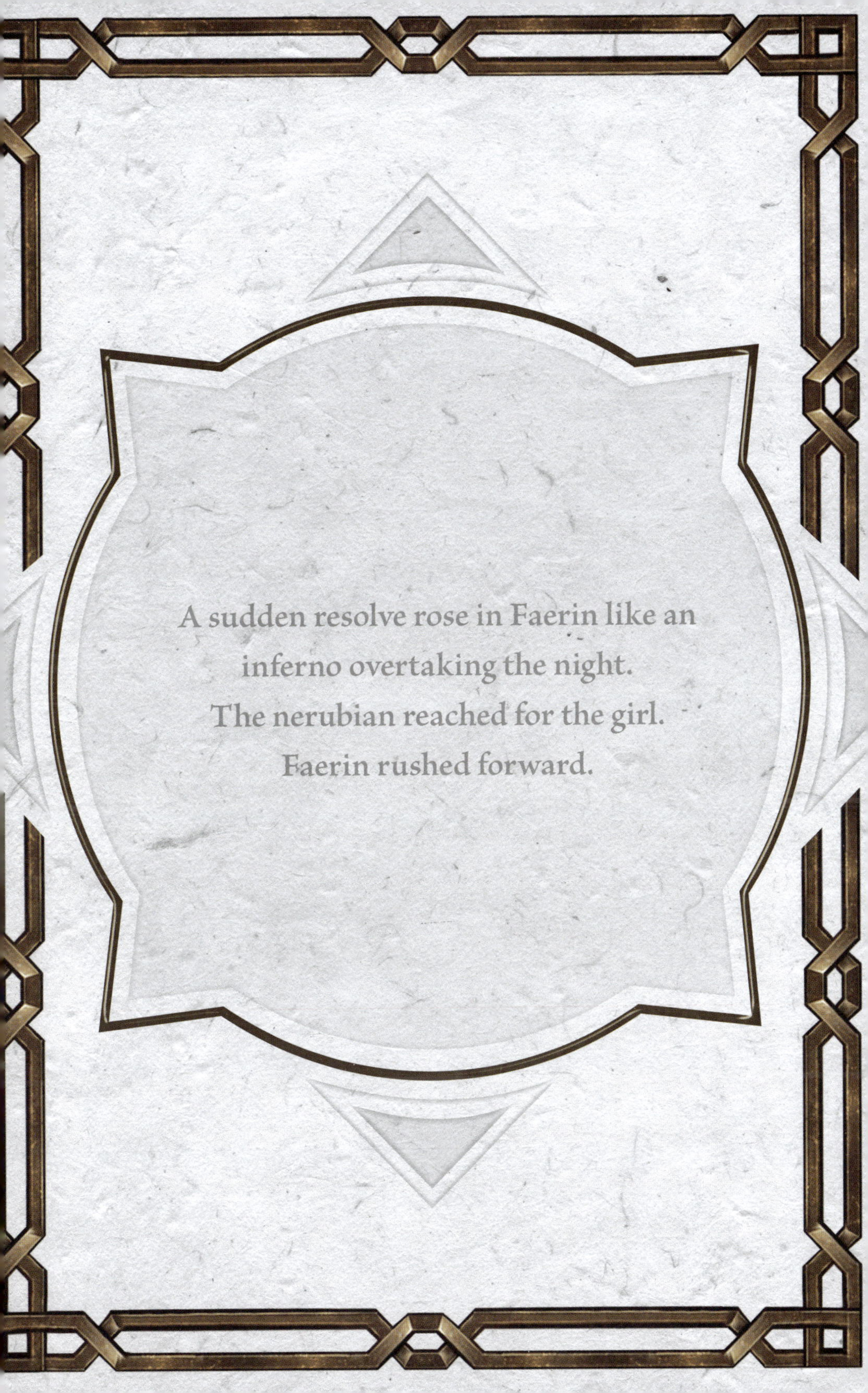

A sudden resolve rose in Faerin like an inferno overtaking the night.
The nerubian reached for the girl.
Faerin rushed forward.

blade, slicing its appendages to ribbons. It clacked and clicked in its death throes, then crumpled with a wet *thump*.

Standing over the body, braced against the other end of the spear, was the paladin who had come crashing through the window. His panted breaths rattled from behind his faceplate, his gaze fixed on Faerin. There was confusion in those eyes as he took in the scene, then slow understanding dawned, followed by the first of many impressed looks she would receive over the coming years.

"You're . . . doing that on your own," he said, his voice low and pained.

Faerin could only nod, slowly lowering her hand. As she did, the dome and the Light at her fingers faded.

Molly whimpered where she'd clutched at Faerin's leg.

"Incredible," the paladin said before a chorus of shouts drew his attention. He turned, hefting his weapon, only for his entire body to sag with relief.

"Forward!" cried a familiar voice, one Faerin often heard softly expressing disappointment in her studies.

General Steelstrike, backed by a contingent of soldiers, swept forward in a methodical rush of blades and arrows. The nerubians still in the streets fled shrieking into the darkness or were felled.

"Thank the Flame." The paladin sighed, then removed his helmet. She recognized him. Ryton Blackholme. He was one of the younger members of the expedition, a talented fighter and just as skilled at molding blades as wielding them. Faerin didn't know every soldier who reported to the general, but she knew the ones who'd made names for themselves. He looked to Molly, then Faerin. "Are either of you injured?"

Faerin managed to shake her head, but little Molly simply remained pressed against her.

"Good," he said, sinking more as the soldiers' shouts drew nearer.

Seeing him relax, the fist of fear around Faerin's heart began to loosen. She'd done it. She'd held fast against the monsters in the dark.

"Faerin, right?" Ryton said, his voice a touch raspy.

She nodded. It was no surprise he knew who she was. As the first and only child in the entire settlement, most were aware of her reputation for giving General Steelstrike no end of trouble.

"You have heart," he continued. "And something more, it seems."

Suffice it to say, neither Sygfraed nor the general were thrilled to hear of Faerin's bravery, both insisting she was not adequately trained for combat and should have stuck to the protocol. But there could be no doubt that more than one life was spared that day due to Faerin's bravery. Because of this, and her blossoming skill in wielding the Sacred Flame, the general begrudgingly let her begin a proper warrior's training.

In the ensuing months, as the orphanage was repaired—the shattered window replaced with fortified wood to form a wall—Faerin found herself spending less and less time there. She was set on a new path now, one that led her to where she stood today.

Her mind continued to bounce from memory to memory, from her first day as a soldier in training, to the day Ryton fought by her side one last time, to the moment she swore the oath to become a Lamplighter, to take the Light with her into the dark.

And now here, where she would ask to take the Light farther.

"Faerin, have you been waiting for me?" called a voice.

For the second time today, she found herself caught off guard. Great Kyron stood a short distance off, their expression amused and curious but pinched with a touch of concern.

Faerin bounded to her feet, nodding her respects. "Great Kyron. I . . . sorry, I didn't mean—I'd hoped to speak with you, if I may."

"Of course." They gestured for her to follow them into the meeting space. It was sparsely decorated, mostly with maps pinned to the walls, each drawn and redrawn to depict enemy and troop movements, both the Lamplighters and the general standing forces.

Faerin had spent much time in this office, for good and not so good reasons. It pricked at something inside her that this might be the last time she and her commander would convene here.

"Is everything all right?" Great Kyron asked as they made their way around the desk to take a seat.

"Yes. That is to s-say, nothing is wrong. *Actively.*" Faerin began, then had to clear her throat when she felt her voice start to crack. She took a slow breath.

Faerin was no stranger to fear. She had known and faced it many times, conquered it many more, but it always managed to rise again.

An undefeatable enemy. An immortal foe. But while fear may have often spurred her into acting, it was faith that ever guided her. It would be no different now.

"There is nothing wrong," she reaffirmed. "But I would like to put in a formal request. Anduin, Alleria, and the others will be returning to the surface soon. I would like to go with them."

The look that crossed Kyron's face wasn't what Faerin expected. She'd braced herself for disappointment, perhaps some incredulity or even anger—though she'd never seen Great Kyron express either. Instead, what she saw was a slight furrow of understanding.

"I had a feeling this conversation was coming."

Faerin couldn't keep her own surprise from dawning. "You . . . you did?"

"Oh yes. For some time now." Kyron bid Faerin sit, which she quickly did. "Having witnessed you these past weeks rally to the defense of not just Hallowfall but the whole of Khaz Algar? Your request is not surprising."

Faerin felt the familiar fist around her heart tighten, but the ache this time wasn't from fear. "Serving my people as a Lamplighter, under you, has been the greatest honor of my life."

"But . . ." Great Kyron coaxed when the silence between them stretched.

"But there is something . . . *more* I must do," she finished. "I'm not entirely sure what that something is, but I know I have a duty to fulfill. Out there. It is a calling I heard even as a child. It's what drove me to leave my life, my family behind. And for a time, it bid me stay here. But now—"

"It draws you elsewhere," they finished.

Faerin lifted her chin, meeting Great Kyron's steady but not unkind gaze. Silence descended once more, and this time Faerin felt she may drown in it.

Now comes the disappointment, she thought.

But Kyron merely regarded her before finally speaking into the quiet. "Faerin, you have been one of our best. That will not change with your location. I have trained many Lamplighters in my time—and I do not believe flattery serves any purpose but to dull a sharp blade—but I have seen your faith bring you this far. If what drew you across the world and into its depths now calls to you again, I believe you would be ill advised not to answer. And while I have no idea where this path may lead you, one thing I *am* sure of . . . is that you will be missed."

The smile that pulled at Kyron's expression eased a tension in Faerin she hadn't realized she'd been holding. With its release she felt the sting of tears. Immediately she wanted to fight them back, to swallow the emotional response for the inappropriate display it may be, but the look on Great Kyron's face told her that wouldn't be necessary.

"Fitting, that one of the empire's most prominent houses is poised to rise in a time such as this. Still, Hallowfall will be that much dimmer," they lamented, bittersweet.

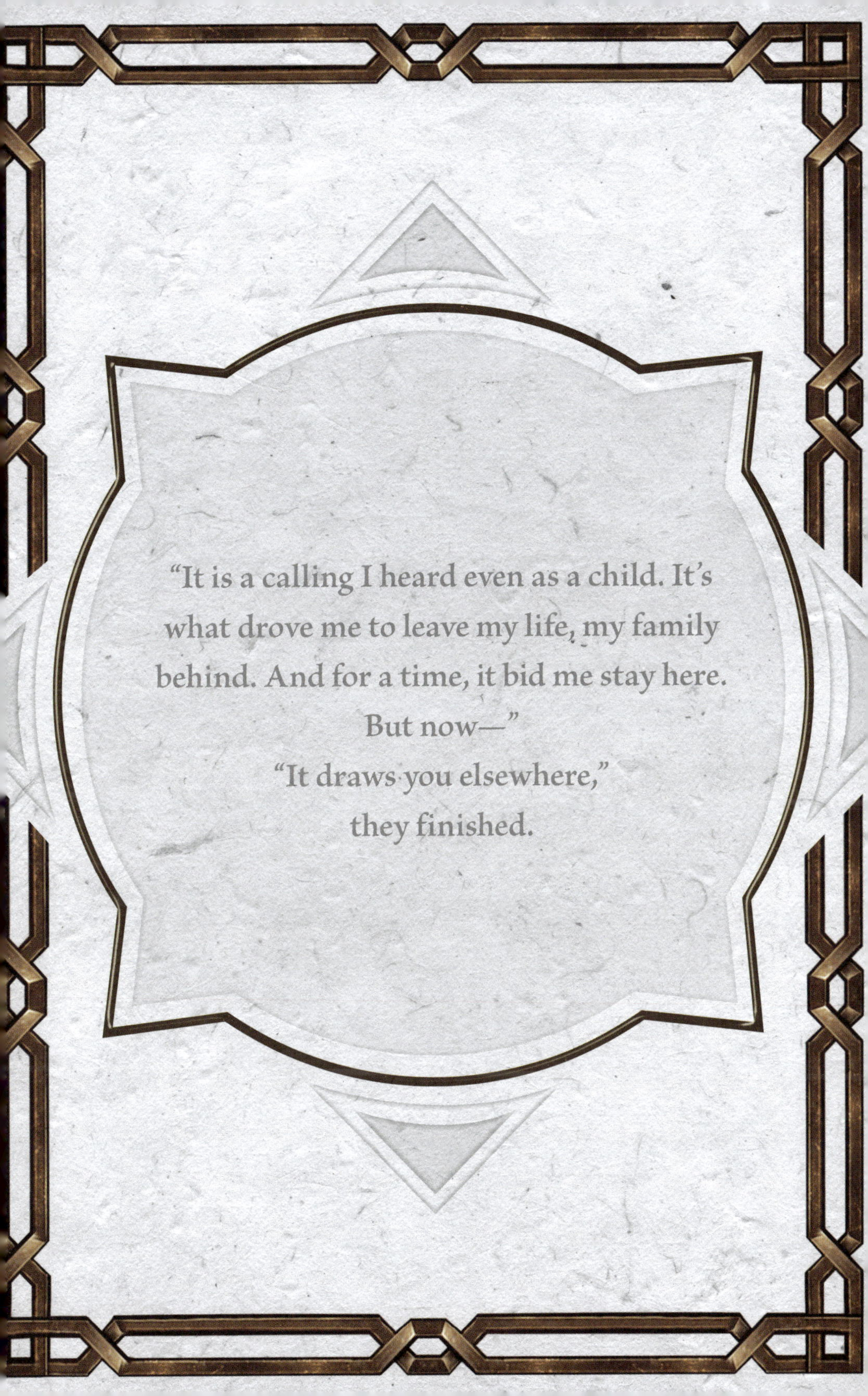

"It is a calling I heard even as a child. It's what drove me to leave my life, my family behind. And for a time, it bid me stay here. But now—"

"It draws you elsewhere," they finished.

Faerin blinked rapidly as she finally allowed the tears to fall in a mix of joy and sorrow. "But the Sacred Flame burns ever on."

Faerin was dismissed to make preparations, which meant the part in all this she was looking forward to the least: saying goodbye.

Most of her fellow Lamplighters were easy to find at the inn where Meradyth said they would be. The whole way there Faerin debated how she would break the news, whether she would take them aside one by one or say her piece to all at once. In the end, she decided to simply get it over with, like setting a bone.

After the words were out of her mouth, there was more silence and staring. Then raucous cheers went up. Everyone congratulated her, offering well-wishes. A few playfully and teasingly groused their jealousies at not getting to go and ultimately decided to drown their collective sorrows in blessed brew. And why not? Though their comrade would be missed, a great victory had been won, with allies from across all Khaz Algar. If there was a time to allow for a little extra frivolity, now was it.

Though there was a brief moment where Meradyth pulled Faerin aside to murmur into the rim of her cup, "I knew it."

"Yes," Faerin sighed, amusedly put upon. "You did."

Meradyth aimed a finger at her. "I always do. And while I'm not happy about this for me, I *am* happy for you. And proud to say I know you and call you friend."

Warmth blossomed in Faerin's chest, and she felt a wide smile break across her face.

Then Meradyth's arms were around her, tight and strong. "Thank you for your honest courage. And for everything else."

Faerin returned the hug as firm as she could. Then it was time to let go.

That night led to another day of goodbyes, amidst packing her meager belongings. She chose to face General Steelstrike next, who was quick to point this out as yet another incident in a long line of undesirable behavior.

"Know that this stubborn refusal to heed protocol will likely lead you into other dangers, dangers beyond . . . my reach." It wasn't said with anger or the usual irritation the general held for Faerin. "Not that you've needed me to save you much at all these days," the general eventually relented with a sag of her shoulders and a heavy breath.

It was in that moment that Faerin got a glimpse of the woman beneath the warrior. The exhaustion that came with the weight of carrying the well-being of an entire community on your shoulders.

"I've needed you from the beginning," Faerin offered from where she stood at attention on the other side of the large table. "I will no doubt need you again in the future, but know I take your lessons with me. Your teaching and guidance have meant the world to me. I just . . . I wanted that to be known."

The two women regarded one another for a moment. Then, surprisingly, it was Steelstrike who broke first. She crossed the space between them and pulled Faerin into a hug so tight she felt lightheaded from it. Faerin returned the embrace, fingers clutching at the fabric draped over her former guardian's armor.

"The strength of the Arathi shines within you," Steelstrike murmured before drawing back to discreetly swipe beneath one eye. Then she straightened and nodded. "Go forth and show the world."

Faerin's next goodbye took her to the stables, where a huge lynx lazed in the doorway, chewing noisily on a dented-in child's ball the orphans had either lost track of or had thrown to the big cats in an attempt to get them to play.

Stepping past the creature—which barely flicked an ear in her direction while it continued to chew—she made her way to a pen in the back, calling in singsong as she went. "Blaaaazeclaaaaaw."

Ryton's lynx lifted her head from where she'd been lazing about. The great cat, more than used to Faerin's comings and goings by now, began to rumble loudly with a purr as the Lamplighter lowered herself to scratch and rub everywhere she could on the creature.

"Who's a good girl? That's you, yes? Yes, you are." Despite her presented aversion to cats, Faerin had come to rather enjoy the great beasts. They were intuitive in a way most people were not.

"I hope you'll understand and forgive me," Faerin said softly, "when I don't return those first few days. Or weeks. I hope you . . . you know that I haven't abandoned you or that I wasn't taken." Her

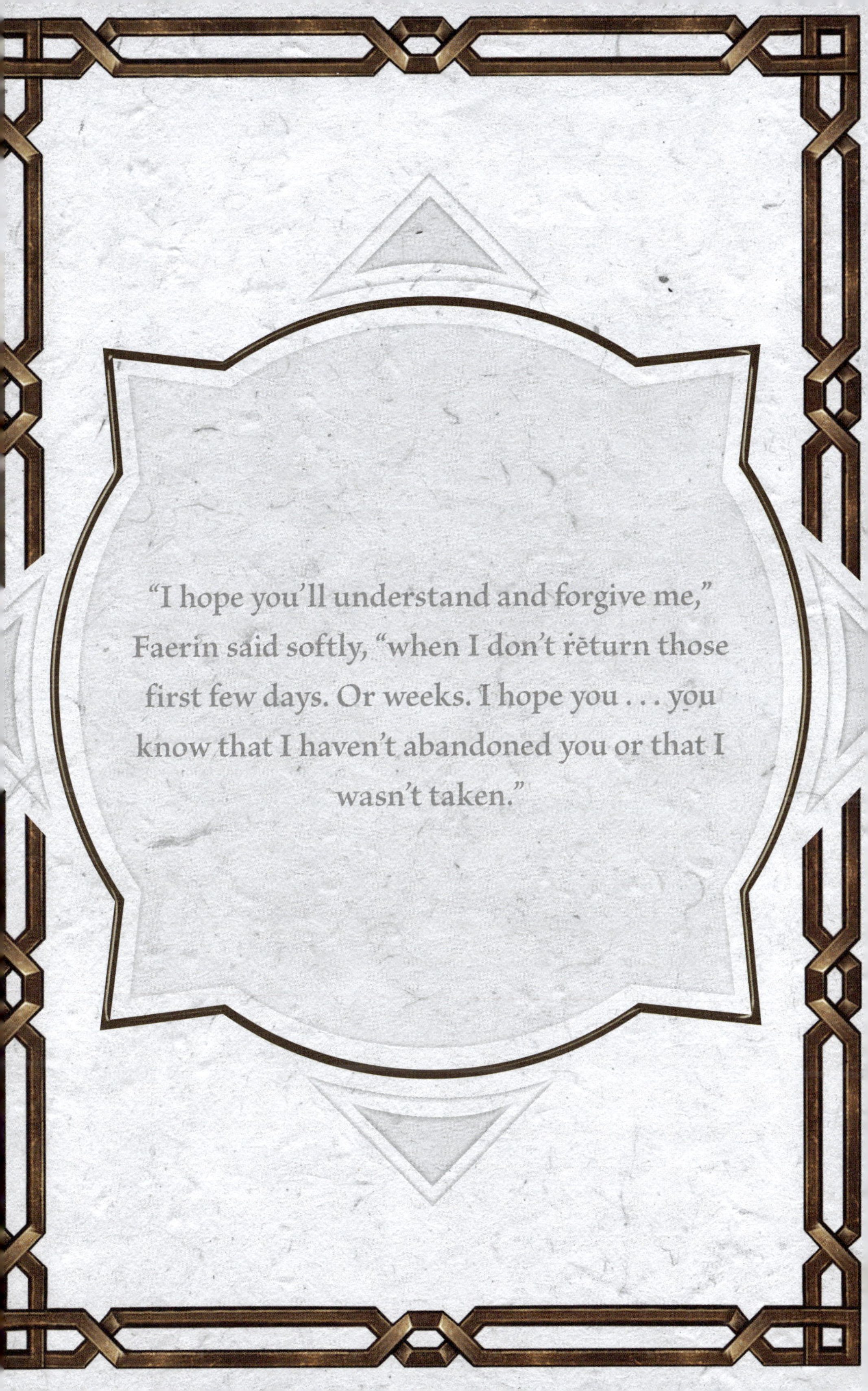

"I hope you'll understand and forgive me," Faerin said softly, "when I don't return those first few days. Or weeks. I hope you . . . you know that I haven't abandoned you or that I wasn't taken."

fingers clutched at a patch of fur, and the lynx rumbled a complaint that made her loosen her hold. Instead, she wrapped her arm around Blazeclaw's neck and buried her face in her fur. "I pray you are comforted. That someone still brings you fresh-caught fish and spring grasses."

She felt the sting of tears again but did not cry. No, she had one more goodbye to get through after this one, and she would need all of her tears for then. So she straightened her back against the wood of the stall, the cat's head resting in her lap while she scratched between its ears.

After an hour or so of more petting and scratching, and at least three helpings of treats, Faerin lifted the strap of her pack and slung it over her shoulder to make the slow trek to the grounds of the priory, where she kept her head bowed and only acknowledged those who greeted her first. The whole of her felt dragged down, as if her legs were made of lead and a stone had fallen into her stomach.

She trod along the paths that just days before had been overrun with misery and shadow, ascended nerubians striking from the dark. The Harbinger had taken their most holy seat of power, and Faerin—along with Alleria, Anduin, and many other champions from the old world—had battled to drive out those last vestiges of the Void's influence. Alleria and her people were blessed to be given back a dear friend once lost. Anduin had finally taken to hear what Faerin had been telling him all along, that the Sacred Flame does not abandon those who need it. And yet, walking down this familiar path, she felt a twinge of bitterness.

It was human, as the saying goes, to feel such things. To know the pain of loss and sorrow as keenly as one would the pain of a knife. But it was not the way of the Arathi, the Lamplighters, to wallow in those feelings. Acknowledge them, yes, but find the courage and strength to move ever forward.

Alleria's friend—Khadgar—had been restored, and for not the first time Faerin found herself wondering why not *her* friends. Why not Ryton or Andari or Molly's parents or any of the numerous others stolen despite the best efforts of her and the other Lamplighters?

She shoved these thoughts aside when she reached her destination, a rise of rock near the bridge to the Dayspring Fields. Faerin stood, staring out at the view, listening to the groan of the waterwheel behind her, watching the airships drift overhead. This had been one of her and Andari's favorite spots. They'd come here for brief moments of respite, to play round after round of Light's Gambit, or sit and talk not as Lamplighters or soldiers, but friends.

In this moment, knowing it might be the last she'd ever set foot here, Faerin felt Andari's presence as if they stood beside her. She tightened her grip on a pair of recently carved and painted Light's Gambit pieces, and the tears she'd mostly managed to tamp down for days flowed free.

"I'd give anything for you to be here," Faerin whimpered into the wind, her head bowed and her arm wrapped tightly around her middle. Her palm ached where her hand fisted around the pieces, wood digging into flesh. "Part of me knows you'd pack my bag and send me off yourself if you were. Maybe even . . . come with me. Maybe I would even ask you." A faint laugh escaped her, and she stepped forward to kneel in the grass, reaching to set the pieces there.

Her fingers brushed the earth, and she thought again of all they'd shared, the time they spent together. Their sacrifice. Their bravery.

"I carry you with me always," Faerin whispered. "Your memory a light unto my feet. Watch over them for me. Protect them where I can't. Flame keep your spirit." Her vision blurry, she pushed herself up onto trembling legs and turned.

Each step fell heavier than the last in some ways and yet lighter in others. This was it. While she knew this was what she was meant to do, and the process had been smoother than she'd expected, it brought into sharp relief the pain of what she was leaving behind. She missed Ryton, who would know what to say or do to assure her. She missed Andari, who would have helped her process everything over a game of Light's Gambit. Knowing the path was one thing, walking it another, and walking it alone . . .

She had often wondered if Queen Craishae had missed the people she left behind when she embarked on her journey to safeguard the world, knowing she may never return. When she bathed in the fiery waters and everything she'd been before burned away.

"Of course she did," Sygfraed had assured her one night when she'd posed the question to him, having spent the better part of days pondering over the parallels between that story and her own. The man then frowned a little. "But sacrifice is not an aspiration. It is an acceptance. Craishae still fought to live, and she lived fully in honor of those who fell before her. Faerin . . . many people draw inspiration from the legends at their end. But I challenge you to draw from the legends as they *began*."

And as Craishae had begun her legend full of hope and determination, so Faerin felt the same burn within her. And with that flame she could take each step farther and farther from her and Andari's special place, from memories of Ryton, the Lamplighters, from the stable and Blazeclaw, from General Steelstrike, from the orphanage and the children there and Sygfraed too, whom she couldn't say goodbye to. Not really. With any luck, the little ones would think of her and know she was off on a grand adventure, like the ones she read to them about. And who knows, with time, perhaps she could bring them back new stories of her own.

The journey to Dornogal was one she'd made before, only this time it felt different. Maybe the sky seemed clearer without the surety that she would be returning to a home underground. Perhaps the air felt crisper now that she knew she would leave these familiar lands and their ways for new places.

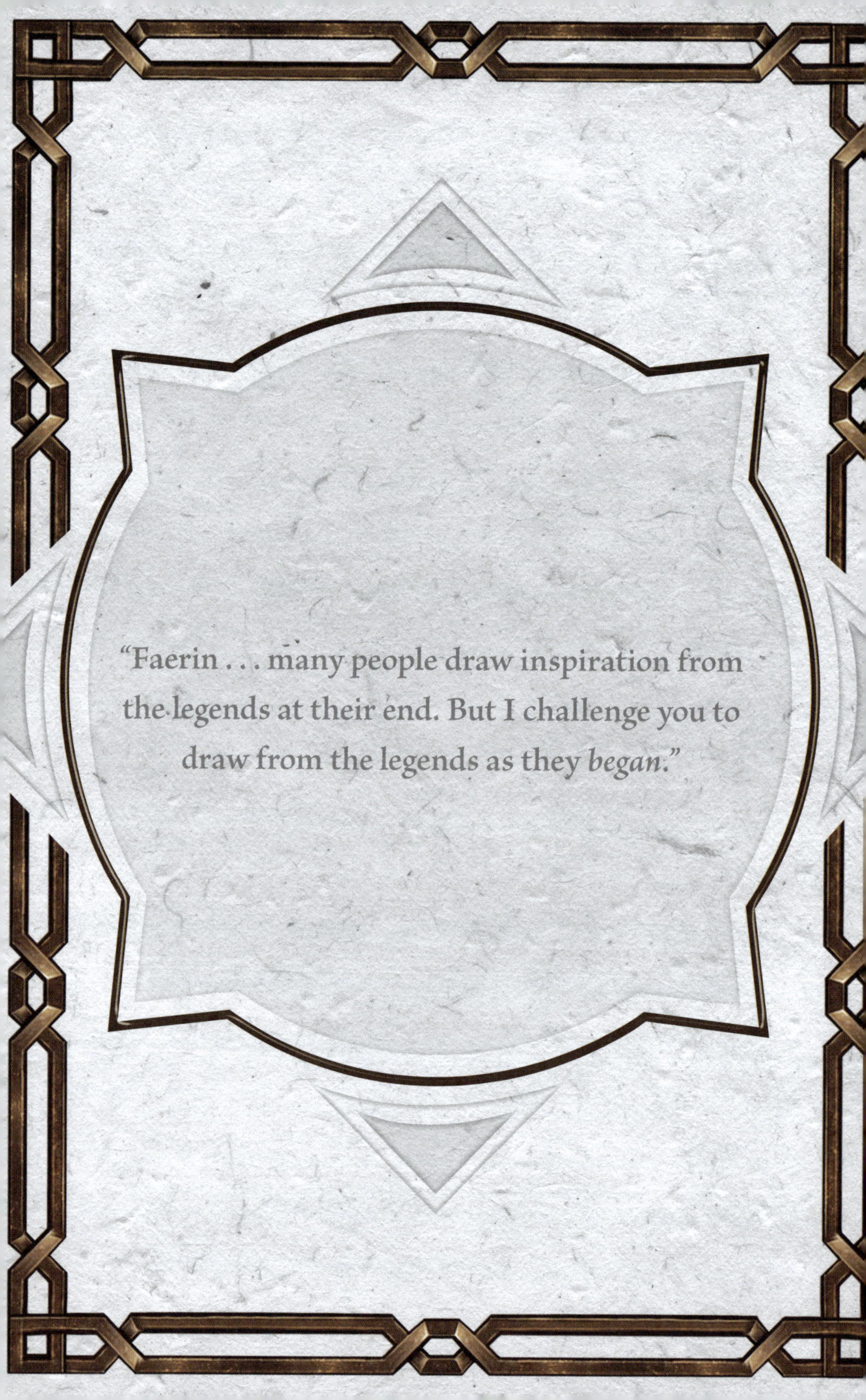

“Faerin . . . many people draw inspiration from the legends at their end. But I challenge you to draw from the legends as they *began*.”

Whatever the case, it caused her to quicken her step as she approached the gathered number who would be making the trek via portal to the old world. Excitement thrummed in her veins, burning similarly yet so very different from the Light, which also hummed eagerly within her.

She spotted Anduin amidst the throng and approached him, and a smile pulled wide at her face when she caught sight of the grin he wore. He seemed . . . brighter, less heavy in a way she knew but could not name.

"Faerin!" he called. "I was beginning to worry if, well . . ."

"If I'd changed my mind about leaving behind my oath, my friends, everything I've known for adventure in a wide new world?" she asked, arching an eyebrow in what she hoped was only *slightly* accusatory.

The way his expression flattened sent delight rolling through her. She laughed and clapped him on the shoulder.

"Easy. I'm still going, with the blessings of everyone I care for and gratitude for all they taught me."

The relief that washed over Anduin was equally amusing. "It's only that I would understand! If you had, that is—changed your mind. I say this while realizing I'm only just now returning from my own adventure into the world."

"And was it what you needed?" Faerin asked, a touch of doubt creeping in just so. "This adventure, I mean, did you find what you were after?"

There was a pause as the man frowned, dropped his gaze briefly, then returned it to her as his smile softened. "I have."

"Faerin." Jaina Proudmoore came to stand next to Anduin, peering at him and then at her. "Good to see you. Anduin was worried you wouldn't make it in time."

"Is that so?" Faerin asked, smirking as the king seemed to lose his tongue a moment.

Anduin cleared his throat. "I-I was just concerned you would have to go through the portal on your own. I wasn't sure if you've traveled by magic before, and it can be disorienting at best your first time. I didn't want you to have to experience something like that alone."

Jaina smirked but said nothing, letting a knowing look do all the talking for her. "In either case, I'm glad you're here and that you've given him a taste of his own medicine."

"Pardon?" Anduin asked, recovering from his brief fluster.

"Now you know what it's like to look after a headstrong noble, prone to doing what they want rather than what they've been counseled."

He huffed faintly. "And what's that supposed to mean?"

"You know very well what it means, *Jerek*."

The bit of color that crawled up the king's neck didn't go unnoticed, but it went unremarked upon as Jaina mercifully changed the subject. "Faerin, you should know, it took some convincing for Danath to agree to this. There is . . . a lot going on back home he'll have to see to almost immediately, same for us. But know that you will still be in the best of hands, and we will be there should you have need of anything."

Faerin nodded, her smile still in place from her previous humor. She had to admit she was disappointed that it wouldn't be Anduin showing her more of the old world, having been the one who shared the most about it. But she understood that he had duties to see to, what with his return and the Harbinger's whereabouts unknown.

Offering thanks as Jaina moved on, Faerin turned her attention to Anduin. Her smile eased a touch higher at one corner. "Jerek?"

He coughed into a fist as the faint splash of red reached his cheeks. He turned, glancing every which way except Faerin's. It was endearing. "That's a story for another time, I think. We're set to leave any moment now. Where is Danath?"

As if summoned by the mention of his name, Danath Trollbane emerged from the gathered number. An old king and soldier, battle worn and ready, he dipped in reverence to Anduin, who quickly returned the bow, then angled around to Faerin.

"You must be Lamplighter Lothar." Danath offered a hand, and Faerin took it. "It's an honor."

"Likewise." She stole a last look at Anduin, who seemed to have recovered well enough.

“I hope the old world lives up to your expectations,” Danath said.

“In truth, I don’t know what to expect,” Faerin admitted. The old world was unknown to her, full of new wonders and dangers alike. But Queen Craishae’s story still echoed in her heart, and that pull at her center settled any and all doubt. The calling that she would answer, same as her ancestor had done. What she didn’t know, the Sacred Flame would guide her through. So she squared her shoulders and lifted her chin. “But I am eager to find out.”

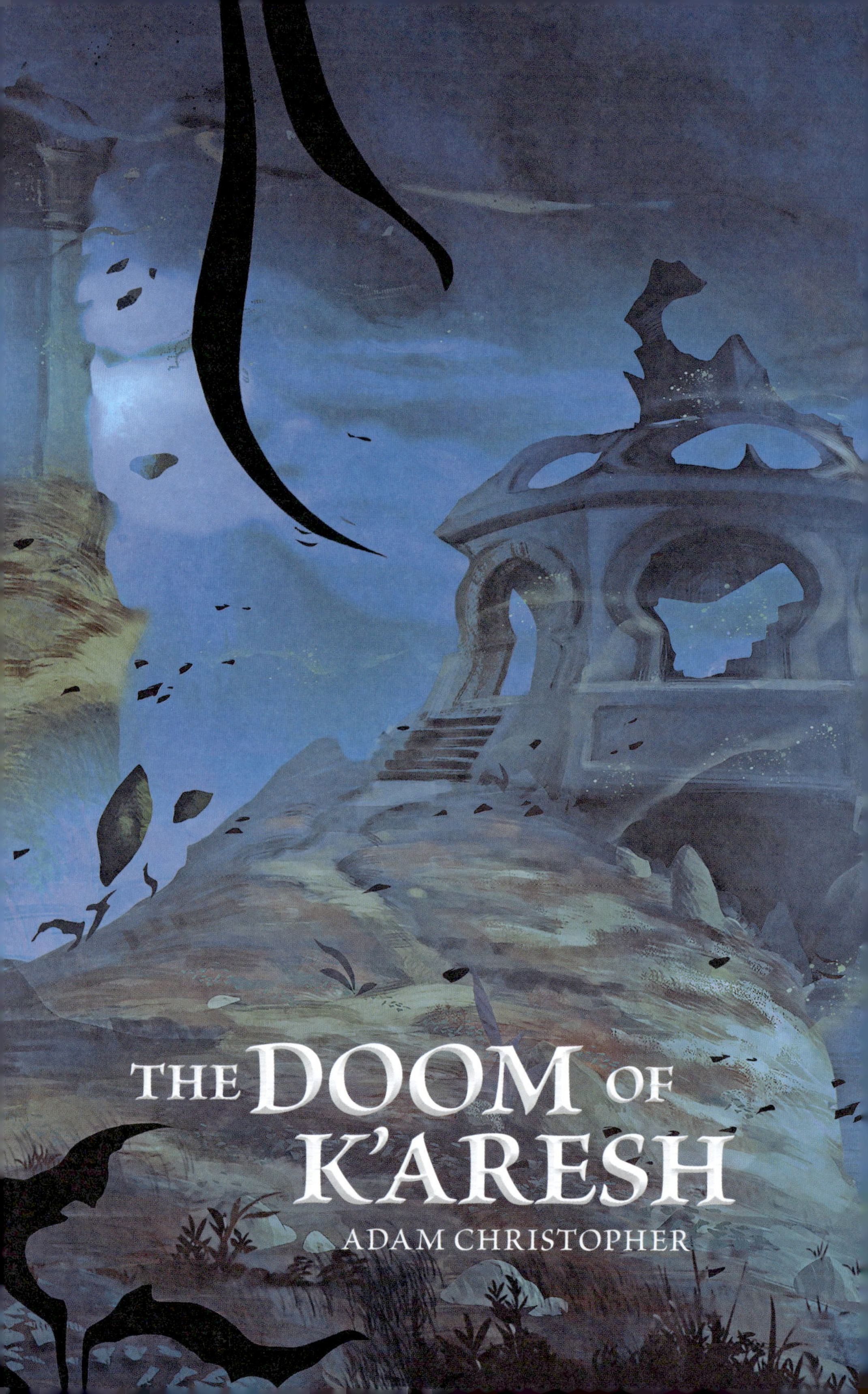
THE DOOM OF
K'ARESH
ADAM CHRISTOPHER

1
The VOICE from the VOID

There was a certain beauty to this place, even she could admit that. A beauty born of tragedy, of horror, but for the moment, Alleria Windrunner pushed such nuance from her mind as she stood on a high, nameless peak at the edge of Telogrus Rift. She stared out into the violet-purple fury of the Void that swirled around the shattered remains of the lost world, seeking . . . perspective. Solace.

Tell Khadgar what we learned. I will return to Dalaran in time.

Alleria's words haunted her. It was avoidance, a sidestepping of her responsibilities. Right now, the new threat to Azeroth felt too big, too abstract—yes, the Harbinger, Xal'atath, was coming, and her world faced a challenge like no other.

As did she. Through the Void, she commanded untold power, but it also went the other way—while the darkness was a part of her, she was a part of *it.* Xal'atath knew this and could use Alleria for some unseen end.

Once more, Alleria felt her connection to the darkness was more a curse than a blessing.

This, against the fact that Azeroth itself sat on the edge of destruction. Alleria knew she had friends and allies to call on, but were they really a match for the Harbinger? This entity that had survived thousands of years, heralded the annihilation of countless worlds? Besides, at this precise moment, she wasn't sure she could face them so soon after confronting the phantom of her love, Turalyon, conjured by Xal'atath to—

To do what? *Kill her?* No, nothing so mundane.

It had been to *unbalance* her. And it had worked. She had played right into the Harbinger's plans. Alleria had been unprepared, and somewhere inside burned the fear that Xal'atath would win.

"I sense a troubled mind."

Alleria looked up from the view of infinity before her to see Locus-Walker slowly approaching. She took a long, deep breath.

"Locus-Walker, I need *answers.* You said you believe Xal'atath seeks for Azeroth the same fate which Dimensius delivered unto K'aresh. I must . . . I must know everything that happened here. You cannot possibly expect—"

Locus-Walker hovered, unmoving, and she knew he would remain there forever, patiently waiting for Alleria to find her center, her moment. Only she wasn't sure she could, not this time.

She lowered her head. She knew what she wanted to say, what she felt she *must* say, but . . . well, hadn't they done this dance before, so many times? She sought to forge ahead, protect her world, but he would give her nothing until she understood the lesson he wanted to impart. This was old ground, well trodden. And yet it was something she couldn't escape. The phantom of Turalyon had admirably demonstrated her need for wisdom.

"I am afraid," said Alleria, finally training her gaze on Locus-Walker. "Of Xal'atath. Of the past. Of what happened to K'aresh. Of what will happen to Azeroth." She paused. "But most of all, I am afraid of *myself.* Of the Void within me. A power I thought I made peace with long ago."

"There is no shame in fear," said Locus-Walker. "The Void is a terrible thing. I will not deny it. That the Void is part of you is something you have learned to live with, even if you can never truly accept it. Just as I must live with my own nature."

Alleria closed her eyes tight. "Perhaps Lothraxion was right," she whispered. "Once you've invited the Shadow into your heart, it ends in madness."

Locus-Walker's laugh surprised Alleria. She opened her eyes to find his ethereal form drifting backward a step, his gold-and-purple spaulders shaking with mirth.

"My pain amuses you?"

"What amuses me, Alleria," he said, tilting his unreadable, bandage-wrapped face, "is that you would remember his words from so long ago but not my own."

"Then tell me again. Speak to me now. I am open to your

counsel." She felt her shoulders sag. "I know I must find my balance again, but I must also know the disaster that looms if I am to avert it."

The two faced each other on the tor for a moment, then Locus-Walker turned away. "Come," he said as he began to descend the slope.

Alleria didn't move. "Where?"

Locus-Walker didn't stop. "We have a task to perform."

"What task? Have we the time?"

At this, Locus-Walker came to a halt and faced her. "Perhaps. Perhaps not. But I believe this quest may be of great benefit to you."

"That is a lot of words to say nothing."

Locus-Walker nodded. "There is a Void revenant somewhere at large here in Telogrus Rift. It is dangerous, and it must be eliminated, but it has concealed itself. The hunt will be restorative—for you, and perhaps for me also. You may gain some perspective on your own nature. You may even repair the trust in yourself that now lies broken."

Alleria frowned. "You promise much. How, exactly, will hunting a creature of the Void help clear my mind?"

"Because while we track, I will tell you a story," said Locus-Walker.

Curiosity piqued, Alleria took a step toward him. Locus-Walker slowed to keep pace beside her.

"It is a tale about balance," he said, "and about my world of K'aresh and the doom that came upon it . . ."

K'aresh was never like your Azeroth. Never green and blue, blanketed by oceans or teeming with growing things. K'aresh was a harsh place, a world of sand and stone and dust. But there was something else—a certain magic—and perhaps aided by that magic, life found a foothold, as it often does. For ourselves, the K'areshi, we loved this hard world, and whatever it lacked, we made. Lessons of survival became our means of innovation until, some millennia later, our society grew into a great web of city-states.

Ma'nussa was the one I called my home. I was a technomancer, a noble class indeed, my life dedicated to studying energy harvest and transference. Our society was built upon oaths, from the lowest nomad to the Oracles themselves, those mighty few who led us in all facets of life. These oaths were no mere fancy; they were the sworn ties that bound us to our work and to one another, a sacred act above no other. To break an oath was to cast aside life itself and to die, alone among the sands.

Each city-state had its ruler—thanks to my status, I was pleased to count Ky'veza, the leader of Ma'nussa, among my closest companions—but it was the Council of Oracles who held authority in all things. The council was led by Salhadaar, High Priest of the Untamed, and when the radiant visions first swept K'aresh, it was his wisdom I sought. When that terrible curse fell upon a number of K'areshi, myself among them, I overcame my fear to pursue its

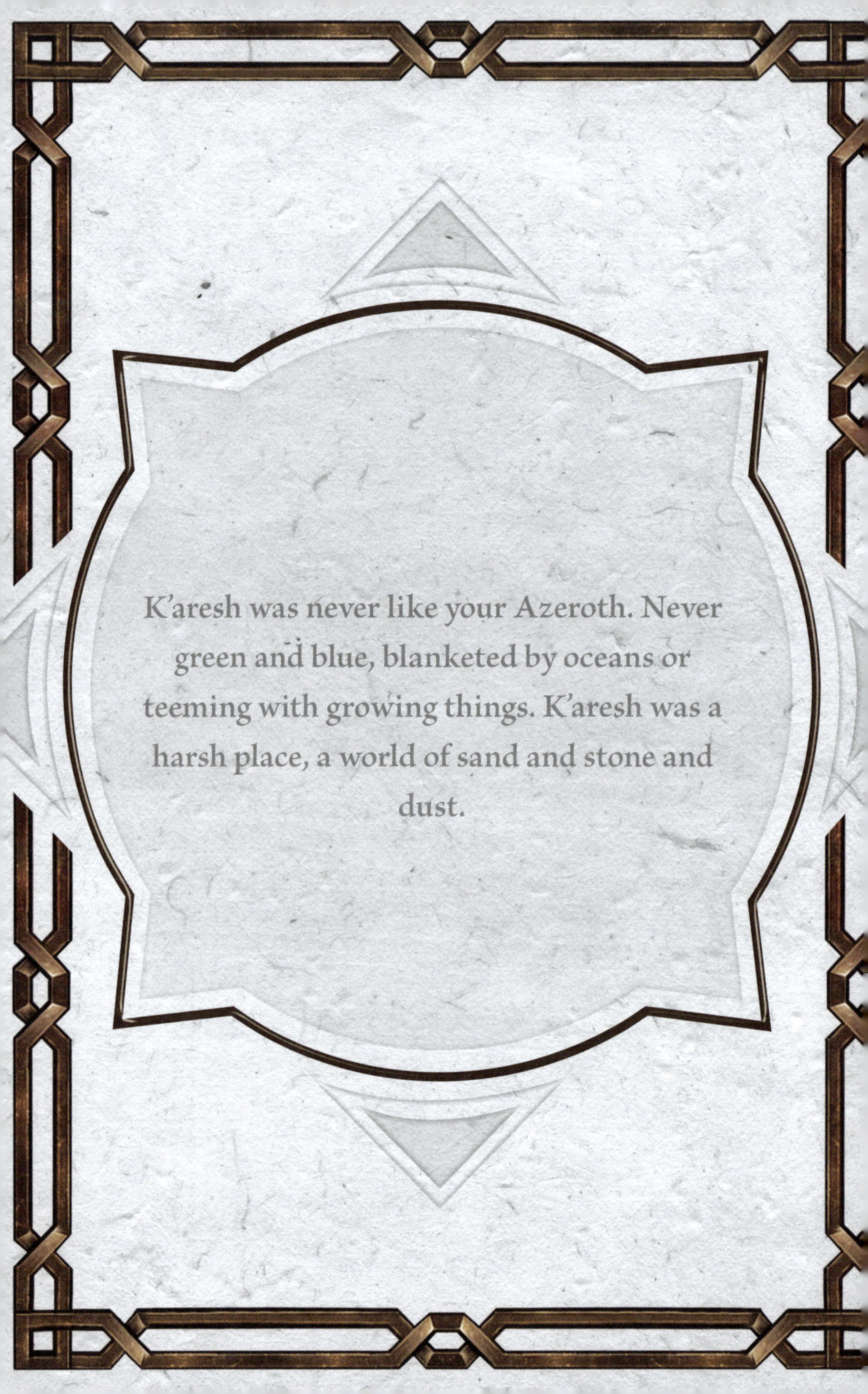

K'aresh was never like your Azeroth. Never green and blue, blanketed by oceans or teeming with growing things. K'aresh was a harsh place, a world of sand and stone and dust.

study. I redirected my laboratories, my observatories, my every effort to focus on the matter. I collated the data, and I made my conclusions. The problem was not a simple one, but I looked to the Oracles. They had guided me as they guided all K'aresh; I knew their advice would be a valuable jewel indeed.

How wrong I was. The meeting of the Oracles was a labor, long in duration, complex in its politics. As the hours ran on, my confidence began to leave me, and when Salhadaar called the council to order for one final time, I knew what he was going to say before he said it.

Yet I had to hear it for myself.

Salhadaar stood, motioning for the table to hush. Around him, the Council of Oracles fell silent, eager to know his final judgment.

I could see the whole council was set against me. All my work, all the data collected from my visorscopes and intrinsic lanterns and many more devices, meticulously compiled and correlated and annotated. Months of toil, all for nothing.

I felt hope failing me as I met the eyes of each representative—there was Salhadaar, and beside him the Soul-Scribe, his closest confidante. Then there was Etries of the Architects and her lackeys, a motley collection indeed. Others I knew by name—those of the Testing I was the least familiar with, they being the least interested in my work—but among the rest I could count on my one true friend, Ky'veza, in whose city the council now sat. Of Bilaal, ruler of Tazavesh, I remained uncertain, although I knew Ky'veza had his ear. The pair sat together and had not yet spoken.

Salhadaar had at least agreed to Ky'veza's request to hold the meeting in her city, rather than insisting I travel to their customary gathering place in Tazavesh. Indeed, he'd heeded my urgent call with rare haste, had sped his entourage across the wastelands with help from the Soul-Scribe, ruler of the wild lands between. The rest of the Oracles had gathered with equal vigor—now staring down at me, seeming all too eager to witness my downfall.

The silence in the chamber was a living thing, thick and moving. I could bear it no longer.

"Forgive me."

At this, whispers raced through the assemblage. Ky'veza looked up, puzzlement clouding her features. I had clearly said the wrong thing.

"We may discuss forgiveness at another time," said Salhadaar. "First we must talk of blasphemy."

The Oracles nodded at one another, impressed with their own wisdom.

"Blasphemy?" Any hope of intelligent debate between peers vanished as the ultimate accusation was so lightly made. I felt my fists curl around the hem of my light summer robe, anger and frustration coursing through me. "The visions that radiate from the Worldsoul are real. I have heard it, and my data prove it!" I gestured to the high shuttered windows of the market guild chamber, quickly co-opted for the council meeting. "Ma'nussa has heard!" I opened my arms to the table. "*You* have heard it, surely!"

"I have heard nothing," came Etries's voice. Her fellows smiled. There was to be no discussion with them. Salhadaar nodded his assent, as did the Soul-Scribe and Bilaal. I turned to Ky'veza, but she would not meet my eye.

"A time comes," Salhadaar said, "when we cannot overlook your conduct. For years, the Oracles have entertained your . . . interest, shall we call it, in the Void. At first it was an amusement, a diversion. That I understood. But now, diversion has become distraction."

"You have taken an oath," said Bilaal, more confident than usual. "We have *all* taken an oath, providing each of us their place and purpose." He stabbed a finger at me. "Your oath is to the technomancers, to study the transfer and transmutation of energy so that we may master it for the benefit of K'aresh. We've not seen a report on your proposed usage of the Reshii Ribbons in months. You neglect your sacred duties, *Void-Sorcerer.*"

I blanched at the epithet. Never before had the Oracles uttered it to my face, but there it was. *Void-Sorcerer.* I had been called worse, but this was a title that filled me with dishonor, and Bilaal knew it.

And yet, I was right to bring my work to the Oracles, I knew I was. The radiant visions were the cry of K'aresh's Worldsoul; this I had confirmed, tracing the source of the visions to the deep heart of our world. I had transformed the abstract to the real, and it was precisely because of my work in decoding the mysteries of the Void that I had been able to achieve this.

My research was, I had argued time and again, an unavoidable part of my oath-sworn endeavors in energy research. One could not exist without the other; to understand energy was to understand all its forms, including the Void. And the Oracles had agreed . . . until I stumbled upon a discovery of great import. One of the K'areshi's greatest cultural artifacts from centuries past—the Reshii Ribbons—were themselves imbued with arcane power. They had such potential to aid in the transmutation of energy that it made the mind reel, if only I could find the key to unlocking their secrets.

With my discovery of the hidden potential of the Reshii Ribbons, my standing had risen among the council, at least for a short while. And so long as my research into the Void did not stray any further and interfere with my oath, they paid little attention to it.

I should have known the radiant visions would change that. To speak of the Worldsoul was to encroach on territory beyond my ken, and the council would see such presumption swiftly dealt with.

"You stand at a crossroads," said Salhadaar. "If you continue to study the Void, then your *real* work will suffer and your oath will be broken."

"And that is something we cannot countenance."

I looked aghast at Ky'veza as she raised her voice at last. She stared back at me, somehow finding the courage to support not her friend but the Council of Oracles.

"Let this be your final warning," said the high priest. "The Worldsoul is beyond the borders of your work. The radiant visions, if such exist, are to be left to those who are expert in such matters.

You are to return your attention to the field of your own expertise and cease all research into the Void. Heed this command, or our next audience will be somewhat more difficult. That I promise."

The hours after that fateful council meeting were but a blur. I had loved Ma'nussa my entire life, yet I saw nothing of it as I stalked the streets, turning this way and that without thought. I found my mind curiously empty after Salhadaar's ultimatum. It was only when I heard the music of the spell-dancers drifting on the fragrant evening air that I realized just how late the hour had grown. Weary, I found my way to the market square and watched the performance of the troupe, who had arrived from the wastelands as part of the Soul-Scribe's caravan.

It was not the first time I had seen them, skirts whirling like spinning tops as their feet kicked sand over colored tiles. Indeed, their traditional dance was a familiar sight in Ma'nussa, the city an ancient resting place on one of the roads the nomads often traveled. And with the nomads came the spell-dancers, who spun for the cheering crowds while their kin collected coin among those gathered.

I had given plenty of coin myself over the years. The freedom in their movements had always been a pleasant escape from the toil of my work, but when I met Krysson, their performance became less an entertainment, more a pilgrimage. We first spoke when she wove between the onlookers to collect coin, taking the place of an absent brother, and at once there was a . . . connection. How or why, I don't think we ever knew. Some mysteries do not need to be solved.

After the night's dance, I waited as I always did when Krysson came to Ma'nussa, under the arches behind the market where the light did not reach, where the people did not walk, not while the night market was at its height. When she found me, she knew at once something was wrong. I rushed us away to a quiet corner, casting a glance here and there to be sure we had not been seen. For me—a technomancer and noble of a proud city-state—to be seen in intimate closeness with a nomad was to invite trouble for us both. Were I in better standing with the council, petitions could be made, backgrounds overlooked, but as I stood in their ire, I wished to spare her the same.

After we had conveyed our love for each other, I shared my troubled thoughts, and we talked long into the night about my work, the radiant visions, and the council.

"Come with me to Tazavesh," Krysson urged.

Her suggestion surprised me. I leaned back against the wall of the alley, and she rested her head upon my chest, her fingers gently following the contour of my face. I sighed and took her hand in mine.

"I will not run," I said.

"I am not telling you to run," she said. "The Oracles will depart for their homes tomorrow, and the Soul-Scribe is going with Salhadaar to Tazavesh."

I laughed. "You suggest I follow the very ones who would condemn this world to its end?"

Krysson pushed herself away from me, her expression stern. "I am saying you need a *rest*, my love. Time away from your work. It will do you good. You can visit the markets there, collect those parts for your laboratory you have been saying you need for weeks now." With a grin, Krysson pulled her cloak around her head and clutched it to her chest like an old crone. "We shall disguise ourselves and shop the market together! No one will look, no one will see!"

She laughed and leaned in and we kissed, and she stayed awhile longer until she knew she must leave. I accompanied her through the darkened city, the two of us playing a game of shadows, our stifled laughter echoing against the closed shutters of the market stalls. At her lodgings, we kissed for a final time, the scent of the desert lingering in the air when she left me.

I was only a scant few paces into my own journey home when I realized I was being followed, and by then it was far, far too late.

As the black bag was pulled roughly from my head, my only thoughts were of Krysson. The Void, the radiant visions, my sacred oath, the final warning of the Oracles, these meant nothing to me beside my love for her. We had been lax. *Complacent.* I cursed my hubris, the very notion that we were being careful. There were too many eyes upon us. And now the price needed to be paid.

The chamber I found myself in was bright, and I blinked to take it in. I had been dragged to a storehouse of some kind, stacked with crates and sacks and all manner of cargoes needed by the market. A quiet, dead space at this hour, the perfect place for my cries for mercy to go unheard.

I was not ready for the end, and as I wondered just how much I would beg for my life, a figure loomed before me and clasped me firmly by the arm. I blinked again, this time in sheer astonishment.

"Ky'veza!"

The smile of the friend I thought had abandoned me was glorious as a sunrise. She squeezed my arm, but I did not hear what she said, such was the roar of blood in my ears. I searched for the ruffian responsible for my kidnap as she too threw back her hood, revealing eyes that glittered like brilliant gemstones in the lantern light. I did not recognize the face, but she bowed her head in respect, before acknowledging someone standing behind me.

High Priest Salhadaar extended his hand. I stared at it—at *him*—and at the group I now saw gathered in an atmosphere of electric excitement. Besides Salhadaar and Ky'veza, I counted five other Oracles, including Bilaal and others too, not from the council but from my own city. There was Allash and Mideches and Darmeto of the technomancers, and beside them another group, two of whom I knew to be merchant-captains of the Ma'nussa market guild and two others I did not recognize. All present, high priest included, were clad in simple brown travel cloaks, the deep hoods proving a more than adequate disguise.

"I see you have met Nari," said the high priest. He had the sense to look somewhat embarrassed as my abductor bowed again. "I had hoped your meeting would be under more *conventional* circumstances, but she is one of my finest covert agents. You will find in her a firm ally."

"As you will in all of us, I hope," said Bilaal. I glanced at him, remembering the cold anger he had directed at me but a few hours before.

Beside him, Ky'veza nodded, perhaps reading the doubt on my face. "Listen to the Ravel," she said, "and all will become clear."

I could only shake my head. "Ravel?" I turned to the high priest. "Is this a dream? Please, tell me what is happening."

"Before we proceed, I must impress upon you the need for secrecy," Salhadaar said. "No one can know of our meeting tonight." He gestured to the group. "*We* are the Ravel. A . . . collection, perhaps, of the sharpest minds in K'aresh. The sharpest, but also the most trusted."

He paused, and I glanced about the room. It was then I noticed an absence, for of the Soul-Scribe, there was no sign.

"The expertise and skill gathered here rivals none," the high priest continued, "and this alliance of friends I formed for one very specific reason."

"Which is . . . ?"

"We *believe* you," said Bilaal simply.

For a moment I wondered whether Nari had not black-bagged me at all, but had, in fact, knocked my mind from my body. Perhaps the bizarre meeting I now found myself in was merely a fevered imagining, as the covert hand of the Oracles carried me off, my body destined to be dumped in a city canal.

"The radiant visions," prompted Ky'veza. "The cry of the Worldsoul. It's all real. We believe you."

"We believe you," Salhadaar continued, "because we have heard it ourselves. We all have. For the moment, the visions are weak, quiet, a melody carried on a distant breeze and, for the moment, nothing more than a curiosity lingering from a half-remembered dream."

"But," said Bilaal, "they grow stronger. And so does the talk, the rumors about them. If we fail to control the situation, we risk widespread panic."

"Which is why you were deceived," said the high priest. "And why I ask now for your forgiveness." He looked into my eyes. "The council meeting was a sham, but one born of necessity. For that I am sorry."

I took a deep breath and tried to understand a twist of events I could not have begun to imagine.

And then I felt something else. A certain . . . lightness in my heart, a weight lifted. Something I had not felt in a long time.

Hope.

"You will kneel."

I gazed at Salhadaar as the high priest pointed to the floor before him. Around the room, the members of this secret society all lowered themselves and bowed their heads.

I knew what this was—an oath-taking ceremony. Once more I wondered if this was a dream, but when the high priest gestured again for me to kneel, I obeyed, my mind racing.

"We hold you in close confidence, friend," began Salhadaar. "Your knowledge is great, your wisdom greater. Will you take a new oath and join our number?"

To receive a new oath was a rare honor, for it signified that the work of my life was not only a great one but that I had achieved a level of mastery few could reach. In my surprise, I found I could not answer, but perhaps there was something written on my face, for Salhadaar smiled as he began the ritual.

"Friend, do you, of your own accord, in the presence of your high priest, hereon swear to dedicate the work of your life to that which K'aresh calls you?"

My voice was weak, but I responded as I should. "I do."

"Do you swear to follow the path of your oath, to dedicate yourself to its guidance, until the work of your life is complete?"

"I do."

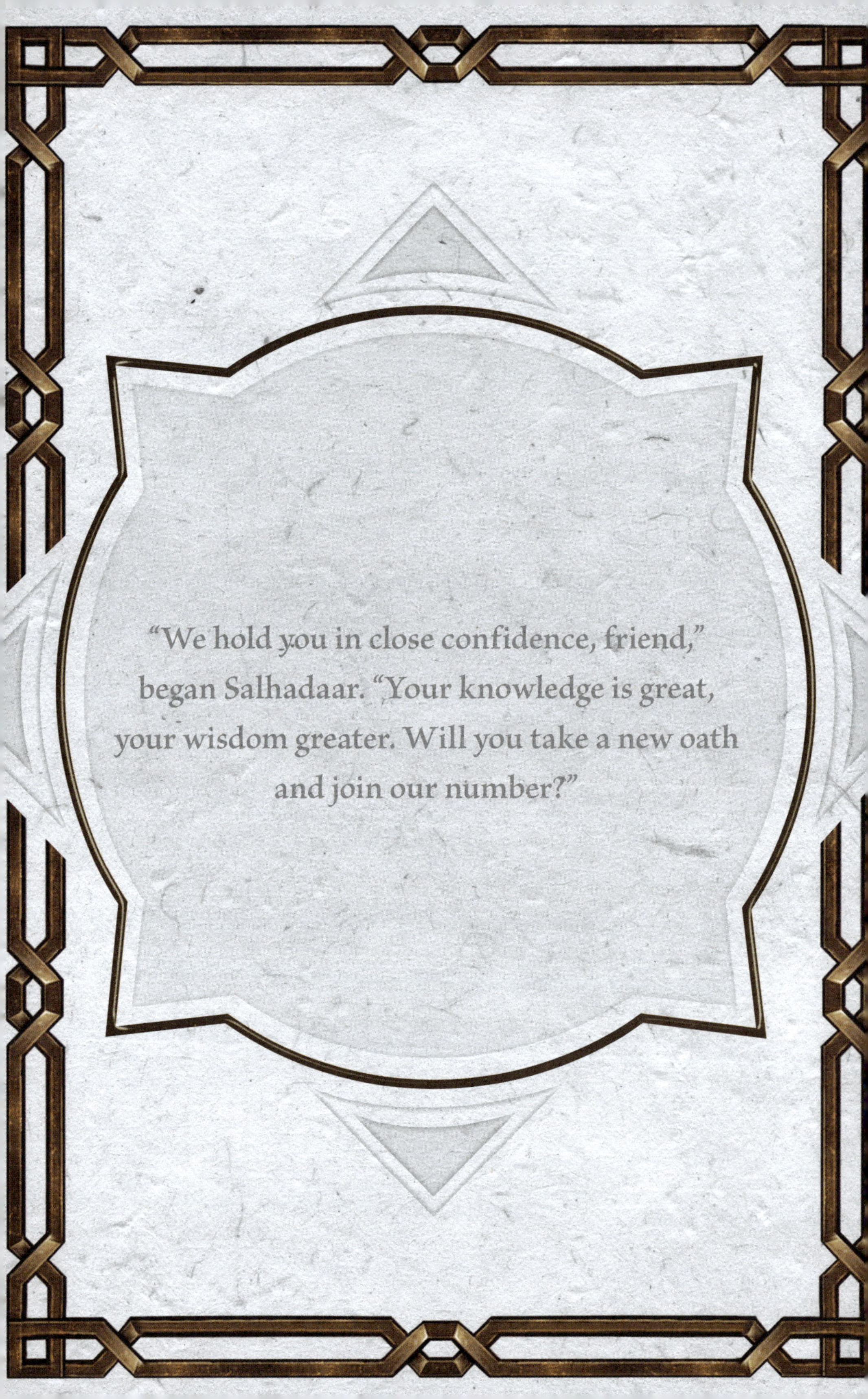

"We hold you in close confidence, friend," began Salhadaar. "Your knowledge is great, your wisdom greater. Will you take a new oath and join our number?"

"Do you promise to forsake temptation and dedicate yourself to the work of your life, mind and body, committing yourself to seeking its meaning and understanding its import, venerating these mysteries until they are mysteries no longer?"

"I do."

"The oath is the path. Guard against all perils that strive to draw you from that path. The oath is the truth. Hold fast against all forces that strive to cast the shadow of deceit upon your journey."

At this I stood before the high priest, as around me the Ravel stood also.

"I name thee the *Locus-Walker*," said Salhadaar, "for this is your truth, as it is mine." And then he smiled.

"Welcome to the Ravel."

As the suns rose beyond the storehouse walls, tendrils of light reaching down between the boards to caress our secret meeting, the Ravel applauded my joining. But as Salhadaar clasped my forearm in warm brotherhood, I heard two things.

The first was a voice inside my mind. I heard Void whispers often, could quell them and push them aside when I needed to, but this voice came louder. I felt fear grip me once more, but amidst these new tides of fate, I controlled myself, pushing aside any emotion as the voice delivered its message to me and me alone.

Beware, Locus-Walker. Beware.

But then I heard something else, and now, so too did my friends. For this sound was a very different thing. The Ravel tensed as one, searching for the source of the cries, the *screams*, the many voices joined in a chorus of terror. Within moments, it sounded as though every soul in Ma'nussa had risen with the suns, only to find some horror waiting.

We rushed outside, and in the early-morning light we gasped in astonishment at the arc of sky above us. The two suns of our world seemed to dim, their warm glow faint and growing fainter. The sky blackened, as though night were falling with impossible speed at an impossible time. At first that darkness was a purple, then it brightened.

Violet, the color of the Void itself.

Beware, Locus-Walker.

The All-Devouring comes.

2
The DEVOURING WAR

The Void roiled in the skies above Telogrus Rift as Locus-Walker led Alleria Windrunner on their chase. She was wearied by the journey, having lost track of how long they'd been on the move. Their hunt had been far from easy.

Telogrus Rift was swarming with creatures of the Void, drawn to this place by the power of the Harbinger. They had managed to evade many beings but had no choice in confronting others that stood in their path. True enough, they had all—so far, at least—been dispatched with ease, but Alleria could not deny how her mind lingered less on the battle and more on the picture of K'aresh that Locus-Walker had painted for her.

They followed a trail that was invisible to the eye, though not to the senses. At first, Alleria merely followed and listened, but as they neared their quarry, she began to feel it, the way the Void seemed to bend around their target. As though a huge boulder had been thrown into a mighty river, the energies of the Void parted around it, the current disturbed, the wake turbulent, unstable.

That sensation had grown ever stronger, and they stopped, hidden behind a shard of rock that rose like a blade from the barren ground of the rift. The rim of the shard was haloed with a bright violet light, betraying the presence of the Void revenant ahead of them.

"Remember," said Locus-Walker, "this creature is far more dangerous than those we have so far encountered. Its heart belongs to me, but it will take the both of us to overcome. Do not underestimate its strength."

Alleria tightened her grip on her bow. "And do not underestimate mine."

The Locus-Walker turned his inscrutable face to hers. "You seek the power to destroy your enemy. But Xal'atath will wield even your own power against you. You must first find balance."

Alleria's face fell. Locus-Walker had promised much would be gleaned from this journey, but right now, she couldn't see any moral or lesson from his potted history of a lost world. What struck her far more was that the powerful being before her—who claimed it best she let go of her every attachment—had once been fallible, emotional. Had once loved and fretted and feared as she now did.

"What . . . became of the K'areshi? Of Krysson?" Alleria asked, knowing it would needle him. "Is she like you now? Or did she fall along with your world?"

Her mentor did not answer. Alleria frowned and was about to

ask again when the violet glow ahead flared brightly and vanished. Locus-Walker stepped out from behind the stone, Alleria at his side, bow raised.

The plain was empty. Of the Void revenant, there was no sign.

Alleria lowered her weapon. "Are we sure that was the one?"

"It was. Did you not feel it?"

Alleria nodded. "Perhaps *it* could feel *us*?"

Locus-Walker drifted a slow circle, scanning the landscape around them. Alleria did the same, her bow at the ready.

Then she saw it. Far away, amidst scattered boulders, a flash of violet, and in her mind, another pull, another tug of the Void.

She opened her mouth to shout, but Locus-Walker flew past her.

Alleria followed at a run.

Beware, Locus-Walker.

The All-Devouring comes.

Those words haunted me, along with that terrible day when the sky had pitched into a purple-tinged night without stars, a night that many feared would prove unending.

And yet, this was not the day of K'aresh's demise. Yes, there was unease. The markets remained closed, not just in Ma'nussa but in every city-state. People locked themselves indoors, fearful of the violet-purple glow that had cast the world into grim, unnatural shadow. Salhadaar convened the Council of Oracles, and many plans were discussed and debated as rumors grew, not just that the sky heralded the end of all things but that the Oracles were in hiding. Unrest churned among those who had seen the radiant visions and knew that action should have been taken long ago.

But it all came to naught. There was disbelief at first, morphing to relief, joy even, as the Oracles emerged and put forward a plan to banish the long and evil night. This plan was not rooted in technomancy, but in a turn to the ancient ways, which brought comfort to the minds who wished to find it. The people celebrated and then, with a resilience worthy of admiration as well as surprise, returned to their daily lives. Either the K'areshi were stronger than I had hoped, or their memories were shorter than I'd expected. Perhaps it was a little of both.

But I understood my new oath, the new work of my life. My resolve had never been stronger.

I had a world to save, and time was running out.

Although our departure had been delayed by the encroaching Void, I accepted Krysson's suggestion and we made a new home in Tazavesh. And while Ma'nussa would forever be *my* city, the months that followed among the bustling markets of Tazavesh were happy ones, and it was to Krysson I owed this joy. Salhadaar had elected to stay in the city, as did the Soul-Scribe. This meant the spell-dancers too had found a fixed abode, the first in many a season. At first, Krysson bristled against this. She and her brothers and her sisters were nomads: a life on the road was *their* oath. To stay in one place was to build a prison for themselves, trapping the very spirits they danced to free.

But while Tazavesh was the true home for neither of us, it was here we found other advantages. We could walk the markets and traffic with the citizenry, and there were no eyes to watch us, no eavesdroppers to whisper. Tazavesh was freer in many ways, it seemed, and its people discarded the norms that had once labeled our relationship taboo.

With the Ravel, the work was as difficult as it was important. True to their word, the Ravel were eager to aid my research, but relocating my laboratory wholesale from Ma'nussa was a bridge too far. The high priest instead gave me a license to use what Tazavesh was most famous for: its market.

The market sprawled as wide as Ma'nussa itself, a town within a town, so large it had its own districts and precincts, the tables and stalls piled with every kind of ware from every corner of K'aresh. In truth, while I had been here before, it still made my head spin with both its size and its beauty—the towering spires, the colored suncloths that stretched between them, spanning impossible lengths; the rich smoke that rose between stalls, carrying the smells of a hundred cuisines from a dozen lands. Distracted as I was by the importance of my work and the doom I had to prevent, I came to rely on Krysson's help in gathering what I required, for she was well traveled and far more at ease dealing with traders and craftsmen than I, able to strike bargains with merchants to whom I could barely offer the simplest of greetings.

The work progressed and Krysson was by my side, and yet there was something very wrong.

Beware, Locus-Walker.

The All-Devouring is coming.

The voice remained.

Over the weeks and months, I had grown used to the radiant visions, had largely been able to put them from my mind as I focused on my work. Of Void whispers, there were many—indeed, from the very moment I first turned my visorscopes upon the Void, I heard the creatures there speak, but *this* voice was that other thing, the one from before, the one that was different, the one that had planted a seed of fear within me, the one that I knew, I *knew*, had sought me out. And as it came again now in the marketplace, I froze.

Locus-Walker, beware.

I stopped, standing before a splendid stall of spun glass from Tingarla, one of the farthest city-states from Tazavesh. The goods commanded a high price indeed, the merchant careful to vet those she thought could afford it even as they approached her table.

Locus-Walker, beware.

The All-Devouring is coming.

He is near.

He is the end.

He is Dimensius.

He is a lord of the Void, and he hungers.

It was Krysson who broke the spell. I recovered my senses and found her apologizing to the merchant, who stared with wary eyes at this nuisance blocking her stall. Krysson pulled me away in a silent daze back to our quarters, and it was there she waited patiently for an answer while I recovered my senses. I told her and she listened, and when my tale was done she considered what I had said with care, her questions and observations astute. This was the first time I had spoken of the voice, and she the first person to know of it.

"It must be related to the radiant visions," she said. "Perhaps your close work investigating the Void opened your mind to . . . something else."

I had no answers, of course, and she had little to say that could comfort me. Conversation then turned to her own news—the spell-dancers were taking to the road once more. Krysson told me she could stay if I wished, but even as she made her offer I knew what my answer would be. She had her own oath to fulfill, as did I.

I promised her I would not allow the fear in my mind to interfere with my work.

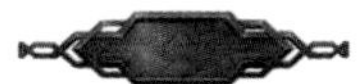

I lost many weeks alone. Yes, I worked and worked hard, but at such a *cost*, forgoing rest and sustenance and any distraction as the voice in my mind pushed aside this happy freedom I'd found with Krysson, replacing it with a fear—and yes, it was fear, despite the promise made to my love—of the mounting danger facing K'aresh. My instruments told me Void energies were accumulating around our world at a truly alarming rate. One day—and soon—these Void energies would do more than strike terror into the K'areshi. They would tear our world apart, laying bare the Worldsoul itself, and our fear only spiced these Void energies as one would prepare ingredients for a meal.

Beware the All-Devouring.

But my toils had not been for nothing. In my weeks of research I had found an answer—indeed, it had been there from the start, but only now had I begun to see it. I could devise a means of protecting K'aresh and its people.

I could save my world—but I could not do it alone.

I needed the Ravel and the full extent of the world's resources to pull off this feat. I met with them regularly to keep them abreast of my progress, but as time passed I saw how they looked at me, and perhaps I could not blame them. I was exhausted but possessed of a feverish intensity even I could recognize as unnerving. The data was complex, decipherable only to myself, a poor salesman on my best day. And the work was not yet complete. Perhaps that was my greatest failing, that I did not give them the solution from the start.

But I wanted to be *sure*. So I waited, and that wait cost me.

And all the while, the voice, the *voice*! What was once a simple warning was now a strange poetry that pulled at my every thought.

Locus-Walker, beware.

The All-Devouring is coming.

After a long stretch of sleeping in my laboratory, barely emerging for meals, I returned home to find Krysson waiting for me. Seeing her was a glorious balm for my troubled mind. She embraced me and held me, and all I could do was stand there and weep.

When I was finished, empty, she pulled away. I moved to kiss her, and she pushed me back with a laugh. She prepared a bath, which was long and hot and wonderful, and I did nothing but succumb to her attentions as she scrubbed and washed the lost weeks away. Then she drained and drew the bath afresh to join me in it, and for a time I forgot about the Void and the Ravel. Krysson even managed to drown out the voice in my mind.

I felt . . . complete. *Whole.* For the first time in weeks, I felt like *myself.* Wrapped in linens, we sat in the warm evening air and drank wine, and she told me of the places she'd been and the dances she'd danced. Why she loved K'aresh, even under the dark Void-touched skies, and why she loved life, and why she loved *me*.

Reunited and restored to my former self, I felt emboldened,

certain of my work and my data. Certain that the solution I had found was the right one.

Tomorrow, they will listen, I told myself. *They will have no choice.*

Krysson saw my mind wandering, of course. "You must tell me what weighs on you," she breathed, a whisper of love and warmth, not of cold echoing darkness.

I took a breath, and Krysson squeezed my hand.

"Time is short," I said. "And I know the name of the threat looming over us."

Krysson cocked her head, concern evident upon her features, but she did not interrupt.

"It is called Dimensius," I said. "It is a void lord, and it is trying to pry apart K'aresh. That is why the Worldsoul cried out to us in the radiant visions. When this being will finally crack open and consume the world I do not know, but it is soon. That is what my data show. The world will be torn asunder, and the K'areshi will die in darkness and pain and terror."

I saw the change in Krysson's features, a hint of that fear I knew so very well, now taking root inside her. I grasped her hand close to me.

"But I can save K'aresh."

Her eyes were wide with wonder. "You can stop a void lord?"

At this I shook my head. "No. And I believe nothing can. Dimensius will pry the planet apart. It is an unstoppable force."

"But you said—"

I squeezed her hand. "I said I can save K'aresh, or . . . most of it.

The K'areshi will live. Whether the void lord will retreat from his meal, seek another target, I cannot know."

I felt my love for Krysson grow in that moment. I watched a transformation in her, her faith—her pride—in me and my work and my oath imparting a strength to her being as it did to my own. She even laughed, softly.

"What do the Ravel say?"

I laughed myself then. "I have yet to tell them."

Krysson pulled herself away and stood, her expression stern. "Time runs out and you have *yet* to tell them?"

I sighed. "It is . . . complicated, my love. We are a group divided. Some believe in me, but others call me Void-Sorcerer, saying it was a mistake for me to join their company." I felt my shoulders slump. "They are tired of problems and want for a solution. But they would smother such an answer in its cradle if I am ill prepared."

Krysson folded her arms tightly and began to stalk the room from balcony to bedchamber, her feet kicking at the carpets as a spell-dancer kicks at sand. I watched in surprise, awaiting a judgment I knew I deserved.

"If they want a solution, give it to them!" she said, not pausing in her strides. "If your calculations on the power of the Reshii Ribbons are finished, then present them." She stopped then and faced me, but this time her expression was warm. "You forget who you are. You are the Locus-Walker. *That* is the oath you swore. *That* is your truth." She walked to the balcony and opened her arms to the darkened city beyond. "We K'areshi are strong, all of us. But the Worldsoul, it called to *you*. You listened, you worked, and you have the answer. You have championed K'aresh even as the greatest among its number humiliated you, then turned to you in secret for help. *You* are the answer."

I did not know what to say. No being had ever made such wild declarations about me, had possessed such unshakeable faith in my worth. Krysson took my hands, pulling me to my feet. She kissed me gently. "You can save the world, my love. That is your truth."

I stared into her eyes and she into mine. I shook in her grasp, barely able to keep myself upright, and yet Krysson stood firm and proud, her strength a wonder of the world.

And she was right. Too long I had lingered, self-absorbed and full of doubt and fear, while the Ravel waited also, their own doubts and fears multiplying by the day.

Enough. *Enough.* I was Locus-Walker, and I was ready.

Let the Void come, for K'aresh would be ready also.

On the way to the Ravel with my final report, I found Nari and Ky'veza. Of the illustrious group, it was these two to whom I was closest, and I greeted them heartily in the market, only to see their open faces clouded with reluctance.

I pulled back the hood of my cloak—the improvement in my form

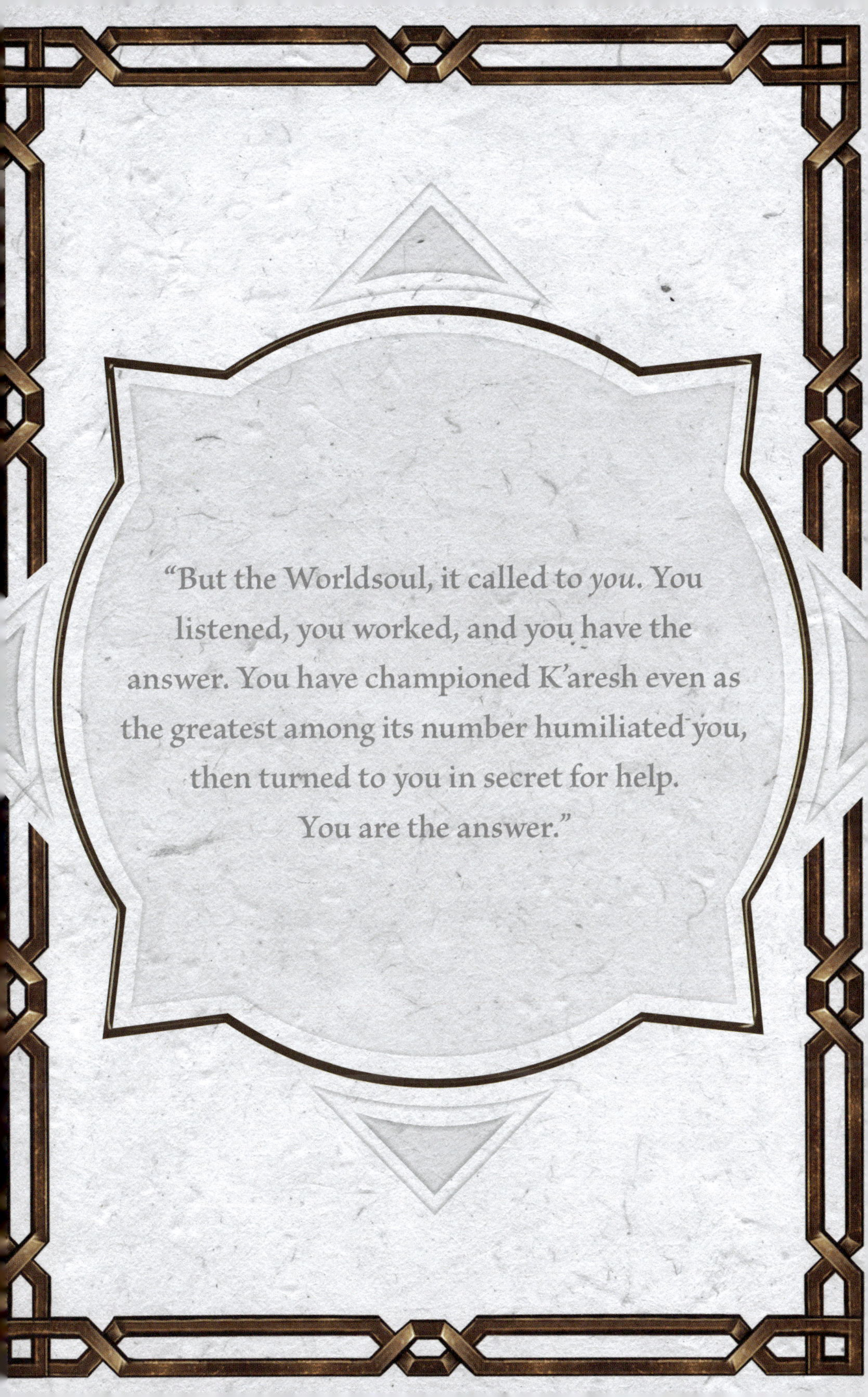

"But the Worldsoul, it called to *you*. You listened, you worked, and you have the answer. You have championed K'aresh even as the greatest among its number humiliated you, then turned to you in secret for help. You are the answer."

must have been obvious, even to my companions, as both beheld me with some measure of surprise. Yet I saw a grimace pass across Ky'veza's face, and I felt suddenly nervous. I clutched tightly the bound findings I was due to present.

"There is *talk*," said Ky'veza, and then she stopped, her eyes falling to the dusty street. I knew this look, the same I saw at that last meeting of the Oracles, so long ago now.

"There are some among the Ravel who wish to distance themselves," Nari said. "From you and your work."

I searched Nari's face, as though the answers to any questions I had were etched there.

Beware the All-Devouring.

"This I know, Nari," I said. "But what has happened? Why the warning now?"

Beware Dimensius.

She paused, seeking the right words. "Your research is hard for the council to understand. You also say that the approaching Void energies will soon begin affecting the planet itself, but we have not seen it; we rely only on *your* data, *your* findings. There are some who whisper that the old ways have been working, that technomancy has nothing more to offer K'aresh. And there are some—"

"There are some who want you out," Ky'veza finished. "They came to us last night. A delegation of those who wish to retract your oath. Those who think of you not as Locus-Walker but as Void-Sorcerer. They will be waiting for you."

I shook my head, but Nari's urgent tone bore into me once more. "Listen! There is still time to right the course, but little of it. You have supporters—we are fortunate to count Salhadaar among them—but even their patience begins to run dry. They need *solutions.*"

I had learned to take Nari's counsel seriously, even more so than that of my old friend Ky'veza. As both a covert agent of the Oracles *and* a member of the Ravel, Nari saw and heard more than any other. People confided in her without even realizing it, and there was none with a better understanding of the current state of play than she.

Beware the All-Devouring.

"I *have* the solution," I said, and not without a little pride. "Here. Look. The work is done. I am ready."

I began to sort my papers until Nari stilled my hand with her firm grip.

Beware Dimensius.

"You are certain?"

Beware this lord of the Void.

I nodded. "It is why I called the meeting today."

He hungers.

"I can save K'aresh."

Nari and Ky'veza exchanged a glance. If they spoke, I could not hear them.

For I was listening to another voice entirely.

At Krysson's urging, I had issued the summons later than usual, and to the Ravel's credit, they responded in kind. As I made my way to the guildhall with Nari and Ky'veza at my side, I thought of their warning. Perhaps the speed of the Ravel's reply was not due to an eagerness to hear my solution, but rather, enthusiasm to witness my downfall.

And despite the detour of my conversation in the market square, we three arrived at the meeting place well before the remaining members of the secret society, as I had intended. Casting aside my customary traveler's cloak, I welcomed my peers one by one when they arrived, noting with some pleasure the shock on their faces at the sight of me, bathed and proper, attired in my finest technomancer robes of gold and purple, the coronet of a nobleman of Ma'nussa sitting on my brow. At this even Bilaal, leader of Tazavesh himself, could not resist a smile, bowing low but with good humor before me, despite the difference in rank between us.

Yes, there was a change in me, and all could see it. It was now on my shoulders to make that change worthwhile. I had spent the preceding months demonstrating the problem to minds that were increasingly closed to me. Now, I would open them once more and show the solution.

"My plan is both a simple one," I began, "and the most complex undertaking K'aresh will ever see." I did not need the binding of parchment I had brought with me, for I could recite every detail of my scheme like a well-loved song. But I had brought something else to aid in my argument, and I took it out now. It seemed light as nothing, a mere strip of silver cloth, smooth, billowing with motion like a gentle river. But when I moved it in my hands, a light shone from deep within, casting arcane beams across the guildhall, pale yet otherworldly, leaving none in doubt as to the nature of the power woven into the very fabric itself.

"The Reshii Ribbons are something we all know," I said. "They are held by most of K'aresh's leaders, symbolic of our ties to the ancient ways. They form part of our history, a reminder of our past. But I say to you now, they are also the key to our future. We know the arcane lives within them, but it is I who have found the secret to calling upon that power." I held the strip up above my head. "Through devices of my design, these sacred artifacts can transmute *any* kind of energy into pure arcane power. This power can be harnessed, funneled through the cores of great reactors, the plans of which I have also drawn."

Bilaal stepped forward. I lowered my hands, showing the Reshii Ribbon to him, and he studied it although at a pace removed, as if he were perhaps afraid to touch it himself. Finally he looked upon me.

"Reactors?"

"Indeed," I said. "It is with these that we will power vast barriers of arcane magic. These barriers can be erected over every city-state across K'aresh. Impenetrable, inviolable, they will shield us."

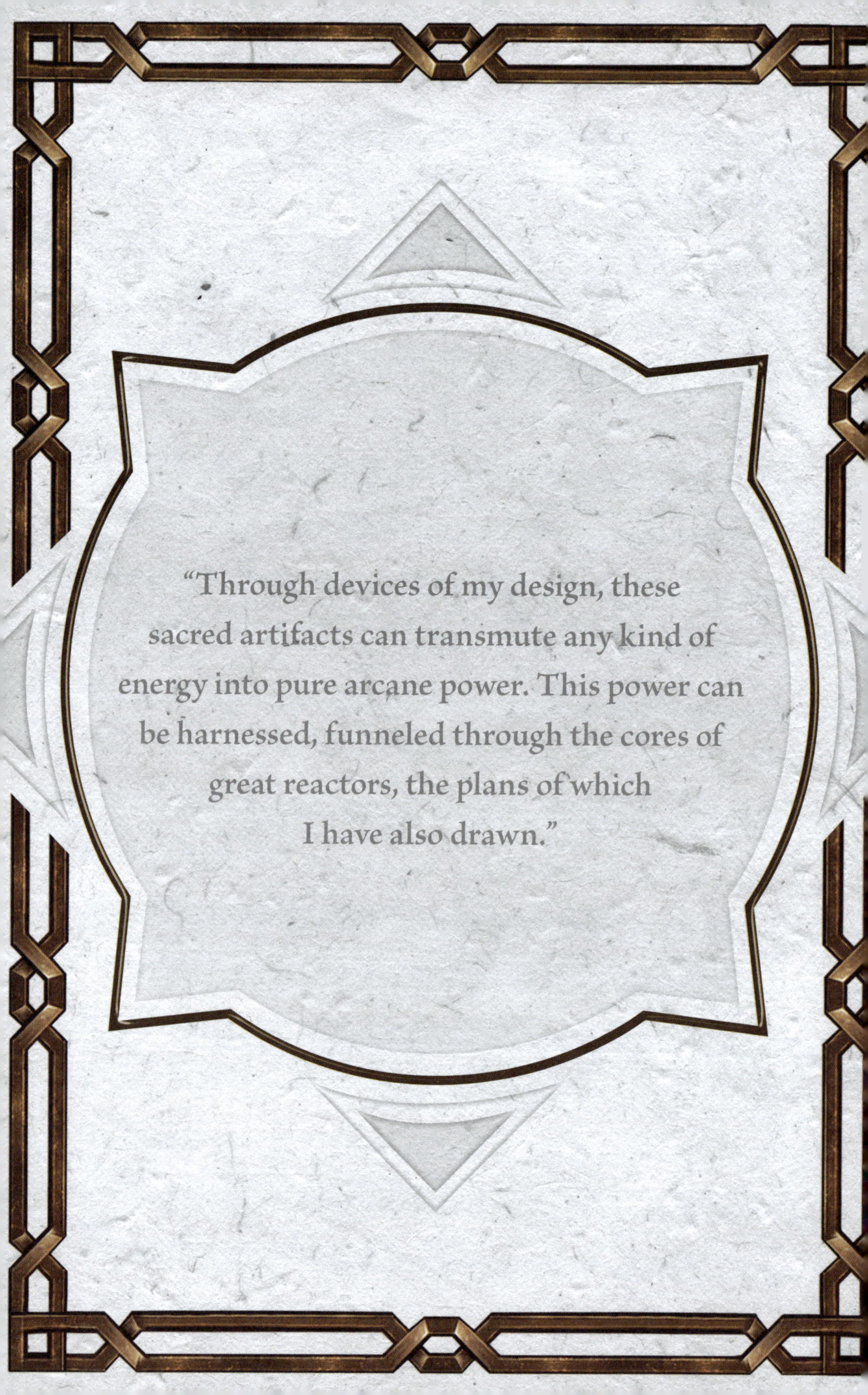

"Through devices of my design, these sacred artifacts can transmute any kind of energy into pure arcane power. This power can be harnessed, funneled through the cores of great reactors, the plans of which I have also drawn."

At this, I turned my gaze upon the rest of the council. "Make no mistake, the Void readies for its great strike. My research tells that this threat that darkens our skies arises from a void lord, Dimensius. This terrible being will crack open our world when it feels the time is right, and we move quicker to that doom with each passing moment. That cannot be prevented." I held up the simple strip of cloth again. "But he will find no matter to feed on. We the K'areshi will survive, safe beneath our barriers."

The Ravel sat in silent contemplation of my proposal. As Nari smiled in her alcove, Ky'veza too made known her approval. She stood from her seat and stalked through the assemblage to grasp my hand in hers.

"It will work," I said. "I know it."

Salhadaar's expression was dark, but I could see he was deep in thought. "The construction of the barriers is work that cannot be concealed," he said at last. "It will require the labor of many."

I nodded. "Then it is time to tell the people. More than us few now see the radiant visions. It scares them, and the Void grows strong upon this fear. You are the high priest. The people look to you and the Oracles for answers. You must tell them everything, and soon, because if we are to protect K'aresh, the magical barriers must be built quickly."

Bilaal sighed loudly. "The planning alone will be substantial, and the only one of us who truly understands what we are to build is *you*." Bilaal glanced at Salhadaar. "To coordinate such a project, I—"

"Let Locus-Walker lead."

The group turned as one to Nari as she stepped from her alcove and into the light. "The Ravel *needs* Locus-Walker. That is why he joined us." She circled the room, gazing upon each member. "We have no time to waste in argument, in debate. We need a leader. Someone to direct our efforts and prepare our world for what is to come."

She stopped before me. Our eyes met and she repeated her conclusion. "Let Locus-Walker lead. If we follow his command, we can be prepared."

There were mutterings around the group. Etries's guffaws were the loudest, but I ignored her. The others bore frowns, but others nodded and soon more were in agreement.

Like me, they accepted Nari's advisement with a noted weight.

Still Bilaal scoffed. "Ridiculous." His eyes appraised me as though I were scrap from a junk stall. "A technomancer of Ma'nussa cannot command the High Priest of the Untamed."

Salhadaar winced, as though in pain. "And yet—"

"You *cannot* agree!" cried Etries. "The Oracles—"

"The Oracles obey my command," said Salhadaar.

"Perhaps . . ." It was one of the merchant-captains, Gez'her. He spoke rarely at our meetings, but always with caution and careful thought. "Perhaps if we study these plans Locus-Walker brings with some care . . ." He turned to me. "If we could perhaps be better educated in your methods, the responsibility of these Reshii Ribbons could be shared."

Ky'veza cut in. "We waste time! You have heard Locus-Walker speak. The Void comes for us, and Dimensius with it. We must act, and act now." She stepped up to Salhadaar, so close he flinched back from her forceful approach. "Say it, High Priest. Give the word, and the work can begin."

Bilaal laughed again. "The people of Ma'nussa must be congratulated for their patience, Ky'veza. But here, your manner is less appreciated than you think."

"Enough."

All attention was on the high priest. His countenance stern. He looked to me, and so authority was conferred with but a simple command.

"It is done already. The Ravel is led by the Locus-Walker. As he commands, so we obey. My final instruction is that the work must begin at once."

Silence reigned, but then, one by one, the Ravel stood and joined my side. Soon only Bilaal and Etries remained stubbornly in place, but with my supporters behind me—high priest included—I stepped forward and held out my hand.

"We do this for K'aresh," I said. "We do this for the K'areshi."

This was enough, for Etries nodded to herself and then took the hand that was offered. Perhaps her decision was enough to convince Bilaal, for as the ruler of Tazavesh sat and stared for a good while longer, finally he joined us. The glare he unleashed upon me as he did so, I did not like, but I put it from my mind.

There was much to do.

To say that K'aresh would never be the same again is to understate matters more than the mind can fathom, for the transformation of our world was both rapid and shocking. By order of the Council of Oracles—driven in secret by my leadership of the Ravel—all effort was made to build my proposed arcane reactors, the K'areshi taking new oaths to commit their paths to this great work.

As the world labored, the voice from the Void continued to speak. At first I tried to ignore it, then I came to embrace it, for I knew I heard it for a reason. It was foolish to ignore the warnings it provided, which also served to strengthen my resolve.

It was the voice that told me the time was coming, that Dimensius was close, that soon the Void would caress the shores of our world before the void lord swallowed us whole.

In truth, there had been dissent among even the people, though perhaps that understates the feeling. Tazavesh and Ma'nussa, Gastalt and Dervashna, and every city-state between was changed forever. The streets and canals, market squares and plazas became a maze of conduits and channels, pipelines and aqueducts that carried not water but the throbbing, humming arcane energy of the Reshii

Ribbons from one great reactor to the next, the entire system a great web powering the barriers that defined our skies.

But public mood was quick to change, because one day, the Void shook the foundations of our world. It was precisely as my calculations had shown and just as the voice had promised. We had completed the job without a moment to spare.

The arcane shield rose above, crackling to life and holding strong whilst the dark power of the Void crashed upon it like grains of sand in a dust storm. The barriers worked, and the K'areshi rejoiced, safe in their homes, in their beloved city-states.

For the first time amidst the backdrop of the Devouring War, it seemed K'aresh could win.

Little was I to know, the survival of my people would come at a terrible cost, and while I had saved the K'areshi from one doom, I had, in fact, condemned them to another fate entirely.

3
ETHEREUM

The years that followed were terrible and dark, both in the hearts of the K'areshi and for K'aresh itself. For while the barriers held and held firm, their dim arcane brilliance and strange warmth were now the only thing that kept our world alive. The twin suns of K'aresh, Meter and Ti'meter, would never again cast their light upon this land nor any other. They had been taken, eaten, *consumed* by Dimensius in his insatiable hunger. K'aresh itself was now alone, trapped in the Void, a prisoner of its terrible lord.

There was, though, something still shining bright within our people, even if our future remained dark as the skies above.

We had *hope*. Hope in ourselves and in the Council of Oracles.

And the Ravel had hope in *me*.

The Void beyond our barriers raged as though a living beast, but the K'areshi found another kind of strength; not content to spectate, they fought back, all aspects—the Untamed, the Exchange, the

Testing, the Architect—united as never before, battling against the unknowable Void with spell and incantation, machine and ingenious device. The Void was a shapeless and fearful horror. But the K'areshi spirit was fierce and undying, something Dimensius the void lord could not anticipate.

And so the barriers held . . . and what started as war soon morphed into siege. Yes, we were protected. Yes, life went on, as best it could.

But how long would we last?

Because the truth was that the very protection we now relied upon came with a terrible cost. Those magical barriers of arcane might had saved our cities, but they were flaying our people alive.

It was called many things at first, but soon all came to know it as simply the Wasting.

I had seen the signs early, and I can only curse my hubris for not taking action sooner. As the barriers were built, so those who worked upon them began to wither and weaken, their skin peeling away, scorched to ash like in a great fire. Perhaps my work, my calculations *should* have been questioned—by myself; by Nari, who was ever-present at my side; by the Ravel, who looked to me for leadership and guidance. Perhaps if they saw what I saw, knew what I knew, and suspected what I *hid* from them, I would have found a solution.

The facts were simple: the vast domes may have appeared solid, but their power was in a state of constant flux, demanding a flow of magic so great it was almost beyond comprehension. My calculations, although terrifying, were correct, and were judged to be an acceptable cost to maintain the barriers over a short period of siege.

But Dimensius had a patience measured not in months or years but in eternities. The longer the siege went on, the more terrible the fate of the K'areshi became.

I consulted with technomancers and mages to find an answer, but as the sheer scale of the problem became more apparent, they began to cloister themselves. They buried their heads not in my data but in crumbling tomes lifted from ancient crypts, in spells and magics from other times and places, as they turned to superstition and ritual to find the answer I could not give them.

The Wasting soon spread, away from the laborers who had the closest contact with the arcane, to the people of the cities themselves. Bodies burned, twisted, shriveled, the flesh charred with no heat as the unending flux of the barriers beat down on the people with the power of too many suns. All the K'areshi, from the Oracles to the nomads of the wastelands, began wrapping their disintegrating forms in layered bindings. In time, the barriers protected city-states populated by faceless, featureless beings.

The K'areshi were strong—but not *that* strong. This was a test like no other, and I feared the Wasting would prove our undoing. The society so carefully governed by the Council of Oracles began unraveling like the bindings that now held our bodies together.

Those whispers of dissent arose once more, but now with a violence previously unseen among the city-states of our world.

First the Wasting, and then . . . chaos. Some who fought the Void lashed their magics against their own kind. Parts of Tazavesh and Ma'nussa, abandoned to the arcane reactors and the conduits that fed them, became battlegrounds, and I watched with sorrow as we descended into a sort of madness. The Oracles, for their part, did exercise a firm hand. It was thanks to them and the K'areshi's deep commitment to their oaths that true anarchy was avoided. But even on peaceful days, there was a tension in the air that could be unbearable.

But perhaps it did not matter, for I had made other errors in my calculations. The truth was the Reshii Ribbons were perfect in their ability to transmute any and all energies—including those of the Void. So while they powered the barriers, channeling energy between the network of arcane reactors that now covered K'aresh, their very nature meant the process was, of its own volition, happening in *reverse* as well. Such was the power of the Void that every attack by Dimensius fed the reactors themselves, the energy absorbed by the barriers and transmuted by the Reshii Ribbons through no design of my own. At first, I was overjoyed; then my elation turned to despair as I realized the fate I had doomed my people to. To be exposed to ever-increasing arcane energy over so many, many years . . . it was *this* that was the true cause of the Wasting.

The barriers would survive; those trapped beneath them would not. Even if Dimensius were one day able to penetrate our defenses, the world he consumed would be a dead one.

"I am afraid."

Krysson lay upon the bed, her face turned away from me. I knelt beside her on the floor, a fresh spool of bandages ready by my side, the shears I used to cut the old bindings away from her body poised over her back. For a moment I remembered the skin beneath those bindings, remembered the feel of it under my fingers, the softness and the warmth, and I wondered if I would ever feel it again.

"My love?"

Krysson adjusted to face me. I looked at her eyes, two glittering jewels shining between the thin slit of her bindings. Her eyes were all I could see of her then, and mine were all she could see of me.

Her words surprised me. Oh, she had spoken before of her fears, as had I. But there was another meaning now. Something I felt too. Krysson feared not for herself, nor even for me, but for the fate of K'aresh and the K'areshi. The thought that all of what we had done was for nothing—that the barriers that had taken so much work had merely prolonged the inevitable—provided another agony. They had condemned our people to a living death, destroying them body and mind before Dimensius came to consume us anyway.

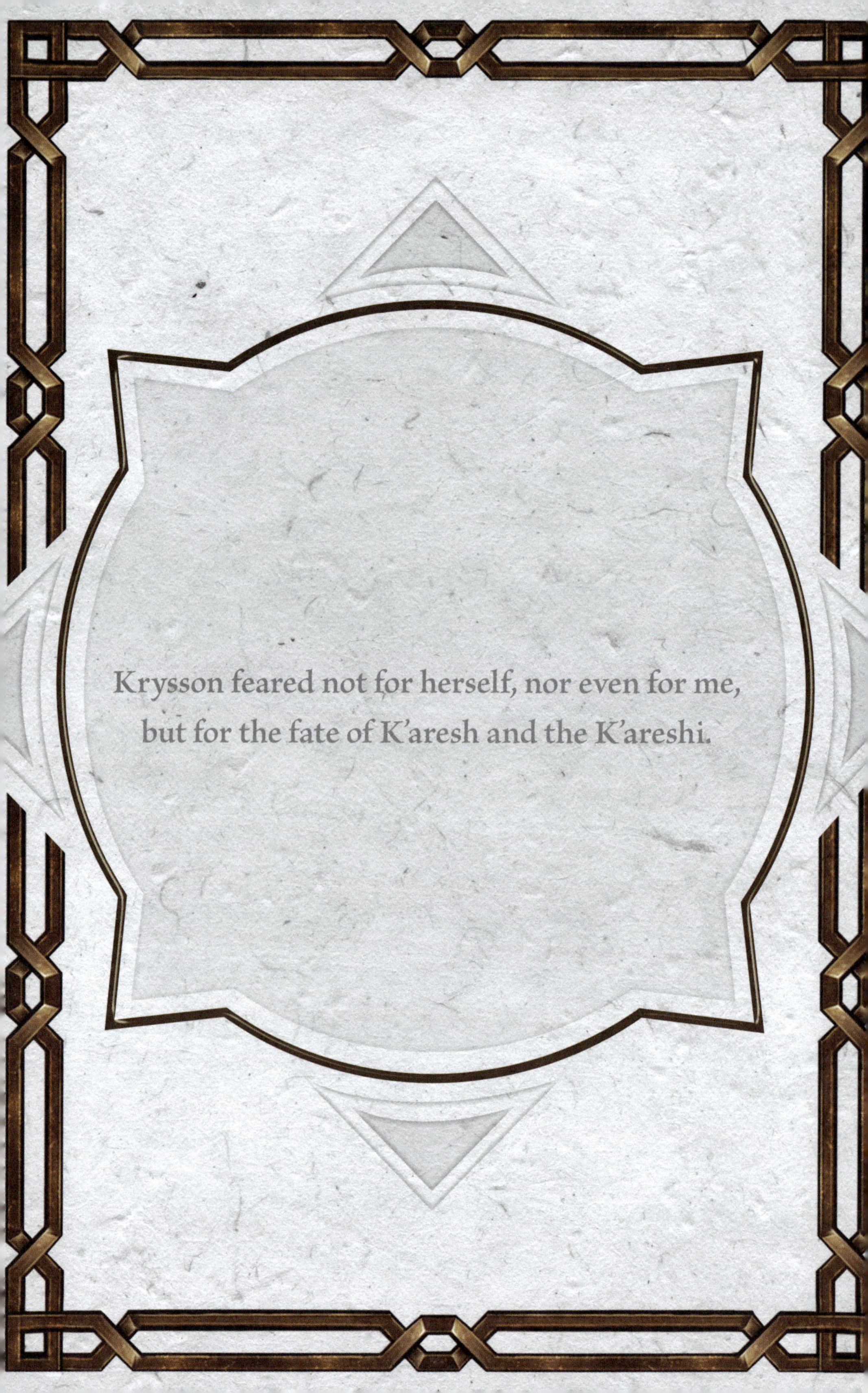

Krysson feared not for herself, nor even for me,
but for the fate of K'aresh and the K'areshi.

Krysson glanced away again. I resumed the task of changing her bandages. I cut the first binding, and Krysson sighed. The bandages were a requirement, but even after all this time, none among my people had grown accustomed to wearing them.

"If we die," said Krysson, "at least we die together."

I kept cutting.

"And at least we die fighting," she continued. "You have served K'aresh well, my love. The barriers have worked."

I stifled a laugh, and, surprised at my own reaction, I paused in my work. "I have protected the K'areshi, only for us to fight among ourselves, to die beneath the source of our protection. And in the end, the inevitable is but delayed. All of what we have done . . . I sometimes wonder why we did it."

"We did it for *us*." Krysson turned on the bed and reached out with a bandaged hand to take my own and squeeze. "We die as *K'areshi*, not as some terrible corruption of the Void. *That*, my love, is perpetual torment. You have saved us from that fate, and for that and many other reasons I have long loved you."

I heard something in my mind then. Not the voice—that I had not heard in many a month—this was a simple sound, a single note . . . no, a single *thought*, drowning out all others, ringing like a bell in my mind. I was fixed to the spot, unmoving, my eyes no longer on hers, but on her back, where the last layer of binding had been revealed. The cloth should have been dark, stained by the decay of the flesh beneath. But instead there was . . .

I could scarcely believe it.

Krysson moved to rise, but I motioned for her to stay where she was. I let go of her hand and she called out in surprise, but I was on my feet at once. I doused the lantern, plunging the bedchamber into sudden darkness.

No, the room was *not* dark! There was a light, and it shone from Krysson herself, pale, faint but present. As my eyes adjusted to the gloom I saw the way the light moved under the bandages, not just on the portion I had exposed but shining through other parts of her body.

It was a light I knew. It was a light *all* the K'areshi had learned about over these last terrible years.

It was the light of the arcane barriers. Krysson's wounds were no longer physical—they were *magical.* The transmutation powers of the Reshii Ribbons had surpassed some threshold, something beyond my calculations, yet again.

No longer beings of flesh.

I froze where I stood, the arcane glow from Krysson's body a ripple across the room, across my body.

Something more.

I listened to the voice in my mind, resisting the urge

Yes, you know. It is the answer.

to turn and face a presence I felt suddenly at my shoulder but

You know it.

which was not there.

But will your people listen?

For the second time in my life, I knew how to save my people.

Salhadaar stared at Krysson. I was ashamed to have asked her here, to show us her glowing flesh, to become nothing but an object of scientific curiosity. But she readily agreed to the task, and I was glad she did, for she was the proof that there was a future for the K'areshi, if not for K'aresh.

Salhadaar waited alongside the rest of the Ravel. We were a smaller group now: many of our peers had succumbed to the Wasting. Those who remained stood wrapped in their bandages, their robes and clothes of office their only true means of identification.

As Salhadaar watched, Krysson withdrew her unwrapped back and, as further demonstration, unwound her left arm. Her blackened tendons were crisscrossed with cracks like one of the ancient stone roads her people used to walk, and from those cracks shone the light of the arcane.

"You are confident in your calculations."

This was Ky'veza, and she did not say this as a question, but a statement. As always, she and Nari were by my side. I could not see Nari smile, not this time, but I imagined the warm expression was still there, beneath her bindings.

I bowed to them, then turned to Salhadaar.

"The Reshii Ribbons are powerful artifacts indeed," I said. "And they have one last secret to unlock." I looked upon the blank, covered faces of my friends. "Do you not see? If we are beings of energy, we will not need this world. We may go wherever we like, anywhere in the Great Dark Beyond. The Reshii Ribbons will not only allow us to survive, they will enable us to become something *more*."

Salhadaar flinched at my words. He glanced at Bilaal, but the two did not speak. While their expressions were unreadable, their body language was as obvious as an open grimoire.

I pressed my case. "The Wasting is unstoppable. It is a by-product of the barriers, an inevitable end to our people. But what if this was not to be? What if we could live on? Transmutation of energy. Transmutation of the *K'areshi*! I say to you now, it is possible!" I held up my hand and tore the bandages from it. The flesh beneath was almost mummified, barely clinging to the brittle bones, but . . . yes, there it was. The glow of the arcane—fainter than Krysson's, but there nonetheless. "We need not be tethered to our physical bodies. With the Reshii Ribbons, we can transmute our very beings into ones of *energy*. We can live on—all of us, and our world too. We can forge a new K'aresh and a new future, free of the barriers, and beyond the reach of Dimensius."

I stopped, and around me the Ravel remained silent. I cursed the bandages we were forced to wear, preventing me from seeing the true reactions of the group. The fact was, I had no more to say. I knew the Reshii Ribbons were the means to our salvation—yet I did not know how. In my mind, I felt ashamed, for I knew the precise mechanism would take time to solve.

And the patience of my peers had worn thin.

Then Nari intervened.

"It is a desperate stratagem," she said. "The final gamble of a dying race."

Salhadaar and Bilaal stirred, glanced at each other once more.

"But," Nari continued, "it is our only hope. For the K'areshi to survive, we have no choice." She gestured to me. "Locus-Walker's efforts have preserved us thus far."

There was muttering at that. Whispers. I felt Krysson take my bare hand in hers, and for the first time in so long, I felt her skin against mine—burned, dry, fragile skin, yes, but for a moment I was lost in happy memories of distant times spent with my love.

It was Bilaal who interrupted my reverie. Perhaps his word was intended only for Salhadaar to hear, but something told me otherwise.

"Blasphemy."

Krysson's grip tightened in mine as a shocked gasp echoed around the hall.

Salhadaar raised his own bandaged hands. "Decorum, please." He looked to me. "I have much to think on." He addressed the Ravel now. "Go. I will call you here again for my final decision."

With that, the Ravel parted.

It was to be for the final time, but I did not know that then.

Word did not come from Salhadaar the next day, nor the day after, nor for several beyond. But I did not wait for his decree—a mere formality, I was certain—for I knew my task was urgent, the work ahead difficult, and that time was not our ally. I therefore started at once to gather what Reshii Ribbons had not yet been used in the arcane reactors. No sooner had I started than the voice came again.

Yes, Locus-Walker. Gather them now, before it is too late.

Not for the first time, I wondered about this voice. Was it real? Or was it merely a facet of my own mind that spoke to me? Because as I collected the Reshii Ribbons, the whisper merely told me what I already knew.

The Reshii Ribbons are the key to the future. The time of the K'areshi's ascendence is at hand.

I could not act alone, and it was to Nari I went for help. Her network of agents was a web that spread across all K'aresh, and gathering the Reshii Ribbons would take many hands.

But it was upon the third day following that Nari returned with troubling news. Her agents had failed in their task, the Reshii Ribbons already gone from their sacred holdings, gathered in number by none other than Salhadaar himself—but she was quick to still my excitement. She doubted the high priest was taking fast action in preparation for what was to come. For on her journeys Nari had heard and seen much. There was rumor and intrigue, news whispered that Salhadaar called himself high priest no longer, that he intended to make a public address on the morrow.

Salhadaar was making plans. And those plans, Nari said, did not feature the Ravel in their undertaking.

I summoned Ky'veza, and Krysson also, for I feared what was to come next and wanted her close. How long our conference lasted, I do not know. But before long a bell sounded across the city—it came from the market square, and we four went with all haste to find the plaza alive with more bandage-wrapped citizens than I had seen together for some time. The news Nari heard had spread, it seemed, and not for the first time I cursed my dedication to my oath, which often cloistered me from the news of the world.

The bell rang a second time, and there was movement on the balcony of the market guildhall. Salhadaar appeared, Bilaal at his side. But there was another with them I had not seen for a long, long time.

"Soul-Scribe," muttered Ky'veza into my ear. "Out from hiding at last." This was true. Since the erection of the barriers, the nomadic peoples of the Testing had become more integrated with residents of the city-states, but even Krysson had not seen the Soul-Scribe for many a month.

Salhadaar spread his arms and the crowd hushed.

"The future of K'aresh hangs in the balance," he said. "I will not lie to you, my people. We have fought long to protect you. We have worked hard to give you the future you deserve. The All-Devouring is a torment without end, and the means of our protection is a suffering we can endure only for so long."

The moment had come, and now, despite the voice in my mind, despite the warnings of Nari, I felt my confidence returning. Salhadaar was doing precisely as we had suggested. The people needed to know what was to come, because after years of struggle and change, this was to be the greatest challenge of them all.

"There is change coming," Salhadaar continued. "Change for all of us. For these last years, you have worked hard and followed the path of your oaths. The Council of Oracles has asked much of you, and the strength of the K'areshi has endured, even as our bodies wither and our numbers dwindle.

"We are soon to face the greatest test of all, and for that reason, we must unite, cast aside our differences, forget our arguments. We have fortitude, we have resolve, and I commit to you now the new oath I have undertaken. For I am no longer your high priest . . .

"I am your high king."

I felt my companions grow tense beside me, even as I struggled to comprehend Salhadaar's meaning, if not his words. To declare himself high king was not a strategy I had expected or understood.

"And as your high king," Salhadaar said, "there are truths I must tell you." At this, he cast his gaze skyward, at the pink dome above that protected us from the boiling darkness of the Void beyond.

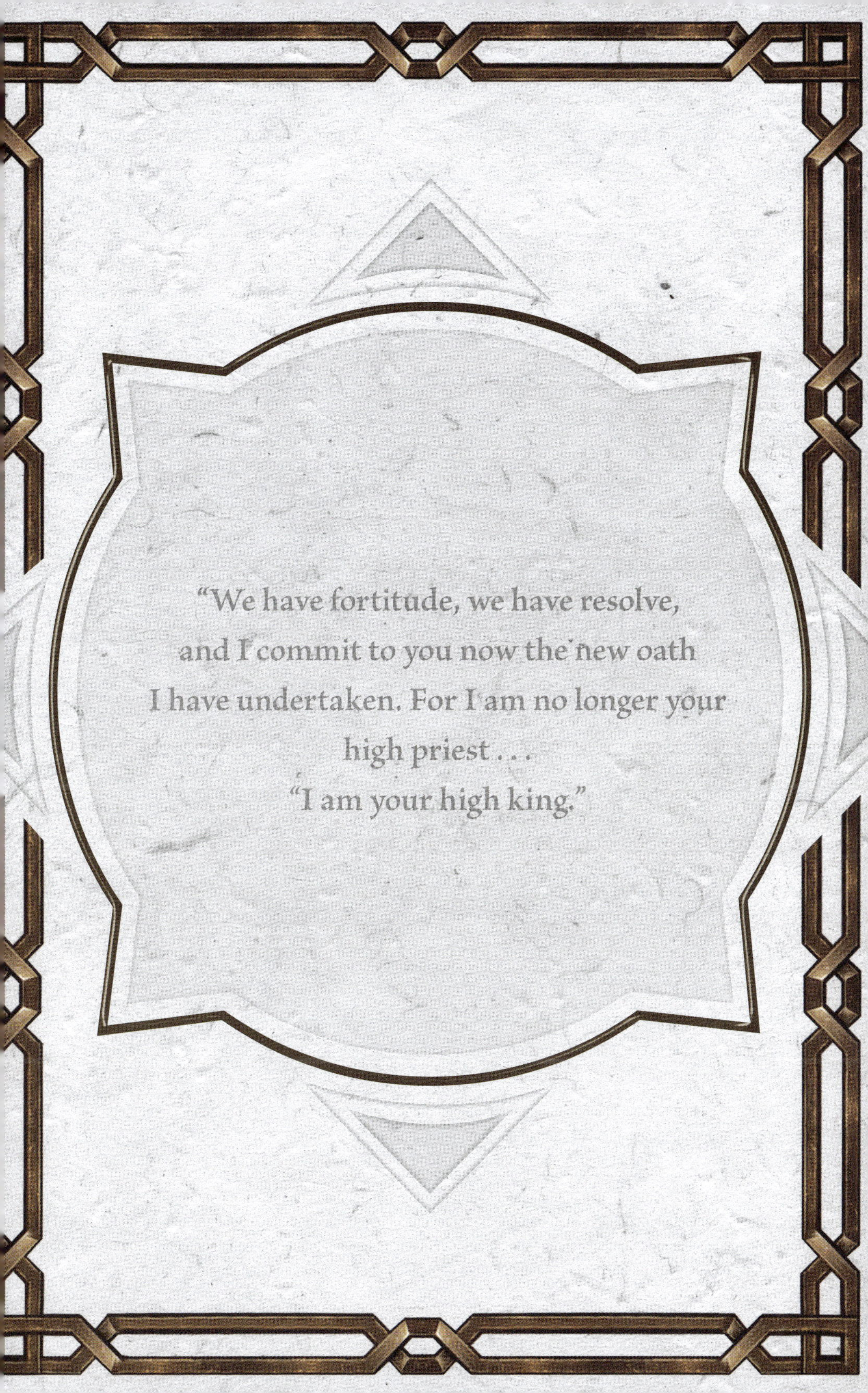

"We have fortitude, we have resolve,
and I commit to you now the new oath
I have undertaken. For I am no longer your
high priest . . .
"I am your high king."

"The barriers both protect us *and* condemn us. We are trapped beneath them as the Wasting destroys us." He stepped forward on the balcony to look down upon his people. "But the Wasting was no accident, my people. There were those among us who schemed and plotted, who designed this fate, who sought the doom of the K'areshi even as we fought for our very survival."

Krysson's grip was tight in mine. I thought of my work, I thought of the preparations we had made, every breath taken to safeguard the future of our people, if not our world itself.

I could scarcely believe what Salhadaar was now saying.

And there, on the balcony above, the newly declared high king was pointing a bandaged hand.

Pointing it at *me*.

"There stands the Locus-Walker," he said. "Void-Sorcerer. Arch-traitor! And there, his comrades, the leaders of a conspiracy that would gift this world to the void lord. They and their friends have met in secret, plotted against us under the guise of saving K'aresh. It is they who have undone us, my people. It is they who have *deceived* us. The Wasting was by their design. They have betrayed us all with their blasphemy!"

And then I felt Krysson's hand pulling on mine. I turned in confusion and, yes, panic, caught in a sea of enemies as the people in the square rounded on us.

"Take them!" This was the Soul-Scribe, her voice loud and sharp, filled with anger and hate.

"Do not let them escape!"

No sooner had the Soul-Scribe cast her order across the crowd than the vast curve of the arcane barrier cracked from horizon to horizon with the sound of a hundred thunderclaps. At once, the crowd ducked, covering their bowed heads with raised arms. And then they looked to the sky. All watched in mute horror as the glassy pink flux that protected Tazavesh split again and again and again, as though it were made not of arcane energy but Tingarla glass.

All stared . . . save for the Soul-Scribe and Salhadaar. As the fear of the crowd turned to a terrible anger directed at my party, I cast a glance upon the balcony of the guildhall. There I saw it—the real traitors, the real conspirators. The pair whispered close, terror the furthest thing from their minds.

And while the barrier crackled and began to fade, the sky restored to the awful purple glow of the Void itself, so the crowd's attention returned to those denounced by their high king.

We were lucky that Nari was with us, Ky'veza too. Their skills in combat were impressive, and although we were surrounded, it was by untrained citizens. My two fierce friends quickly pushed the rioters aside, allowing the four of us to flee the square intact. Nari led the way, her intimate knowledge of the city and its secrets a boon as we sought sanctuary. My mind roared with noise, and it was all I could do to follow, my hand never leaving Krysson's.

But now the entire city was against us. Every alley and

thoroughfare led us to citizens, all angry, some armed, the high king's decree having been heard across the land, the message echoed and amplified by the Council of Oracles.

As we ran, I soon realized that I was a liability, slowing down our escape. We stopped in a shadowed corner, and I outlined my plan. Krysson had to be kept safe, and Ky'veza promised to be her guardian. Despite the high king's betrayal, I knew I had work to do, that there still might be a chance, however slight, to use the Reshii Ribbons and save the K'areshi. In this task, Nari would protect and aid me.

And so we separated, our farewells hasty, with a promise to meet when it was safe. And then I watched Ky'veza and Krysson as they vanished into an alley.

And then I too ran, as all around us, the city fell to riot and the sky darkened and the Void roiled, and what hope I once had vanished along with the barriers that protected us.

On a high plateau of Telogrus Rift, Alleria Windrunner stopped in her tracks.

"And?"

Locus-Walker turned from surveying the way ahead and drifted back toward his pupil.

"You have a question?"

"I have many," said Alleria. "Aren't you going to tell me what happened next?"

Locus-Walker paused. "There is little to tell," he said. "Nari and I succeeded in our task, eventually."

"Eventually?" Alleria sighed. "I must know more than that!"

"Must you?" Locus-Walker asked. "The Reshii Ribbons saved us. Our people were transmuted into beings of energy. Dimensius closed in and K'aresh was consumed. There was nothing the K'areshi could do to stop it, but we survived, in a way."

Alleria felt her jaw slacken in surprise. "And Krysson? What happened to her? And what happened after the high king denounced you? You speak now as though it all meant nothing to you."

"Much happened," said Locus-Walker, "to many people. Of Krysson, I never saw her again. Of Nari and Ky'veza . . . of Salhadaar and the Soul-Scribe . . ."

He trailed off. Alleria looked firmly at him, her hands clasping and unclasping the grip of her bow in frustration.

"That is a story for another time," he said finally. "The K'areshi survived. Some of them, anyway."

Alleria shook her head. "They survived and yet you have abandoned them, isolating yourself. What for? Penance? Shame? Fear? Surely they need you now as they needed you then."

"And there," said Locus-Walker, "your aim is so very wide of the mark, archer."

Alleria sighed in frustration. "Your history lesson was perhaps less useful than you think. Did you mean to balance my mind through sheer distraction?"

"It is your *tethers* that make you unbalanced, Alleria. Release these things that weigh you down, these people you care about. This is holding you back from becoming who you're meant to be."

"The people I care about? Like you did with Krysson? With Ky'veza?"

Locus-Walker came closer. "Perhaps you *do* understand. It was not the story of K'aresh that was the lesson—though it was the information you demanded of me—it was the story of *Krysson*. Through her tale I had hoped to show you that some paths are meant to fork, that some destinies are not designed to be so entwined. That some futures exist, but they must exist apart. To find your truth, you must see this and you must decide, balancing the good of your people, the good of your kin, against the good of *yourself*."

Alleria stared at Locus-Walker, trying to untangle his message. There *was* wisdom there, she knew—

"There!"

Alleria spun. They were no longer alone on the plateau. They had found the Void revenant.

Or rather, the Void revenant had found *them*.

The creature towered over them, a living, spinning storm of Void energy, purple smokelike eddies of dark power rising from its armored shoulders, from which sprouted six ragged, bladelike wings. Hunched over, its face hidden by a heavy iron mask that revealed nothing but a gaping maw lined with jagged teeth. Glowing power rimmed its terrible form like a cursed hoarfrost that left spots dancing in Alleria's vision. She blinked them away and, readying herself for battle, felt her heart thud in her chest, in her ears . . .

No. The sound, it was not her fear, her reeling thoughts. It was a *voice.* A whisper, calling out across the infinite distance of the Twisting Nether. The voice pulled at her, altogether alien and yet at once instantly familiar.

Alleria turned away from the creature. She saw Locus-Walker behind her, hovering motionless, his gaze upon the revenant. As she watched, he held out a hand toward it, but the gesture was peaceful, almost . . . friendly.

Locus-Walker knew something about the revenant he hadn't told her. It was a creature, he had said, more powerful than the others they had encountered but the same in nature. Yet *how* he knew it was on Telogrus Rift, *why* it was so important to dispatch, he had never said.

The voice called again. In Alleria's mind it sounded like a woman's, although perhaps it was just an echo of her own.

But . . . could Locus-Walker hear it too? Was *that* how he knew the creature was here?

And then the voice was gone, and the sudden silence in

Alleria's mind rang out like a bell. She glanced at Locus-Walker, saw his outstretched hand curl into a tight fist.

"Now," he said. "The time is *now.*"

Alleria turned slowly, pulling her bowstring back, hard. She felt it dig painfully into her bottom lip, felt the way her hand stretched the skin of her face back, baring her teeth. She sighted along the length of the arrow, aiming for the creature's heart.

But she did not fire.

"*Alleria*, quickly now," said Locus-Walker. "Fire, before it knows."

Alleria lowered her bow. "I want to know who it is before I kill it."

She expected perhaps another lecture, another lesson wrapped in a riddle. Instead, Locus-Walker snarled and flew forward, pushing Alleria to the ground as he launched his attack. Alleria rolled in the dirt and saw the Void revenant spin and begin to lengthen, the power of the shadow growing inside it as it focused its attention at the oncoming attack. Within moments, it was twice the size it had been, dwarfing Locus-Walker before it.

Alleria stood. She sighed, then gritted her teeth, took her aim, and fired her arrow.

The battle was short but fierce, and then Alleria and Locus-Walker were alone on the plateau once more, the Void energies of the revenant evaporating like colored smoke back into the Twisting Nether. All that remained of the creature was its heart, the pulsing core of Void energy hovering in the air before them.

Alleria slung her bow over her back and reached for the heart, feeling the slight tug of the Void on her hand as she went to take it. She knew what she had to do. She had done it before. Locus-Walker had shown her.

"Stop."

Alleria dropped her hand. "I thought—"

"I told you before. This one belongs to *me*." Locus-Walker drifted forward as Alleria stepped back. She felt her heart thud in her chest again.

She *had* to know.

"This creature," she whispered. "This revenant of the Void . . ."

"Ask your question."

Alleria reached forward and took the heart in her hand. She squeezed, feeling it buzz uncomfortably, the electric tang of the Void as it seemed to surge, invisibly, around her. The voice called out again. Maybe it was her own voice. Maybe it was an echo of the Void.

Or maybe it was the echo of someone else entirely.

"Do you know who this creature was once?" she asked.

Locus-Walker's hand curled once more into a fist.

"That belongs to *me*," he said.

"I know it does," said Alleria. "It always did, didn't it?"

Locus-Walker did not speak.

"You are wrong, Locus-Walker," said Alleria. "My strength—my *balance*—comes precisely from those I love. They are not a weight that needs to be countered lest I be dragged down. My love for them is not a thing to be purged so I can be pure of mind and sure of focus. My strength comes from them." She stepped closer to Locus-Walker, holding the Void heart in her hand. "That was where *your* strength once came from too. You told me the story of two loves on a dying world, and I felt that love across the ages. You claim to teach me, but it is *you* who have forgotten the lesson. It is true that the future has many paths, and there is another open to me now. A path I fear you never saw back then."

Alleria opened her hand. The Void heart floated in the air, glowing with an impossible halo of violet, and drifted slowly toward Locus-Walker.

"Or perhaps you flinched away from it," said Alleria. "I do not know. It was not my story to tell."

With that, she spun on her heel. "I must return to Dalaran. Khadgar awaits my report." She looked over her shoulder. "Perhaps now you will think about the lesson *I* have given *you*."

She walked off across the barren plateau as the Void flashed above her, and Locus-Walker was alone with his thoughts, alone with his past. Before him, the Void heart floated.

A long moment passed before Locus-Walker reached out and took the Void heart. He paused only for the span of a breath, and then he consumed it, and it was gone.

And with it, the memory of a love from another time.

ABOUT THE AUTHORS

ADAM CHRISTOPHER is the *New York Times* bestselling author of *Star Wars: Shadow of the Sith* and *Stranger Things: Darkness on the Edge of Town*. He has also written official tie-in novels for the hit CBS television show *Elementary* and the award-winning *Dishonored* video game franchise Co-creator of the 21st century incarnation of Archie Comics superhero The Shield, Adam has written for Greg Rucka and Michael Lark's *Lazarus* series from Image Comics and Big Finish's *Doctor Who* universe. A contributor to the internationally bestselling *Star Wars: From a Certain Point of View* anniversary anthology series, Adam has also written for the all-ages *Star Wars Adventures* comic from IDW. Adam's original novels include *Made to Kill* and *The Burning Dark*, among many others, and his debut novel *Empire State* was both a *SciFi Now* and *Financial Times* Book of the Year.

ANDREW ROBINSON is a prolific animation writer and creator who has worked for companies like Marvel, WB, Hasbro, Cartoon Network, Sony, and others on IP like Transformers, Spider-Man, Avengers, Young Justice, G.I. Joe, and more. Since joining Blizzard Entertainment in 2014 he has written animated shorts, songs, world-building lore, comics, and short stories for all their games, and is eager to bring Blizzard's fans more

L. L. MCKINNEY Named one of *The Root*'s and BET's 100 most influential African Americans, Leatrice "Elle" McKinney, writing as L. L. McKinney, is an advocate for equality and inclusion in publishing and the creator of the hashtags #PublishingPaidMe and #WhatWoCWritersHear. Elle is a lover of comics, anime, video games, sci-fi, and fantasy, and strives to push these mediums toward representation that better reflects the diverse world we live in. An adamant HeiHei stan living in Kansas City, she spends her free time with her family or plagued by her cats—Sir Chester Fluffmire Boopsnoot Purrington Wigglebottom Flooferson III, esquire, Baron o' Butterscotch, and Lord Humphrey Blepernicus Zoomerson Wailingshire Toboeans Chirpingston IV, Breaker of Things I Love. Or Chester and Humphrey for short. Her works include the Nightmare-Verse books, the award-winning *Nubia* graphic novels through DC, Marvel's *Black Widow: Bad Blood*, and many more.

"Heartlands" written by Adam Christopher,
illustrated by Brush Sauce Studio and Denis Rogic
"The Tipping Point" written by Andrew Robinson,
illustrated by Matt Hubel, Jeff Parrot, Anastasiia Poliakova,
Tina Wang, and Dragonfly Studios
"Faith & Flame" written by L.L. McKinney,
illustrated by Zoltan Boros and Catarina Pulli
"The Doom of K'aresh" written by Adam Christopher,
illustrated by Cynthia Sheppard and Gabriel Gonzalez
cover art by Andrii Shvyrov N-iX Games

EDITED BY

Chloe Fraboni, Sydney King

DESIGN & ART DIRECTION BY

Corey Peterschmidt

PRODUCED BY

Brianne Messina, Valerie Stone

LORE CONSULTATION BY

Sean Copeland

GAME TEAM CONSULTATION BY

Raphael Ahad, Abigail Manuel, Nicholas McDowell,
Chris Metzen, Aaron Olson, Justin Parker, Stacey Phillips,
Korey Regan, Stephanie Yoon

SPECIAL THANKS

Holly Longdale

BLIZZARD ENTERTAINMENT

Senior Director, Consumer Products: **FUNG THAI**
Manager, Publishing: **PETER MOLINARI**
Associate Manager, Consumer Products: **CHANEE' GOUDE**
Senior Director, Story & Franchise Development: **VENECIA DURAN**
Senior Manager, Writing & Books: **MATTHEW COHAN**
Senior Producer, Books: **BRIANNE MESSINA**
Associate Producer, Books: **VALERIE STONE**
Editorial Supervisor: **CHLOE FRABONI**
Senior Brand Artist: **COREY PETERSCHMIDT**
Associate Manager, Creative Development Production: **JAMIE ORTIZ**
Producer, Lore: **ED FOX**
Lore Historian Lead: **SEAN COPELAND**
Associate Historian: **IAN LANDA-BEAVERS**